MW01147972

THE
SAVAGE BOY

NICK COLE

ISBN: 978-1-949731-08-8

Published by Galaxy's Edge Press

INTERMEZZO

For those who loved

The Old Man and the Wasteland,

You will find this novel a bit different.

This time the Apocalypse is personal.

I thank you in advance for this brief indulgence.

God willing, we may yet hear more of the Old Man.

CHAPTER 1

You take everything with you.

That is the last lesson. The last of all the lessons. The last words of Staff Sergeant Presley.

You take everything with you, Boy.

The Boy tramped through the last of the crunchy brown stalks of wild corn, his weak left leg dragging as it did, his arms full. He carried weathered wooden slats taken from the old building at the edge of the nameless town. He listened to the single clang of some long un-used lanyard, connecting against a flagpole in the fading warmth of the quiet autumn morning.

He knew.

Staff Sergeant Presley was gone now.

The last night had been the longest. The old man that Staff Sergeant Presley had become, bent and shriveled, faded as he gasped for air around the ragged remains of his throat, was gone. His once dark, chocolate brown skin turned gray. The muscles shriveled, the eyes milky. There had been brief moments of fire in those eyes over the final cold days. But at the last of Staff Sergeant Presley there had been no final moment. All of him had gone so quickly. As if stolen. As if taken.

You take everything with you.

The cold wind thundered against the sides of Gas Station all night long as it raced down from mountain passes far to the west. It careened across the dry whispering plain of husk and brush through a ravaged land of wild, dry corn. The wind raced past them in the night, moving east.

A week ago, Gas Station was as far as Staff Sergeant Presley could go, stopping as if they might start again, as they had so many times before. Gas Station was as far as the dying man could go. Would go.

I gotcha to the Eighty, Boy. Now all you got to do is follow it straight on into California. Follow it all the way to the Army in Oakland.

Now, in the morning's heartless golden light, the Boy came back from hunting, having taken only a rabbit. Staff Sergeant Presley's sunken chest did not rise. The Boy waited for a moment among the debris and broken glass turned to sandy grit of Gas Station, their final camp. He waited for Sergeant Presley to look at him and nod.

I'm okay.

I'll be fine.

Get the wood.

But he did not. Staff Sergeant Presley lay unmoving in his blankets.

The Boy went out, crossing the open space where once a building stood. Now, wild corn had grown up through the cracked concrete pad that remained. He crossed the disappearing town to the old wooden shamble at its edge, maybe once a barn. Working with his tomahawk he had the slats off with a sharp crack in the cool, dry air of the high desert. Returning to Gas Station, he knew.

Staff Sergeant Presley was gone now.

The Boy crossed the open lot. Horse looked at him, then turned away. And there was something in that dismissal of Horse that told the Boy everything he needed to know and did not want to.

Staff Sergeant Presley was gone.

He laid the wood down near the crumbling curb and crossed into the tiny office that once watched the county road.

Staff Sergeant Presley's hand was cold. His chest did not rise. His eyes were closed.

The Boy sat next to the body throughout that long afternoon until the wind came up.

You take everything with you.

And...

The Army is west. Keep going west, Boy. When you find them, show them the map. Tell them who I was. They'll know what to do. Tell them Staff Sergeant Lyman Julius Presley, Third Battalion, 47th Infantry, Scouts. Tell them I made it all the way — all the way to D.C., never quit. Tell them there's nothing left. No one.

And...

That's the North Star.

And...

Don't let that tomahawk fly unless you're sure. Might not get it back.

And...

These were all towns. People once lived here. Not like your people. This was a neighborhood. You could have lived here if the world hadn't ended. Gone to school, played sports. Not like your tents and horses.

And...

There are some who still know what it means to be human — to be a society. There are others... You got to avoid those others. That's some craziness.

And...

"Boy" is what they called you. It's the only thing you responded to. So "Boy" it is. This is how we...

Make camp.

Hunt.

Fight.

Ride Horse.

Track.

Spell.

Read.

Bury the dead.

Salute.

For a day the Boy watched the body. Later, he wrapped Staff Sergeant Presley in a blanket; blankets they had traded the Possum Hunters for, back two years ago, when their old blankets were worn thin from winter and the road, when Staff Sergeant Presley had still been young and always would be.

At the edge of the town that once was, in the golden light of morning, the Boy dug the grave. He selected a spot under a sign he could not spell because the words had faded. He dug in the warm brown earth, pushing aside the yellowed, papery corn husks. The broken and cratered road nearby made a straight line into the west.

When the body was in the grave, covered, the Boy waited. Horse snorted. The wind came rolling across the wasteland of wild corn husks.

What now?

You take everything with you.

Horse.

Tomahawk.

Blankets.

Knife.

Map.

Find the Army, Boy. All the way west, near a big city called San Francisco. Tell them there's nothing left and show them the map.

When he could still speak, that was what Staff Sergeant Presley had said.

And…

You take everything with you.

Which seemed something more than just a lesson.

CHAPTER 2

The road and the map gave the number 80. For a time he knew where he was by the map's lines and tracings. He alone would have to know where he was going from now on.

I followed him from the day he took me. Now I will need to lead, even if it is just myself and Horse.

Horse grazed by the side of the broken and cracked highway.

The short days were cold and it was best to let Horse eat when they could find dry grass. The Boy considered the snow capped mountains rising in the distant west.

Sergeant Presley would've had a plan for those mountains.

You should be thinking about the snow, not about me, Boy.

The voice of Sergeant Presley in his head was strong, not as it had been in the last months of his life when it was little more than a rasp and in the end, nothing at all.

You're just remembering me as I was, Boy.

I am.

You can't think of me as someone who can get you outta trouble. I'm dead. I'm gone. You'll have to take care of your-

self now, Boy. I did all I could, taught you everything I knew about survival. Now you got to complete the mission. You got to survive. I told you there'd be mountains. Not like the ones you knew back east. These are real mountains. They're gonna test you. Let me go now and keep moving, Boy.

The sun fell behind the mountains, creating a small flash as it disappeared beyond the snowcapped peaks. Horse moved forward in his impatient way. The Boy massaged his bad leg. This was the time when it began to hurt, at the end of the day as the heat faded and the cold night began.

Sometimes it's better to drive through the night, Boy. Horse'll keep you warm. Better than shiverin' and not sleepin'. But stick to the roads if you do go on.

The Boy rode through the night, listening to Horse clop lazily along, the only sound for many hours. He watched his breath turn to vapor in the dark.

I should make a fire.

The Boy continued on, listening to Sergeant Presley's voice and the stories he would tell of his life before the Boy.

Ah got caught up in things I shouldn't have. You do that and time gets away from you. It shoulda taken me two years to get across the States. Instead it's taken me almost twenty-five or twenty-eight years. I've lost count at times. How old are you, Boy? You was eight when you come with me. But that was after I'd finished my business in Montana. That took me more than twenty to do. Maybe even thirty. Nah, couldn't have been that much.

We fought over San Francisco maybe ten years. After the Chinese kicked us out of the city and dug in, that's when the general sent us east to see if there was anyone left in D.C. My

*squad didn't make it two weeks. Then it was just me. Until
I met you, and that was up in Wyoming.*

*I spent three years fighting in a refugee camp up near
Billings. That's where I lost my guns. After that it was all the
way up to Canada as a slave. Couldn't believe it. A slave.
I knew that camp was doomed from the start. I should've
topped off on supplies and food and kept moving. Cost me
all told seven years. And what I was thinking going back to
get my guns after, I couldn't tell you to this day. I knew there
was no ammo. I didn't have any ammo. But having a gun…
People don't know, see? Don't know if it's loaded. I musta
walked a thousand miles round-trip to find out someone had
dug up my guns. Stupid. Don't ever do anything stupid, Boy.*

Later, the Boy limped alongside Horse thinking of
"Reno" and "Slave Camp" and "Billings" and "Influenza"
and "Plague" and especially "Gone," which was written
next to many of the places that had once been cities. All
the words that were written on Sergeant Presley's map.
And the names too. In the night, the Boy and Horse entered a long valley. The old highway descended and he
watched by moonlight its silver line trace the bottom of
the valley and then rise again toward the mountains in
the west. Below, in the center of the valley, he could see
the remains of a town.

*Picked over. Everything's been picked over. You know it.
I know it. It is known, Boy. Still you'll want to have your
look. You always did.*

For a long time the Boy sat atop the rise until Horse
began to fidget. Horse was getting crankier. Older. The
Boy thought of Sergeant Presley. He patted Horse, rubbing his thick neck, then urged him forward not thinking about the slight pressure he'd put in his right leg to
send the message that they should move on.

CHAPTER 3

The Boy kept Horse to the side of the road, and in doing so he passed from bright moonlight into the shadows of long-limbed trees that grew alongside the road. He watched the dark countryside, waiting for a light to come on, smelling the wind for burning wood. Food. A figure moving in the dark.

At one point he put his right knee into Horse's warm ribs, halting him. He rose up, feeling the ache across his left side. He'd smelled something. But it was gone now on a passing night breeze.

Be careful, Boy.

Sergeant Presley had avoided towns, people, and tribes whenever possible.

These days no good ever comes of such places, Boy. Society's mostly gone now. We might as well be the last of humanity. At least, east of Frisco.

On the outskirts of a town, he came upon a farmhouse long collapsed in on itself.

I can come back here for wood in the morning.

Down the road he found another two-story farmhouse with a wide porch.

These are the best, Boy. You can hear if someone's crossing the porch. You can be ready for 'em.

The Boy dismounted and led Horse across the overgrown field between the road and the old house.

He stopped.

He heard the soft and hollow *hoot, hoot* of an owl.

He watched the wide night sky to see if the bird would cross. But he saw nothing.

He dropped Horse's lead and took his crossbow from its place on the saddle. He pulled a bolt from the quiver in his bag and loaded the crossbow.

He looked at Horse.

Horse would move when he moved. Stop when he stopped.

The Boy's left side was stiff. It didn't want to move and he had to drag it to the porch making more sound than he'd wished to. He opened the claw his withered left hand had become and rested the stock of the crossbow there.

He waited.

Again the owl. He heard the leathery flap of wings.

Your body will do what you tell it to, regardless of that broken wing you got, Boy.

The Boy took a breath and then silently climbed the rotting steps, willing himself to lightness. He crossed the porch in three quick steps, feeling sudden energy rush into his body as he drew his tomahawk off his belt.

Crossbow in the weak left hand, waiting, tomahawk held high in his strong right hand, the Boy listened.

Nothing.

He pushed gently, then firmly when the rotten door would not give. Inside there was nothing: some trash, a stone fireplace, bones. Stairs leading up into darkness. When he was sure there was no one else in the old farmhouse he went back and led Horse inside. Working with the tomahawk he began to pull slats from the wall, and then gently laid them in the blackened stone fireplace. He made a fire, the first thing Sergeant Presley had taught him to do, and then closed the front door.

Don't get comfortable yet. If they come, they'll come soon.

He could not tell if this was himself or Sergeant Presley.

The Boy stood with his back to the fire, waiting.

When he heard their call in the night, his blood froze.

It was a short, high-pitched ululating like the sound of bubbling water. First he heard one, nearby. Then answers from far off.

You gotta choose, Boy. Git out or git ready.

The Boy climbed back onto Horse, who protested, and hooked the crossbow back into its place. He pulled the tomahawk out and bent low, whispering in Horse's ear, the ceiling just above his head.

"It'll be fine. We can't stay. Good Horse."

Horse flicked his tail.

'I don't know if he agrees,' thought the Boy, 'but it doesn't matter, does it?'

The face that appeared in the window was chalk white, its eyes rimmed in black grease.

That's camouflage, Boy. Lets him move around in the night. These are night people. Some of the worst kind.

The eyes in the window went wide, and then the face disappeared. He heard two quick ululations.

More coming, Boy!

The Boy kicked and aimed Horse toward the front door. Its shattered rottenness filled the Boy's lungs as he clung to Horse's side and they drove through the opening. He saw the shadow of a man thrown back against a wooden railing that gave way with a disinterested crack.

Other figures in dark clothes and with chalk-white faces crossed with black greased stripes ran through the high grass between the road and the farmhouse. The Boy kicked Horse toward an orchard of ragged bare-limbed trees that looked like broken bones in the moonlight.

Once in the orchard, he turned down a lane and charged back toward the road. Horse's breathing came labored and hard.

"You were settling in for the night and now we must work," he whispered into Horse's twitching ears.

Ahead, one of the ash-white, black-striped figures leaped into the middle of the lane. The figure planted his feet, then raised a spear-carrying arm back over his shoulder.

The Boy tapped twice on the heaving flank with his toe and Horse careened to the right, disagreeing with a snort as he always did.

'You wanted to run him down,' thought the Boy.

They made the road leaping a broken fence. He stopped and listened. The Boy could hear the ululations behind them. He heard whistling sounds also.

Down the road quickly, get outta Dodge now, Boy!

He took the road farther into town, passing the crumbling remains of warehouses and barns long collapsed. Stone concrete slabs where some structure had burned down long ago rose up like gray rock in the light of the moon. Sergeant Presley had always spoken simply at such places.

Gas Station.

School.

Market.

Mall.

The Boy didn't know the meaning or purposes of such places and possessed only vague notions of form and function when he recognized their remains.

In the center of town he saw more figures and brought Horse up short, hooves digging for purchase on the fractured road. The Ashy Whites formed a circle and within were the others. The Ashy Whites were standing. The others sat, huddled in groups.

"Help us!" someone cried out and one of the Ashy Whites clubbed at the sitting figure.

Behind him, the Boy could hear the ululations growing closer. Horse stamped his hooves, ready to run.

"Rumble light!" roared a large voice and the Boy was suddenly covered in daylight — white light like the "flashlight" they'd once found in the ruins of an old car factory. It had worked, but only for a day or so. Sergeant Presley had said light was once so common you didn't even think about it. Now…

No time for memories, Boy!

Horse reared up and the Boy had to get hold of the mane to get him down and under control. Once Horse was down and settled, the Boy stared about into the blackness, seeing nothing, not even the moonlight. Just the bright shining light coming from where the Ashy Whites had been.

An Ashy White, large and fat, his face jowly, his lower lip swollen, his eyes bloodshot, stepped into the light from the darkness off to one side. He was carrying a gun.

What type of gun is this, Boy?

When they'd found empty guns Sergeant Presley would make him learn their type, even though, as he always said, *They were no good to anyone now. How could they be? After all these years there ain't no ammunition left, Boy. We burned it all up fightin' the Chinese.*

Shotgun, sawed off.

The Ashy White man walked forward pointing the shotgun at Horse.

What will it do? he heard Sergeant Presley ask.

Sprays gravel, short range.

The Ashy White continued to walk forward with all the authority of instant death possessed.

There can't be any ammunition left. Not after all these years, Boy.

He kicked Horse in the flanks and charged the man. Pinned ears indicated Horse was only all too willing. Sometimes the Boy wondered if Horse hated everyone, even him.

In one motion the Boy drew his tomahawk.

The man raised the weapon.

Don't let it go unless you mean to, might not get it back, Boy. He always heard Sergeant Presley and his words, every time he drew the tomahawk.

He'd killed before.

He'd kill again.

He was seventeen years old.

The world as Sergeant Presley had known it had been over for twenty-three years when the Boy whose own name even he had forgotten had been born on the wind-swept plains of what the map had once called Wyoming.

You strike with a tomahawk. Never sweep. It'll get stuck that way, Boy. Timing has to be perfect.

Jowls raised the shotgun, aiming it right into the Boy.

There can't be any ammunition left, Boy. The world used it all up killing itself.

And the Boy struck. Once. Down. Splitting the skull. He rode off, out of the bright light and into the darkness.

CHAPTER 4

He could hear the Ashy Whites throughout the night, far off, calling to one another. At dawn there were no birds and the calls ceased.

Boy, Sergeant Presley had said that time they'd spent a night and a day finding their way across the Mississippi. *Things ain't the same anymore.*

They were crawling through and along a makeshift dam of river barges and debris that had collected in the mud-thickened torrents of the swollen river.

You probably don't know what that means, d'ya? The mosquitos were thick and they had to use all their hands and feet to hold on to anything they could as the debris-dam shifted and groaned in the treacherous currents. It felt like they were being eaten alive.

If I'd fallen into the water that day what could he have done to save me?

But you didn't, Boy.

I was afraid.

I knew you was. So I kept telling you about how things were different now. About how sane, rational people had gone stark raving mad after the bombs. About how the strong oppressed the weak and turned them into slaves. About how the sick and evil were finally free to live out all of their canni-balistic craziness. And how sometimes, just sometimes, there might be someone, or a group of someones who kept to the good. But you couldn't count on that anymore. And that was why we were crossing that rickety pile of junk in the river rather than trying for the bridge downstream. You smelled what those people who lived on the bridge were cookin' same as I did. You knew what they were cooking, or who they were cooking. We didn't need none of that. The world's gone mostly crazy now. So much so, that all the good that's left is so little you can't hardly count on it when you need it. Better to mistrust everyone and live another day.

Like these Ashy Whites out in the night looking for me.

Seems like it, Boy.

Many times he and Sergeant Presley had avoided such people. Horse knew when to keep quiet. Evasion was a simple matter of leaving claimed territory, crossing and recrossing trails and streams, always moving away from the center. The town was the center. Now, at dawn, he was on the far side of the valley and he could make out little of the town beyond its crisscross roads being swallowed by the general abandonment of such places.

You almost got caught, Boy.

But I didn't.

We'll see.

He waited in the shadows at the side of a building whose roof had long ago surrendered inward, leaving only the walls to remain in defeat. The warm sunshine on the cracked and broken pavement of the road heading west beckoned to him, promising to drive off the stiffness that clamped itself around his left side every night.

They'll assume you're gone by now, Boy.

The Boy waited.

When he hadn't heard the ululations for some time, he walked Horse forward into the sunshine.

Later that morning he rode back to the town, disregarding the warnings Sergeant Presley had given him of such places.

Whoever the Ashy Whites were, they had gone.

And the others too, huddled within the circle of the Ashy Whites — that voice in the night, a woman he thought, calling for help.

Who were the others?

The answer lay in the concrete remains of a sign he spelled S-C-H-O-O-L.

School.

This had been their home. The fire that consumed it hadn't been more than three days ago. But the Boy knew the look of a settlement. A fort, as Sergeant Presley would have called it. The bloated corpses of headless men lay rotting in the wan morning light.

This is where those who had huddled within the circle of the Ashy Whites had lived all the years since the end of the things that were.

Before.

He found the blind man at the back of the school, near the playground and the swing sets.

Remember when I pushed you on a swing that time, Boy? When we found that playground outside Wichita. We played and shot a deer with my crossbow. We barbecued the meat. It could have been the Fourth of July. Do you remember that, Boy?

I do, he had told Sergeant Presley in those last weeks of suffering.

It could have been the Fourth of July.

The blind man lay in the sandbox of the playground, his breath ragged, as drool ran down onto the dirty sand, mixing with the blood from the place where his eyes had once been.

The Boy thought it might be a trap.

He'd seen such tricks before, and even with Sergeant Presley they'd nearly fallen into them once or twice. After those times and in the years that followed, they'd avoided everyone when they could afford to.

He got down from Horse.

"There's no more to give!" cried the blind man. "You've taken everything. Now take my life, you rotten cowards!"

The Boy walked back to Horse and got his water bag. Not much left.

He knelt down next to the blind man and raised his head putting the spout near his lips. The blind man drank greedily.

After: "You're not with them, are you?"

The Boy walked back to Horse.

"Kill me."

He mounted Horse.

"Kill me. Don't leave me like this. How…" The blind man began to sob. "How will I eat?"

The Boy atop Horse regarded the blind man for a moment.

How will any of us eat?

He rode off across the overgrown field and back through a broken-down wire fence.

That's everything you need to know, Boy. Good. Tells you everything you need to know. Supremacists. Coming down out of their bunkers in the North. Don't know these guys, but they're probably worth avoiding. Probably here slavin'.

Probably.

Go west. Get into the Sierras before winter. The mountains will be a good place to go to ground for winter. It's hard to live in the mountains but there'll be less people up there. You plan, you prepare, and you'll do just fine. Come spring, you cross the mountains and head for Oakland. Find the Army. Tell them.

In the days that followed, the Boy rode Horse hard across the broken and barren dirt of what the map called Nevada. On the big road, Freeway, which he kept off to his right, he passed horrendous wrecks rusting since long before he'd been born. He passed broken trucks and overturned cars, things he'd once wanted to explore as a boy. Sergeant Presley would often let him when they'd had the time for such games — the game of explaining what the Boy found inside the twisted metal, and what the lost treasures had once meant. Before.

Hairbrush.

Phone.

Eyeglasses.

There was little that remained after the years of scavenging by other passing travelers.

The winding, wide Freeway curved and climbed higher underneath dark peaks. Roads that left Freeway often disappeared into wild desert. Sometimes as he rested Horse he would wonder what he might find at the conclusion of such lonely roads.

At one intersection the rusting framework of a sign crossed the departing road. From the framework three skeletons dangled in the wind of the high desert, rotted and picked at by vultures.

Probably a warning, Boy. Whoever's up that road doesn't want company.

It was a cold day. Above he could see the snowcapped peaks turning blue in the shadow of the falling sun. Later that night as he rode down a long grade devoid of wrecks, snow began to fall and he was glad to be beyond the road-sign skeletons.

He made camp in the carport of a fallen house on the side of a rocky hill that overlooked the winding highway. He stacked rubble in the openings to hold in the warmth of his fire.

CHAPTER 5

She and her sisters came out that night, south out of the desert wastes ranging up toward the road. Winter was coming on fast, and they needed to make their kills soon and return south to their home near the big canyon. They had hunted the area lean of mule deer and for the last week had been reduced to eating jackrabbits. Far too little and lean for a pride of lions.

Did she think about what the world had become? Did she wonder how she had come to be hunting the lonely country of northern Nevada? Did she know anything of casinos and entertainments and that her ancestors had once roamed, groomed and well fed, behind glass enclosures while tourists snapped their pictures?

No.

She only thought of the male and their young and her sisters.

Tonight the wind was cold and dry. There was little moonlight for the hunt. If they could only come across a pack of wild dogs. It would be enough to start them south again. Once they were south, they would have food in the canyons. And if they had to, they could always search the old city. There was always someone there, a lone man digging among the ruins. There was always someone hiding within the open arches and shredded carpets, the overturned machines and the shining coins spilled out as though carelessly thrown down in anger.

She topped the small line of hills and saw the dark band of the highway heading west. They had always regarded this road as the extent of their northern wandering. Now they had to turn south.

Her sisters growled. She watched the road, looking for a moving silhouette in the darkness. One sister came to rub her head with her own.

Let's return. He is waiting.

And for a moment she smelled... a horse.

They had taken wild horse before.

When she was young.

Running down the panicked mustangs.

There had been more than enough.

She scented the wind coming out of the east and turned her triangular head to watch the curve of the road as it gently bent south along the ridge line.

There was a horse along the road.

CHAPTER 6

In the late afternoon of the next day the Boy rode alongside the highway listening for any small sound within the quiet that blanketed the desolation of the high desert.

There is nothing in this land. It's been hunted clean.

The Boy, used to little, felt the ache in his belly beginning to rumble. It had been two days since the last of a crow he'd roasted over a thin fire of brush and scrub wood.

So what's that tell you, Boy?

Death in some form. Either predators who will see me as prey or poison from the war.

That's right, he heard Sergeant Presley say in the way he'd always pronounced the words "That" and "is," making them one and removing the final "t."

A place called Reno is in front of me. Maybe another day's ride.

All cities are dead. The war saw to that, Boy.

Some cities. Remember the one called Memphis. It wasn't poisoned.

Might as well have been, Boy. Might as well have been.

The big roar came from behind them. Horse turned as if to snarl, but when his large nostrils caught the scent of the predator he gave a short, fearful warning. The Boy patted Horse's neck, calming him.

I've never heard an animal make a sound like that. Sounds like a big cat. But bigger than anything I've ever heard before.

He scanned the dusty hills behind him.

He saw movement in the fingers of the ridge he'd just passed.

And then he saw the lion. It trotted down a small ridge kicking up dust as it neared the bottom. For a moment the Boy wondered if the big cat might be after something else, until it came straight toward him. Behind the big lion, almost crouching, a smaller lion, sleeker — no great mane surrounding its triangular head — danced forward, scrambling through the dusty wake of the big lion.

He wheeled Horse about to the west, facing the place once called Reno, and screamed "Hyahhh!" as he drove the two of them forward.

CHAPTER 7

'The idiot,' thought the lioness. She'd only made him come along so he could roar at just the right moment and drive the horse into her sisters and the young lying in wait ahead. Instead he'd cried out in hunger at the first sight of the meaty flanks of the horse. She could hear the saliva in his roar. The cubs would be lucky to get any of this meal.

His cry had been early and she knew from the moment the horse began to gallop that her run would never catch the beast. For a short time she could be fast. But not for long. Not in a race. Her only hope now was that her sisters and the young were in a wide half circle ahead, and that the horse would continue its course into their trap.

'The idiot,' she thought again, as she slowed to a trot. 'He's only good for fighting other males. For that, he is the best.'

The Boy raced down alongside the ancient crumbling highway, but Horse was slowing as the ground required caution. A broken leg would be the death of them both. He reined in Horse hard at an off-ramp and sent them down onto an old road that seemed to head off to the south. Ahead, a slope rose into a series of sharp little hills, the ground smooth, windblown sand and hardpack. He spurred Horse forward up onto the rising slope. At the top he stopped and scanned behind him.

In the shadow of a crag, he could see the big lion doggedly trotting along the ridgeline. Ahead of the lion, crouched low and crawling, the sleeker lion had stopped. The Boy could feel its eyes on him.

"It's us they're after, Horse. I don't think they're going to take no for an answer."

Horse snorted derisively and then began to shift as if wanting to turn and fight.

That's jes big talk, Boy! Those lions'll kill him dead and you with him. Don't pay no attention to him, Horse's jes big talk. Always has been.

Ahead to the west he could see a bleached and tired city on the horizon. But it was too far off to be of any use now.

And it could be poisoned, Boy. Radiation. Kill you later like it did me.

The Boy turned Horse and raced below the ridgeline, skirting its summit. They rounded the outmost tip of the rise, and beyond it lay a vast open space, empty and without comfort.

The ground sloped into a gentle half bowl and he could see Freeway beyond.

I should never have left the road. We could have found a jackknifed trailer to hide in. Sergeant Presley said those were always the best places to sleep. We did many times.

He patted Horse once more on the neck whispering, "We'll sprint for the road beyond the bowl. We'll find a place there."

Horse reared impolitely as if to say they should already be moving.

Halfway down the slope at a good canter, watching for squirrel and snake holes, places where Horse could easily snap one of his long legs, the Boy saw the trap.

There were five of them. All like the sleeker, maneless lion. Females. Hunters. They were crouched low in a wide semicircle off to his right. All of them were watching him. He'd come into the left edge of their trap.

You know what to do, Boy! barked Sergeant Presley in his teaching voice. His drill sergeant voice. The voice with which he'd taught the Boy to fight, to survive, to live just one more day.

Assault through the ambush.

Horse roared with fear. Angry fear.

The Boy guided Horse toward the extreme left edge of the trap, coaxing him with his knee as he unhooked the crossbow, cocked a bolt, and raised it upward with his withered left hand.

Not the best to shoot with. But I'll need the tomahawk for the other.

The sleek females darted in toward him, dashing through the dust, every golden muscle rippling, jaws clenched tight in determination.

This is bad.

The fear crept into the Boy as it always did before combat.

Ain't nothin' but a thang, Boy. Ain't nothin' but a thang. Mind over matter; you don't mind, it don't matter.

The closest cat charged forward, its fangs out, and in that instant the Boy knew it would leap. Its desire to leap and clutch at Horse's flanks telegraphed in the cat's wicked burst of speed.

The Boy lowered the crossbow onto the flat of his good arm holding the tomahawk, aimed on the fly, and sent a bolt into the flurry of dust and claws from which the terrible fanged mouth and triangular head watched him through cold eyes.

He heard a sharp, ripping yowl and kicked Horse to climb the small ridge at the edge of the bowl. On the other side he could see frames of half-built buildings below on the plain before the city.

Half-built buildings.

Construction site.

Maybe houses being built on the last day of the old world. Houses that would never be finished.

If I can stay ahead of them for just a moment...

Horse screamed and the Boy felt the weight of something angry tearing at Horse's left flank.

One of the female lions had gone wide and raced for the lip of the ridgeline. Once on top, it had thrown everything into a leap that brought it right down onto Horses's flank.

The Boy cursed as he swiped at the fierce cat with his tomahawk. But the lioness had landed on Horse's left side and his axe was in his right hand. The Boy batted at the lioness with the crossbow. It's mouth was open, its fangs ready to sink into Horse's spine, The Boy shoved the crossbow into the cat's open jaws. Gagging and choking, the lioness released Horse's torn flesh as its paws attempted to remove the crossbow. It fell away into the dust and Horse continued forward. Already the Boy could feel Horse slowing. His own feet, bent back onto Horse's flanks, were dripping with warm blood.

"Don't slow down," he pleaded into Horse's pinned ears, doubting whether he was heard at all. "Just make it into those ruins."

When Horse didn't respond with his usual snort, the Boy knew the wound was bad.

CHAPTER 8

The Boy drove Horse hard through the drifting sand of the old ruins. Rotting frames of sun-bleached gray and bone-white wood, warped by forty years of savage heat and cruel ice seemed to offer little protection from the roaring lions now trotting downslope in a bouncing, almost expectant, gait.

They wove deeper into the dry fingers of wood erupting from the sand of Construction Site. The Boy heard the crack of ragged wooden snaps beneath Horse's hooves. He hoped they might find a hole or even a completed building to hide in. But there was nothing. Behind them he could hear the cats beginning to growl, unsure how to proceed through the rotting forest of ancient lumber. The Big Lion gave a roar and the Boy knew they would be coming into the maze after them.

Near the far edge of the spreading ruins, the Boy found a half-constructed bell tower ringed with ancient scaffolding over a narrow opening. It was their only hope. He steered Horse in under the rickety scaffolding still clinging to its long unfinished exterior. In the shadowy dark he dismounted Horse and raced back outside. He swung his tomahawk at the ancient scaffolding, cutting through a rusty bar with one stroke. He stepped back inside once he'd smashed the other support bar. The scaffolding began to collapse across the entrance as he saw the Big Lion come crashing through the warped and bent forest of dry wood, charging directly at him.

The scaffolding slanted down across the entrance as shafts of fading daylight shot through the dust.

The Big Lion crossed the ground between them in bounds.

Focus, Boy.

The Boy reached up and crushed another support with his tomahawk and more abandoned building material came crashing down across the entrance. Dust and sand swallowed the world and the Boy closed his eyes and didn't breathe. Horse screeched in fear as the Boy hoped the collapsed scaffolding would be enough to block the entrance.

When he opened his eyes he could see soft light filtering through the debris-cluttered opening.

He put his good hand on Horse, conveying calm where the Boy felt none, willing the terror-stricken animal to understand that they were safe for now.

Then he looked at the wound.

Claw marks straight down the side. The whole flank all the way to the hock was shaking. He took some of his water and washed the wound. Horse trembled, and the Boy placed his face near Horse's neck, whispering.

"It will be okay.

"I will take care of you."

The wound is still bleeding, so I'll have to make a bandage.

He poured some water into the sand and made mud. He didn't have much water, but it was vital to get the bleeding stopped.

He can't bleed forever, Boy.

When the mixture was ready he packed it into the wound, steadying Horse as he went, murmuring above the lion's roar as he applied the wet mud.

She paced back and forth outside the never-to-be-finished bell tower.

Horse was definitely inside. She could smell it. She could smell its fear.

At the top of the bell tower, fifteen feet high, she could see narrow arches. If she could leap from another structure she might get in there and make the kill.

The male rose up on his hind legs and began to bat away at the collapsed opening. Wood splintered and cracked as he put all of his four hundred pounds onto the pile of debris. As usual he tired quickly and went to lie down, content to merely wait and watch the entrance. The sisters came up to him one by one, trying to reassure him that all would be well, but he seemed embarrassed — or frustrated. Normally expressive, his great face remained immobile, which the young usually took for thinking. But she knew he was merely tired and mostly out of ideas and generally unconcerned at how things might turn out.

She knew him — and loved him.

She paced away from the tower and then turned, gave two energetic bounds, and leapt. She almost made the top. Her claws extended, ripping into the dry stucco of the bell tower, revealing ancient dry wood beneath.

She began to climb toward the opening, and a moment later a sheet of stucco ripped away and she fell backward.

There is wood like a tree underneath. 'Once this skin is off,' she thought, 'I'll be able to climb in.'

She began to stand on her hind legs and rake her claws down the side of the tower as chalky stucco, dry and brittle, disintegrated.

As if not to be outdone by her sister, another of the females began to dig at the base of the tower like she might for the making of a den. Now it would be a race. Who would get to the horse first? The male would like that. He would reward whoever got in first. It was his way.

The sun was going down. It would be a long night.

CHAPTER 9

Horse had stopped trembling. He seemed resigned now to the tight space and had stopped threatening to fight present conditions. The Boy climbed atop Horse and reached for the high arched openings just below the roof. Leveraging himself upward, he was able to climb into them.

Below, the lions were instantly aware of him. Multiple pairs of glowing dark eyes watched him. By the barest of moonlight he could see them lying about while the one who had been digging at the base of the tower stopped.

If I had my crossbow I could pick her off.

Never mind what you don't have, Boy. You better start thinking about a jailbreak, otherwise…

The Big Lion roared loudly, opening its mouth and showing its fangs as it turned its head, throwing the roar off into the hills. When the lion finished it stared straight at the Boy.

The Boy listened to the echo of the roar bounce off the far hills, its statement reminding him of the vastness of the high desert and how alone he was within it.

'So that's how it is,' thought the Boy. 'All right then, no surrender.'

One of the females suddenly ran forward, leapt, and almost caught the edge of the arched opening. The whole bell tower shook and Horse cried out in fear. The lion slid down as her claws raked the stucco off, revealing the dry wooden slats beneath.

This thing was not well constructed in the Before, and these hard years since haven't improved it. You would tell me to stop and think, Sergeant.

He removed his tomahawk from his belt.

The feline turned and charged the tower again. The Boy waited and as it made its leap he slammed the tomahawk down into one paw. The beast screeched and threw itself away from the wall.

That should give me some time.

The Lioness watched the Boy for a moment, the contempt naked in its cool eyes, then lay down apart from the others, and began to lick the wound. The Boy could not tell how badly he might have hurt it.

He lowered himself down into the dark, finding Horse with his dangling feet. Then he gently let himself down onto Horse's back. He sat there, letting his eyes adjust to the darkness.

I've got to do something about the digger next. If I can do something about her, maybe they'll get the point that I'm not coming out. Maybe then they'll go away.

You sure about that, Boy?

The only thing else I can think of is to strike at them as they come through the sand under the wall.

It seemed a thin plan, but looking at the four walls and Horse, what else could he do?

For the rest of the night he listened to the digger. Occasionally the lions would growl and he thought it best not to go up into the high arched openings.

If I remain invisible to them, then maybe "out of sight, out of mind" as you used to say, Sergeant?

Or…

If they can't mind me, then I won't matter to them.

And it was there in the dark that the Boy realized Sergeant Presley had been full of knowledge. Full of words and wisdom. Those things were a comfort to him in the times he and Sergeant Presley had been in danger.

I'm young. I haven't had all the years it takes to acquire wisdom. Now death is closer than it has ever been.

Everyone dies, Boy, even me. Maybe it's not as bad as you think.

Soft, pale light shone through the arched windows above. The night had passed and though he had not slept much, the Boy felt as though he'd slept too much. As if some plan of action should have occurred to him in the hours of darkness. But none had and he cursed himself, not knowing what the coming day might bring.

He heard a roar, far off, then another one and another, almost on the heels of the echo of the first.

More lions?

Trouble always looks for company, Boy. Always.

Then I'll be ready. Whatever it is, the best I can do is to be ready.

He climbed to the top of the bell tower and looked out from the arches. The Big Lion, the male, was on his feet and staring into the darkened west. A thin strip of red dawn cut the eastern desert in half like a hot knife.

The Boy followed the Big Lion's gaze into the dark and saw three male lions, smaller — not by much, manes almost as big — pacing back and forth in the dark.

The females were drawing the cubs back from the Big Lion.

If there is going to be a fight, the newcomers might not know I'm here. If they win, then this could be good for me.

She limped toward her mate.

Had she ever been special to him?

She liked to think so. She liked to think there was something special between her and him that her sisters had never known. Would never know.

She'd seen him fight other males before. The desert was full of their kind. The mule deer and wild animals had been abundant in all the years she had known and the prides had grown large. And now, from some unknown pride much like her own, the young lions had come to find mates for themselves among her pride. Just as he had once found her.

Limping forward to stand behind him, she could at least do that for the love of her existence. She could at least do that. But when he turned, she saw the flash of anger in his eyes, warning her to get back, and maybe something she had never seen before. Fear.

He roared again. It was his way and his answer to the challengers. His roaring anger at the horse within the bell tower had most likely summoned these challengers out of the dark. She knew his roar, beautiful and safe to her, had cost them all.

She lay down in front of her sisters, between them and her mate — their mate — and watched.

When the battle started in earnest, it transformed from a storm to a whirlwind in the space of a moment. The newcomers, baiting the big male half heartedly, as though they might leave at any moment, suddenly came at him at once, silent, focused, hopeful.

His great claws pinned the first and he sank his jaws into the back of his challenger's neck. She heard the crunch of bones and knew that one was finished, though it continued to flail wildly, its claws drawing blood across her mate's belly.

Another challenger circled wide and landed on her mate's back after a great pounce. The challenger was unsure what to do next. The third came in hard at his flank and began to tear away great strips of fur and skin with claws that looked long and sharp.

Here was their leader, she thought. He had been smart enough to wait.

The male shook the one in his mouth as he tried to draw his victim upward.

She cried out for him to be done with that one and to handle the other two, but her cries were drowned out by his as he roared and whirled on the leader. He batted at the flanker, who tumbled away and then turned the momentum into something to fling itself right back at the male.

The challenger on his back held on for dear life and she could sense the fear in that one. That one didn't have it in him to sink his fangs into her mate. He was the runt. He would never have a pride of his own.

The male pinned the lion he'd cast off; it was his technique, she knew, to use his size to subdue and strangle his enemies. Enraged, he crushed the leader beneath him and tore out his throat.

Her paws, kneading the soft sand of the desert, relaxed. She knew he had won. He would be wounded, badly if the blood streaming down his belly was any indicator, but he had at least beaten these challengers. She was proud of both him for his strength and herself for her faith and love.

Thunder broke across the darkness like dry wood split sharply.

Thunder was what she'd thought the sound was, and for a moment she'd expected lightning. But the sudden white light that would illuminate the land never came. Instead she watched him roll off his foes in a great spray of blood.

The Back Biter rolled away, confused. For a moment the runt raised a paw as if he might step this way or that, flee or attack. Then another bolt of thunder erupted, and a fraction later the Back Biter's head exploded.

In the wind she found a new horse and acrid smoke; a mule also.

Her sisters were fleeing into the night.

The young whimpered.

She turned back to him and crossed the short space to his body. Her eyes were on his mane and the face that had once expressed so many thoughts to her. So many thoughts that she knew she had never known him completely.

He was still.

Asleep.

Beautiful.

Noble.

Even when she heard the thunder erupt again, near and yet as if part of a dream she was only waking from, she watched his face.

The bullet struck her in the spine.

And she watched him.

She watched him.

She watched him.

CHAPTER 10

"All my skins is ruin't!"

Early light had turned the night's carnage golden. The Boy listened to the man below.

"This one, that one over there! Hell, Danitra, all of 'em." Then, "Maybe 'cept this one."

The Boy listened from the shadows of the bell tower.

You be careful now, Boy! There's little good left in this world.

"Might as well come out!" thundered the voice. "Seein' as how I saved ya and all such."

He knows I'm here. And he has a gun. Not like the rusty "AK Forty-sevens" and broken "Nine mils" we would find sometimes. His gun is different, like a polished piece of thick wood. As though it were different and from some place long ago.

For all that Sergeant Presley had tried to explain about guns to the Boy, he'd never guessed one would've made such a sound, like the crack of distant thunder from under a blanket.

He patted Horse and climbed up into the high arched openings once more.

"There ya're!" roared the man.

He was barrel-chested and squat. He wore dusty black leather and a beaten hat, hair dark and turning to gray. He stopped his cutting work to look up from one of the lions, holding a large knife in his bloody hand.

"These are mine," he said and turned back to his business with the hide. "Any more in there besides you?"

The Boy said nothing.

"That means nope," said the stranger.

"My horse."

"Well, you better get down and get him out of there."

The Boy continued to watch the man as he skinned the lion, swearing and sweating while he made long, sawing cuts, then stood, wiped his knife, and pulled back a great streak of hide.

"C'mon boy. I got work to do. No one else here but me and my horse and Danitra. She's my mule."

He set to work on the next lion.

"This one's even worse than the last! That was a mess. Coulda done that better myself. What tribe you with, boy?"

The Boy said nothing and continued to watch.

"You with them tribes out in the desert?"

The Boy remained silent.

"Well, pay it no mind. I've got to get these hides off and cut some meat. So if you don't want to be a part of that then I'll ask you to get your horse out of there and move along." The man stood staring at the Boy, his bloody knife hanging halfway between forgotten and ready.

"My horse is injured."

The man wiped the knife once again on the leather of his pants and spit.

"Well, get him out of there and let's take a look. I know a thing or two about horses."

The Boy climbed down the side of the bell tower using the wooden slats exposed after the attacks of the lions. At the bottom, he began to remove the debris blocking the entrance as the man returned to skinning the dead lions.

"It's bad." The man spit as he ran his hands across Horse. For a moment Horse grew skittish, but the man talked to him in a friendly manner and Horse seemed to accept this as yet one more thing to be miserable about.

"Not the worst. Best we can do for him is get him up to the river, the other side of Reno. Good water there. We can clean the wound and get him ready for the fever that's bound to come. If he can survive that fever, then, well maybe. But fever it'll be. Always is with them cats."

'I'm not ready to lose Horse,' thought the Boy. 'It would be too much for me right now. First you, Sergeant, and now...'

Ain't nothin' but a thang, Boy! You do what's got to be done. Without Horse you'll be finished in a week.

"Name's Escondido. I'll lead you up to the river — goin' that way myself and I'll show you the path through Reno. Now get to work and help me with these hides, then we'll be movin' on out of this forsaken planned community of the future."

The Boy stared at the ground.

"That's what you was holed up in when I found you," said the man called Escondido as he pointed first to the bell tower and then the rotting timber. "Someone was building a neighborhood here on the last day. Never got finished. See all that rotten wood? Frames for houses. This bell tower was probably the fake entrance. Make it seem like something more'n it was. They would have called it some name like Sierra Verde or the Pines. Probably something to do with the bell tower. Bell Tower Heights! Yes siree, that's what they woulda called it. Old Escondido knows the old people's ways. I was one of 'em, you know. I lived in a house once. Can you believe that, boy? I lived in a house."

I've got to do whatever it takes to save Horse.

"How far is this river?"

"Be there by nightfall. We don't want to be in Reno after dark, that's for sure."

"Reno wasn't nuked?" "Nuked" was a Sergeant Presley word.

"No. But it looks like a big battle was fought there out near the airport. So the city might as well have been nuked. Strange people live in them old casinos now. Had a partner used to call 'em the Night People, 'cause they get crazy and howl and cause all kinds of havoc at night. Last two or three years when I crossed over the Sierras I liked to avoid Reno. Got into a bad spot there one time about dusk. It was a bad time, even with my guns."

The Boy followed Escondido's gaze to a bent and broken horse. Its hair was matted and lanky, and it cropped haphazardly at what little there was to be had, as if both tired and dizzy. In the worn leather saddle, the Boy saw two long rifles.

"That horse ain't much to look at. But best part of him is he's deaf, so when my breech loaders go off he don't get scared and run off."

The Boy worked for the rest of the morning scraping the hides of the lions as Escondido finished the skinning and then cut steaks from the female. He built a small smoky fire and the meat was soon spitted and roasting in the morning breeze.

"We got to eat these now. It'll be a long day getting through Reno. Then we still got to ride up into the hills to reach the river."

Once the mule, Danitra, as Escondido called her, was saddled with hides, they sat down next to the fire and ate.

"How much water ya got? asked Escondido through a mouthful of meat.

"Not much. I'll save it for Horse."

"There's no water worth havin' between here and the river, so keep that in mind. Don't go gettin' thirsty. I'll trade you some for that old Army rucksack you got there on your horse."

The Boy continued to chew, putting Escondido's offer away until later, hoping the heat and dust would not force him to trade Sergeant Presley's ruck for a mouthful of water.

They rode out of the bloody camp. Escondido's nag could do little more than trot and so the pace was slow. Escondido filled the silence of the hot afternoon with conversation and observations, all the while watching the crumbling remains of the world for shadows and salvage.

"Was tracking them lions for three days before they got onto your big one. I heard him roar and I knew I'd lost 'em. Couldn't get a shot off on 'em all night. But I knew I had to find 'em before they got into that fight. Hides'll be ruined and Chou'll make his usual fuss 'bout it and all. Still I got ways and means. What tribe did you say you was with?"

When the Boy didn't answer, Escondido continued on.

"My family came from out of the South. I had another name. Prospero, my mother used to call me. But, in the little refugee camp we started out in, they called me Escondido. That's where my family had been before the bombs: a place called Escondido. Tried to ask my papa where that might be. All he said was that it was gone now. A fantasy place."

And...

"I cross over the mountains beginning of summer every year. This year I got a late start. Mountains is gettin' weirder every year. You know about the Valley? No, don't make no difference, you don't look like them people. Say, was you born that way or'd you get bust up when you was little?"

And...

"What was you doin' out here? This part of the desert ain't safe. Though for that matter, what part is?"

Don't tell anything about ye'self, Boy.

"You don't say much, do you? Is that your tribe's way? Don't say much?"

It was afternoon by the time they crossed onto the dusty streets of Reno. Buildings lay collapsed or shattered to little more than rusting frames that groaned in the sudden gusts that came in off the desert.

In the silence of late afternoon, shadows turned to blue and Escondido continued to talk in a low whisper though he would stop when they passed piles of rubble and twisted metal that lay across the wide thoroughfare leading into the heart of the darkened city.

"The people, the tribes, savages all up in the mountains, everywhere I've gone, they wear hides to show what mighty hunters they are. Now up at the trading post in Auburn, everybody wants hides so they can trade with them savages. Them lions, if'n they'd been perfect, woulda fetched a high price from old Chou. That's a shame. A perfect shame."

Ahead, each of them could see the rising pile of bleached casinos crumbling around a bridge that rose over the wide avenue they would follow. A bridge that connected two of the ancient palaces and seemed to loom over the road like the wingspan of some prehistoric dead bird.

Escondido withdrew one of the rifles from its saddle holster and rested the butt on his thigh as he gave a soft *chick, chick* to his nag.

The he looked at the Boy and drew his finger to his lips.

CHAPTER 11

Cities ain't got nothing left for you, Boy.

And yet, Sergeant, I've always wanted to go into them. To know what's in them.

Places where you might have lived, Boy, had things been different.

Sergeant Presley's voice seemed to ignore Escondido's whispered commentary and remembrances as they led their horses through the dust and rubble.

I try to find myself in them, Sergeant Presley. I try to find who I might have been.

Why, Boy?

It might tell me who I am, Sergeant.

"I come through here must've been something like five years ago with a partner. Dan was his name." Escondido's face looked gray and dusty in the last orange light of day. His mouth, full of crooked teeth, hung open, sucking at the dry desert air.

The Boy could hear Escondido's heavy breathing.

They entered the long, crumpled stretch of casino row. Hollow-eyed windows gaped blindly down on them from along shell-dented walls.

"Said he might go in and jes' take a look around. I tells him it's jes' not done, Dan. Jes' not done."

They passed a burned U.S. Army tank poking its melted barrel out from a storefront whose sign had long since been scoured to meaninglessness.

M-1 Abrams, thought the Boy.

"Toughest hour of my life was waitin' for Dan to come out. I sat there holding that horse of his for the longest time. We'd had a good haul in lions that year. What was the point of going in?"

Ahead, a sweeping bridge spanned the gap between two casinos like a broken arm reaching out from the wreckage of a terrible accident to touch another victim.

"Worst part's just ahead," muttered Escondido.

Escondido cocked back the hammer on his long rifle.

This is what I mean, Boy. Told you not to get caught up in things and here you are, caught up.

I could answer you, he thought to Sergeant Presley. But you would tell me I was crazy. You would tell me that you are dead and the problems of this life no longer concern you. Wouldn't you?

"I waited an hour and he never come out," whispered Escondido.

The laughing started.

One voice cackled, clear and very near at once.

Moments later two others responded, as if only politely and at a mediocre jest.

Then another burst out, hysterically almost.

Finally the rest were laughing uncontrollably.

Sniggering.

Guffawing.

Giggling.

Snickering.

Hooting.

Wailing.

Sobbing.

Moaning.

Crying.

Laughter careened across the broken casino walls.

Laughter was everywhere.

"Keep straight on!" yelled Escondido over the echoing din.

For a moment there were almost-shadows within the recessed gloom of the buildings high above. Not quite, but almost.

Leading Horse, the Boy pulled his tomahawk from his belt.

"They won't come out. Never do. But you don't want to go in after 'em all the same," warned Escondido.

They crossed the shadow of the broken bridge and a sink crashed to the dusty pavement behind them.

Horse reared and snarled fearfully.

The Boy held him around the neck, whispering softly.

"I know. I know. I know," he said over and over.

Once they were almost out from underneath the broken walkway, Escondido muttered, "I think that's what all the silliness is about. Trying to get us to come in and take a look."

A scabbed face, pale and haunted, appeared for a moment behind dusty shards of broken glass three stories up. Whether it was a man or a woman, who could say.

They passed on and the laughter seemed to fade in quiet increments. Finally there is a single painful scream.

In the hours that passed between the ruins of Reno and the river, Horse began to favor his unhurt legs, limping with the left hind leg. The Boy knew a powerful infection had already set in.

"He can't go much farther," said the Boy.

"He'll have to. Another few hours to the foot of the mountains and then the river. I won't sleep down here tonight."

They rode on, passing through lonely crumbling hills in the weak last light of day. When the sun finally fell behind the lowest of the Sierra Nevada, the land turned to purple and the smell of sage hung heavy in the shadows.

"Another hour and we'll be alongside the river. Once we're to it my hunting lodge won't be much farther on. I won't waste a bullet on your horse. Load 'em myself and there's precious few left now. Understand?"

The Boy said nothing as darkness settled across the lonely spaces that surrounded them. They heard the river long before they saw it, babbling in the moonlight. Its wide curves followed an old broken highway off to one side. Long, flat swathes of calm river erupted, burbling, over stones, and beyond that, small waterfalls marked their climb up alongside the river's fall.

Horse was badly limping when Escondido stopped. They were on a wide turn below a small pass. The river, off to their left, was little more than soft noise. Escondido seemed to rise for a moment off his horse's back, smelling the wind. The Boy tasted the night air also and found charred wood.

When they came to the river crossing that led to Escondido's lodge, the Boy could see the charred remains of wood and stone from across the rock-filled river.

On the other side Escondido said nothing and climbed down from his nag. He walked into the midst of the burnt timber and ash. "Still warm." He laughed. "Thought they'd burn me out, they did."

The Boy got down off Horse and began to inspect the wound again. When he touched it, Horse danced away from him. He removed his pack and led Horse down the river. The water was cold, startlingly cold as he washed Horse's wound. At first Horse wouldn't stand for it, but as the cool water numbed the heat in the wound, the big horse tolerated the cleansing.

By the time the Boy led Horse back up to the clearing where once the lodge watched the creek and the highway beyond, Escondido had built a fire.

"I'm gonna tell you something you don't want to hear," said Escondido above the clatter of a pot he set on the fire. "I'm lit out at first light. I'm done with this side of the mountains. It ain't safe and it's gittin' a lot more dangerous. Time was it was just me between here and the Hillmen. Now all them southern tribes is comin' north, just itchin' fer a fight with the Chinese. This is my last hunt. Tomorrow I ride for Auburn. After that, who knows? There's a widow for me somewhere, I guess."

They watched the fire. Escondido cut branches from a sapling and roasted strips of lion meat.

"This part's the part you ain't gonna like. So here it is. That horse needs to rest and even if he does that, ain't no guarantee he's gonna make it. In two days or sooner we'll have snow and if his infection is gonna come, it'll kill him before we make it within the gates o' the outpost."

They were silent, each watching the meat and fire, the wood turning to ash, the orange coals beneath.

Escondido rose to turn the strips of lion and settled back down onto an old blanket.

"I come here twenty seasons musta been. Every summer I'd cross them mountains above us and come down here to hunt. First few days I got the place in order, then I had a whole operation to set up. Shoulda seen it. Hides tannin', big porch I like to set on of an evenin'."

"There was no trade in hides with the Hillmen 'fore the Chinese set up the outpost there in Auburn. Hillmen coulda cared less about lion hides. The whole bunch of 'em was different in every way. Lived out in the woods and only came together once a year when they'd get up a hunt or needed to fight one of the other tribes. I finally figured out why they called themselves the Hillmen when me and Danitra set up camp near the old school the year before it burned down. One night I was havin' a look for anything useful and I saw that their old football team was called the Hillmen. Now they live alone out in the deep woods mostly, but they still think of themselves as some old football team from before the bombs. It was how they told the difference between them and strangers. Crazy, huh? But not really — makes more sense than some of the other tribes."

The fire popped and the aroma of roasting meat caught the night's breeze as sparks rose into the dark sky.

"Not much fat in lion," noted Escondido.

Then…

"I'll miss this place for the rest of my days."

The mule honked at some ground squirrel. Escondido watched the forest for a long moment, his coal-black eyes wide in the dancing light of the fire.

"So, if you could ride with me, I don't think you'd make it. Or more to the point, I don't think yer horse'd make it. So I'm leavin' you. Sorry. That's the way it has to be."

When the Boy failed to protest, his face calm, almost asleep in the firelight, Escondido said, "I'll show you a few things in the morning, maybe even some bushes that'll help with the healing. If you get to work on a shelter, you'll be ready if them tribes come back lookin' for me. Most likely they'll take to you more than they ever did me. They're tribal like you. Don't like city people like me. Hate the Chinese, they do. But you, you'll be fine I suspect."

They ate the lion and fell asleep near the fire. The night came on cold and the Boy dreamed of faces in windows. His last thought before he closed his eyes beneath the broken crystal of night was of faces. He remembered faces, though he did not remember who they belonged to. What was Sergeant Presley's face like? He wondered and for a moment he could not remember its shape. But when he thought of the Sergeant's rare smile, the face came back to him. And he was asleep.

CHAPTER 12

Snow fell and had been falling since they first woke. Now it was coming down steadily. High above, white clouds had replaced the startling blue of morning. Escondido, on the far side of the river and rounding the curve of the old highway that wound its way up across the pass, did not turn to see the Boy one last time, and then he was gone.

The wind rushed through the pines and made the only sound of the place where once Escondido's hunting lodge stood.

You got to prioritize, Boy!

And he did. The Boy knew he had to get moving. There were three things to do.

Make a shelter.

Gather healing herbs for Horse.

Find food.

But for a long moment he stood there. It was so quiet in between the thundering gusts of wind that shook all the pines at once that he could hear snowflakes landing on the ground all around him. Or so he thought.

Escondido left him with a simple knowledge of the area's herbs and inhabitants. The lions wouldn't come up

56

this far and they didn't like the cold anyway. There were some wolves. But wolves were wolves. There was a way to handle them. Then there was the bear: a mother brown bear, one of the worst kind. Two seasons ago, Escondido related, she had two cubs. This year he didn't see the cubs. But the bear lived in a cave upriver at the top of a small conical hill. A small mountain even.

"You'd be wise to steer clear of her altogether. The brown are the worst. Man-eaters."

Horse was on his side now. HIs large dark eyes were weak and milky. Often he would raise his head to make sure the Boy was near. But even that act seemed too much for him.

So what do you do first, Boy? Make a plan. Get moving. Get to work. Do something. Make a decision. If you don't, circumstances will decide for you. The enemy loves to tell you what to do.

It was the voice of Sergeant Presley, heard over a thousand camps at morning, in the frosty nights of Michigan when they'd barely survived. Down South, crossing the big river, he'd heard the Sergeant plan and tell him to do the same.

It's all you got now, Boy!

The Boy gathered herbs. He found most of them not far from the river. Most of them were dying as winter came on.

Will that affect their potency?

Don't matter, Boy. It's all you got right now.

He spent the rest of the morning mashing the herbs and slowly adding water until all became paste. He boiled the paste for a while, per Escondido's instructions. He applied the hot paste after having taken Horse to the river to clean the wound once more in the icy water, in which Horse's legs gave out for a moment and he stumbled, casting a look at the Boy as if they were both embarrassed to the point of death. After, when the paste was hot and went on Horse's wounded flank, after Horse lay down, his eyes resigned to the smoking fire, the Boy murmured, "I didn't see that. Let's just forget about that." The Boy covered him with his only blanket.

Afternoon, thin and cold, settled across the little river. There was no warmth left in the big stones and a breeze could be seen in the pines atop the surrounding mountains.

The Boy began to hack at the burnt lumber of Escondido's lodge, salvaging any usable beams for shelter. There weren't many. Near the river, he found fallen trees and in dragging them, he was soon exhausted.

If I had Horse right now this would be easier.

When night fell, what he had was little more than a two-sided lean-to. The open side faced the mountain wall that rose above their camp. Moving Horse within the lean-to, the Boy built a fire. Later he gathered loose wood from the forest floor and brown grass for Horse.

It was night now and he didn't mind the dark or the forest. He had known such places his whole life.

CHAPTER 13

In the night, keeping the fire high, face burning hot, body and back cold, the Boy sat staring into the shifting flames. Occasionally he simply watched Horse. He tried to make a plan for the coming morning beyond this endless freezing night.

Fishing in the river.

Food.

Traps.

How to improve the shelter.

The snow was coming down thick and silent. It hissed as it fell into the fire.

Even with the fire, it was cold. But Horse slept and that was good. Or at least the Boy hoped it was good.

On nights like this, when it was too cold, Sergeant Presley would talk, telling him things, teaching him. Sometimes they would break camp and simply walk to keep warm. The Boy remembered walking in the freezing rain outside Detroit.

Later he remembered the heavy warmth of late summer when they finally reached the Capitol in Washington, D.C.

Sergeant Presley's Mission, he'd called it.

They'd come upon the old Capitol the day before, broken buildings overgrown by blankets of green. Cracked highways had fallen into swampy water thick with flies and insects.

I got to go in there, Boy, and there ain't no use you comin' in with me, said Sergeant Presley on that long-ago day.

It was hot and sticky in the late afternoon. Summer. It had been raining for much of the week.

Let's make camp and then I'll go in and look for what I got to find— what I know won't be there. But I'll go in all the same.

They'd been living well that year. They'd fought for Marshall and his men the spring before. A range war in Pennsylvania. When the war was over, they'd been granted permission to move on into Maryland. When they'd gone from the warlord Marshall and his expanded kingdom, they'd had good clothes and supplies. They'd found nothing but wild people after that — abandoned farms and shadows in the thick forest and overgrown towns. The small villages and loose power that men like Marshall had held over the interior lands between the ravaged cities would not be found along the devastated ruin of the eastern coast.

One morning, in the center of a town that had burned to the ground long before the Boy had been born, standing in the overgrown weed-choked outline of an intersection, Sergeant Presley said, *If there is anyone here, I'll find them in the Capitol — or in the President's bunker below the White House.* They were both looking at an old fire hydrant that had been knocked out into the road. The road was covered in hardened dirt that had once been muddy sludge.

Who am I kidding? Sergeant Presley had suddenly erupted into the silence of the place. *There ain't anybody left. There wasn't since it all went sideways and there hasn't been since. I know that. I've known it all along!*

His shouted words fell into the thick forest turning to swamp. An unseen bird called out weirdly, as if in response.

But orders are orders, he'd said softly, his sudden rage gone. *And someone had to come and find out. Once I know, we'll head back to the Army in Oakland. We got to cross the whole country. You up for that, Boy?*

Sergeant Presley had smiled at him then.

The Boy remembered, nodding to himself.

Still, it'd be nice if someone was there. That'd be something, Sergeant Presley had said.

But there hadn't been.

Now, beside the fire in the mountains as the first big snow of winter came on, almost to the other side of the country, the Boy knew there hadn't been anyone in the old Capitol or at the President's bunker beneath the White House.

Sergeant Presley was gone all that next day.

In the morning the Sergeant had put on some special gear they'd found in a place called Fort. They'd spent two weeks looking through the place, scouring warehouses that had long since been looted, searching through ash and rubble. Finally, in a desk drawer they'd found the gear Sergeant Presley had been looking for.

Some clerk probably got told to bring in his MOPP gear in case things went that way in those days. So he brings it in and his section sergeant checks it and then sends him off to do paperwork. And now I'm gonna wear it and hope the charcoal and other protectants are gonna hold out long enough to get me to the White House without getting radiation poisoning.

When he'd left, wearing the dull green cloth and rubber shoes, fitting the gas mask and hood over his head, Sergeant Presley had looked like a monster.

He was gone all that day.

Sitting by the fire, the Boy couldn't remember what he'd done after that. Probably exploring with Horse.

In the swarming-insect early evening, outside the Capitol in the swamp camp, it was misty. The gloomy ruins of the Capitol faded in the soft light of dusk. It looked like a dream. The Boy remembered that in the last moments of light, the Capitol, whatever it had once been, looked like a dream castle — like something that might have once had meaning for him. Like things that seem so important in a dream, but when you awake, those things seem of little value and you can't imagine why they'd held such a place in the dream.

That was what the Capitol had looked like to the Boy in those last moments of daylight.

In the early evening of that long lost waiting-day, Sergeant Presley had finally come up the hill to their camp above the swamp. Threading his way through the tall grass, Sergeant Presley took off the bug-eyed gas mask. He dropped or threw the mask off into the sea of silent yellow grass. He tore off the suit, coughing. Crystal droplets of sweat stood out in his short curly hair.

The Boy gave him water from their bag, then some of the cakes they always made back then.

Still hot in there. Sergeant Presley coughed.

The Boy said nothing.

"Hot" meant forbidden. If sometimes they saw a city on the horizon, like the one by the big lake, its tall towers skeletal and bent, Sergeant Presley would simply say *still hot.* And sometimes he would add, *When you're an old man, if you live long enough, you can go in there. But I never will.*

Sergeant Presley drank more water and coughed.

I woulda brought you somethin', but it's too hot in there. I swear I came right up on a bomb crater. Must've been low yield. But hell if it didn't go up twenty degrees. I look around and everything is black ash. Even the marble on one of them old government buildings, the House I think it was called, had turned black.

He coughed again.

'He will never stop coughing,' thought the Boy. That was when the coughing had started. That day everything changed, though at the time neither of them knew it.

Sergeant Presley knew it, he suspected. But he didn't say anything.

Sergeant Presley coughed again.

Made it all the way to the White House.

He coughed and then drank, swallowing thickly.

There was never anything there. It wasn't a direct hit. See, back then our enemies were fighting unconventionally. Dirty-bomb strikes by remote-controlled aircraft launched within our borders. Terrorists. They went after Washington early on. We knew that. It wasn't until later, when China got involved, that we didn't know for sure what had really happened anywhere. After that it was just plain dark everywhere.

He chewed numbly on the cake, staring at their wispy fire. The Boy watched him, saying nothing.

The bunker was a deep hole. Must've used the Chinese equivalent of a J-Dam on it. I saw one of those take out the TransAmerica Building in Frisco. I'll show you when we get there. Anyways, they must have used a "bunker buster" on it. Then, whether before or after, there must have been a nuclear strike, probably an airburst. Whole place was cooked.

He coughed, choking on the cake.

Now the Boy looked up at the night sky. It had stopped snowing. The stars were out, shimmering in the late night or early morning. His face was hot. He stood up and walked to the cliff wall.

He leaned against it, feeling the cold stone on his back.

You should sleep, Boy. Tomorrow's gonna be a long day.

'I wish,' thought the Boy, 'that all of the days that had been were long days. I wish you were here.'

He did not hear the voice of Sergeant Presley and wondered if he had ever heard it. Or if he would ever hear it again.

As he walked back to the fire, a pebble fell off the side of the cliff and the Boy turned, staring up into the heights. His shadow loomed large against the wall. He saw his powerful, strong right arm and when he moved the withered left arm, it looked little more than a thin branch.

He stared at the wall and its many shadows. For a moment he could almost see a man.

The man was sitting. Hunched over. Staring sightlessly out into the world. His hand was holding something up to his mouth.

A cake.

It was as though he was looking at Sergeant Presley on that hot, sweaty, and very long day outside the ruins of the Capitol.

Sergeant Presley, sitting, tired, sweating. Eating a cake. Alive.

He turned back to the fire after staring at the image for too long. But he wished it were true. He wished Sergeant Presley were here with him now, across the country. Almost to the Army. Alive.

He picked up a piece of burnt wood from Escondido's lodge.

He turned back to the cliff wall.

And he began to draw that long lost day. Sergeant Presley at the end of his mission. At the end of his country. At the beginning of the end of his life.

CHAPTER 14

At first light he checked the river. In a pool off the main channel he spotted three trout lying in the current, close to the bottom. He watched them for a long while, listening to the constant, steady crash of the river downstream.

The backs of the trout remind him of broken green glass bottles he'd once seen in a building where he and Sergeant Presley had slept for the night. *Wine bottles,* Sergeant Presley muttered simply, as an epitaph over the heap of green glass. The Boy remembered holding a piece up, examining it in the wavering light of their fire. *Careful,* Sergeant Presley had warned him. *Don't cut yourself, Boy.*

He found a long piece of driftwood waiting on the rocks by the river, left by the springtime flooding of that year. He returned to camp with the driftwood and after inspecting Horse's wound, which looked bad and worse now in the bright light of morning, he dug out wet grass from underneath the snowfall and laid it near Horse's head. Horse seemed not to notice.

He laid more wood on the fire, its wetness making white smoke erupt into the cold air.

The Boy sat down next to the smoking fire with the driftwood stick lying away from his body. Taking one end of the wood, he cut long peels of bark away from himself and soon the white flesh of the wood underneath lay exposed. He fed the soft peels of wood into the fire as he continued to bring the stick to a point. In the end, it became a sharp spear.

He returned to the pool and waited. There was no sign of the broken-wine-bottle-colored trout. He sat on his haunches watching the gentle current drift along the bottom of the rock-covered pool.

Later, one of the fish entered the pool. The Boy waited, watching it move first one way and then another. He got little flashes of white from off its belly as it turned. Finding the current, the emerald-colored trout settled into it. After a moment, when the Boy knew it would be sleeping, he raised up, leaning over the pool, the spear drawn back over his good shoulder, the point just above the surface of the water.

He waited.

He felt a breath enter his lungs and as he let the air go, when there was little left in him, he plunged the spear through the surface, catching the trout in the back, just behind its head. It bent to the left, sending up a splash of water with its wide tail, and the Boy hauled it from the pool, amazed at his prize. Its rainbow-colored flanks fell away from its wine-bottle back, the white belly pure and meaty. It was a creature of beauty.

When the catch was gutted and spitted over the smoking fire, the Boy made more herb paste and applied it to Horse's wound, wiping away the oozing pus as best he could.

He'd tried to lead Horse to the water before doing this, but the animal wouldn't even bother to raise his head, much less stand.

"Okay, rest then," said the Boy and heard the croak in his voice against the deafening fall of water over rock.

When the fish was cooked, he walked while eating, back to the drawing of Sergeant Presley on the cliff wall. He'd worked on it late into the night, immune to the cold. When he'd returned to the fire, he'd felt frozen. The heat stung his skin as it warmed him. He'd thought the drawing had been complete, but now looking at it in the late-morning light he could see where features would need to be added — filled in and shaded.

In the afternoon he tried to improve the shelter, but other than laying green pine branches across the top, there was little that could be done.

You've got to find better shelter, Boy! If this lodge was here from before the war then chances are there are others like it.

The Boy had seen many buildings from Before built in clusters; the towns they had passed through and the cities he had wanted to visit. Clusters.

In the afternoon he walked upriver with his tomahawk and knife. His withered left side felt stiff, but he concentrated on its movements, controlling it, willing his leg to step over fallen logs instead of dragging as it would've liked to if he'd ridden Horse for days at a time.

He heard a loud twig snap underneath his feet.

Too loud, Boy! No go.

Everything Sergeant Presley had taught him had been graded. When the time had come for the Boy to perform a task, the standard for pass or fail was always "good to go" or "no go." He'd hated when Sergeant Presley wrenched his mouth to the side and said, *No go.*

Upstream the river began to curve to the north, winding through a series of rapids. Off to the left he could see the steep, conical mountain Escondido had warned him of, where at the top a bear made its den.

It was winter now. Bears should be asleep.

There were no other lodges, or if there had been, what remained of them could not be found.

It was hard to imagine the world as a place where people could either live in cities or in the forest. What was so special about cities?

You always wanted to go there, Boy.

I did. I wanted to know what was in them.

And…

What would I have been like if I had lived in one?

Standing at the bend in the river, feeling his withered leg and arm stiffen in the late-afternoon cold as the sun fell behind tall peaks to the west, he thought of people he once knew and could not remember.

They had always lived in the cold plains. His first memory was of running. Of a woman screaming. Of seeing the sky, blue and cold in one moment, and the ground, yellow stubble, race by in the next.

Sergeant Presley had rarely mentioned "your people."

Not like in tents, not like your people.

All gone over to animals, not like your people.

They don't ride horses, like your people do.

That night the temperature dropped and the snow came down in hard clumps without end. He lay next to Horse, who moved little and whose breathing was shallow. At one point, the Boy was so cold he thought he should surely die.

When he awoke in the morning everything was covered in snow.

The best time to do something about a thing is to do it now, Boy!

We won't last out here another night.

When Horse opened his eyes they fluttered.

You won't make it out here like this, will you, Horse?

He laid his hand on Horse's belly, feeling the heat both comforting and sickening at once.

He knew what he had to do. He had known it in the freezing night when the snow had stopped falling and the wind rushed through the pines, seeming to make things even colder than when the snow had fallen. Even the sound of the icy water falling along the rapids seemed to make the world colder.

The Boy had known in the night what he must do.

He'd waited for Sergeant Presley to tell him not to do it.

"You would say," he thought aloud, pretending to be Sergeant Presley's voice. "You would say it was fool's business. That's what you would say."

He waited, listening to the rush of the water in the river.

He looked upriver, his eyes falling on the small, steep, conical mountain.

You would say that.

Ain't nothin' but a thang, Boy. Mind over matter. You don't mind, it don't matter.

You would say that also.

You got to kill that bear, Boy. No two ways about it.

CHAPTER 15

That morning he collected three long poles of fresh wood that wouldn't snap. Working with his knife he sharpened the ends into stakes, hardening them in the fire until the tips were black.

By noon he'd fed Horse, who ate little of the fire-dried grass the Boy had placed before him. He sat by the fire putting a fresh edge on the steel tomahawk Sergeant Presley had given him. Its bright finish was a thing made in the past, never to be seen again. Often, when they had encountered strangers, he'd seen their eyes fall to it, wanting it for their own.

Laying aside the sharpened tomahawk, he gave the knife an edge. They'd made these knives at the Cotter family forge. Sergeant Presley's knife lay wrapped within a bundle the Boy had carried away from the grave on the side of the road surrounded by the wild corn that had seemed to grow everywhere, a bundle the Boy had no desire to open.

You might need it for this one, Boy.

But the Boy couldn't see what an extra knife might do for him. He knew if his plan was a "no go" and he found himself down to his own knife, there wouldn't be much hope left in an extra knife.

That's right, Boy; work smarter, not harder. Knife work is hard work.

Let's hope it doesn't get to that.

The last thing the Boy would need for his plan would be what was left of the precious parachute cord. There was less than thirty feet of it now. As a child, the Boy had always been fascinated by the large coil, amazed at it, as he always was of the things from Before. There had been so much of the parachute cord, it had once seemed endless, always coiled about Sergeant Presley's shoulder to hip as they walked. One time Sergeant Presley had even made a knotted section of it for him to play with, muttering, *Merry Christmas*, as he'd handed it to the Boy on that long-ago winter day. Years passed, and traps and snares and other bits that could no longer be salvaged had reduced the large coil to less than thirty feet.

The Boy withdrew the last of it from his pack.

I don't want to use even this, but if I have to I will.

He thought of the bear.

He'd seen bears killed. The Cotter family hunted them for sport and meat. He'd followed one hunting party and watched them run down a small, fast black bear that was more interested in getting away than fighting. In the end, it had played dead until they'd put a bolt under its left shoulder blade.

They had seen big bears in the Rockies. Most of them had kept their distance, or charged, only to veer off. Horse was good for scaring things away. Once Horse went up on his hind legs, most animals knew he wasn't interested in running.

He looked at Horse.

Are you dying too? Like Sergeant Presley?

He patted the big brown belly; Horse stirred only slightly.

"I'm going to clear out a place for us to hole up in through the rest of winter." Then, "I'll be back."

He went down to the river and speared another of the broken-wine-bottle trout. Gutting and filleting the trout, he laid its body out on planks of charred wood over the embers of the fire. After eating the fish he collected his gear, shouldering the three heavy poles and placing the thin coil of rope over his head to hang down from his neck.

Everything was moving too fast.

He could feel the tomahawk hanging from his belt, the knife in its sheath at his back.

What am I missing?

Mind over matter, Boy.

You don't mind, it don't matter.

He climbed the conical hill, hauling himself up its snow-covered granite ledges. He avoided any pines that grew out of the rock, knowing them to be untrustworthy because of the shallow soil they grew in.

He found the cave just underneath the top of the hill. It would be a useless exercise if the cave was too low for Horse to squeeze into. What would be the use of dislodging the bear only to find his shelter too small? But the cave was like a wide frown on a mouth. It was tall enough at its highest point for Horse. Getting him up here would be another story — collecting wood also.

It's not ideal, but it's all I have.

You're assuming victory, Boy. First you got to kill that bear. But it's good you're thinkin' about tomorrow all the same.

A wide, flat ledge lay before the opening and below that, a sheer drop to the river below. He set the poles down, laying them gently in a crevice running through the cold gray granite. The poles came together, echoing, and the Boy waited, unsure what he would do if the bear were suddenly to appear.

I'll attack her.

That would be bad, Boy.

But what else was there to do? If she chases me I won't get away. If I attack, maybe she'll run.

In the moment that followed, the Boy could hear only the distant sound of the river below.

On a thick tree, stunted and growing out of the rock, he could see the deep indentations of the bear's claw marks.

What do you know about your enemy, Boy?

It's a bear.

A sow.

Cubs two years back, which means they've left.

I don't know if it's a grizzly or one of the browns, which are the worst. Too bad it's not one of the black ones.

And you would ask me about the battlefield. That's what you would ask me next, Sergeant Presley.

Where you gonna fight, Boy?

He looked at the flat ledge. It wasn't more than twenty feet wide and as much across.

I could make a trap, but I don't know where. I'd have to get her down the hill and chasing me.

Deadfalls are the best, Boy.

To do that, I'll have to get her down the side of the mountain and into the forest. Even then, the ground is frozen. It would take me a day or two to make a pit. One more night like the last and we won't make it.

So it's the ledge then, Boy.

I go in hard with a spear. If she's asleep I put one into her. I back up, grab another and put it in. By the time I get to the third...

You'll be at the at the edge of the cliff. That drop'll do the job, Boy.

She'll have to have a reason to go over.

If you've put three spears into her, Boy, you'll be the reason. All she can think of at that point is wanting you dead and then going back to sleep.

Here's what you do, you anchor the parachute cord and tie it about your waist, Boy. Wait until the last second and she'll follow you over.

Numbly he took the coil of rope off his neck. His heart was beating quickly.

He told himself to calm down. To stop.

Just do this. Don't think too much about it.

He crept toward the frowning entrance of the cave. There was a short drop inside. On the floor below, he could see a shapeless mass in the dark. The cave smelled of animals. He listened. He heard nothing. He waited, watching the shapeless mass. His vision narrowed as he stared hard, willing the details to be revealed.

He blinked and looked away as his vision began to close to a pinpoint. His heart was pounding in his ears.

Stop.

He crawled back out onto the ledge.

The drop was a good two hundred feet into the rapids.

I'm not really going to do this, am I?

Mind over matter, Boy.

He played the rope out, tying it about his waist.

They don't make this stuff anymore. Airborne Ranger gear, Boy. Best ever.

You'd said that, every time you brought it out, Sergeant. Every time we made a trap or a snare, you said that.

I was proud of what had once been. Proud that someone had made parachute cord. I had no right to be, Boy. But I was proud all the same.

The Boy searched the underside of the ledge.

A few feet below the edge and off to the side, a rugged little pine jutted out from the rock wall.

It's all I have.

To the west, large clouds, gray and full, rolled across the high peaks.

More snow tonight.

It will be very cold.

He climbed down the cliff face.

He loved to climb.

For a boy who had been born crippled and could not run as others did, climbing was an activity where the playing field leveled.

He had always climbed.

The Boy clung to the side of the rock wall. He spent more rope than he would have liked securing it to the pine. But he had to.

When he'd climbed back onto the ledge his muscles were shaking.

I need water and I've forgotten to bring the bag.

What else am I forgetting?

He felt fear rise again as he cupped a handful of snow and put it in his mouth.

In just a moment I'll have to do this.

Stop.

Mind over matter, Boy.

I don't mind. It won't matter.

That's right, Boy. That's good.

A strong wind came off the mountain peaks above and whipped long hair into his green eyes.

He brushed it away.

What else am I forgetting?

When he picked up the first pole it felt too light.

It felt hollow like he could break it across his knee.

He laid it down just in front of the cliff's edge, pointing toward the frowning mouth of the cave.

The second pole felt heavier. He placed it at the entrance.

When he went back for the third, it felt lighter than the second and he switched it out. 'I'll want the heaviest one first,' he thought.

Crouching low and entering the cave, he felt the rope pull taut at his waist.

It won't reach. I won't be able to get close enough to make the most of the spear.

He undid the rope about his waist and changed to a slip knot.

This is how it works, he told himself.

Change of plans, he'd heard Sergeant Presley say.

Change of plans.

He laid the loop of rope at the base of the second pole.

When you fall back to this position, you slip the rope around your right wrist, Boy.

What about the left?

I can't trust that side.

What else am I forgetting?

Stop, he told his heart.

Stop.

He crept into the cave, the tip of the spear dead center on the sleeping mass.

There was a moment.

A moment to think and to have thought too much.

He felt it coming. He'd known it before at other times and knew it was best to stay ahead of such moments.

He drove the spear hard into the mass.

An instant later it was wrenched out of his hands as the bear turned over. He heard a dry snap of wood echo off the roof of the cave as he retreated back toward the entrance.

For a moment, the Boy took his eyes off the bear as he slipped the loop about his wrist and grabbed the spear, making sure to keep the trailing end of the parachute cord away from the end of the pole.

In that moment he could hear the roar of the bear. It filled the cave, and beneath the roar he could hear her claws clicking against the stone floor as she scrambled up toward him.

When he looked up, following the blackened tip of the spear, he found the grizzly's head, squat, flat, almost low beneath the main bulk of her body. She roared again, gnashing a full row of yellowed fangs.

He jabbed the spear into her face and felt the weapon go wide, glancing off bone.

He backed up a few steps and planted the butt of the long pole in the ground.

The grizzly, brown, shaggy, angry, lurched out onto the ledge. It rose up on its hind legs and the Boy saw that it might, if it came forward just a bit, impale itself on the pole if it attacked him directly. He adjusted the pole right underneath the heart of the raging bear.

The bear made a wide swipe with its paw smashing the pole three quarters of the way to the top.

In the same instant that the pole was wrenched from the Boy's grip, and as if the moment had caused an intensity of awareness, he felt the slip knot, its mouth still wide, float from off his wrist.

Stick to the plan, Boy! You can't change it now.

He'd heard that before.

His back foot, his good leg, planted at the edge of the cliff, the Boy raised the final pole.

The bear on hind legs wallowed forward.

The Boy checked to make sure the parachute cord was really gone.

It was.

The moment that hung between the Boy and the bear was brief and startlingly clear. To have questioned what must be done next would have been lethal to either.

The Boy loped forward and rammed the pole straight up and into the chest of the bear.

'There is no other way but this,' he thought in that moment of running.

'No other way but this.'

He felt the furry chest of the bear meet his grip on the pole.

He pushed hard and felt the arms of the bear on his shoulders. He felt a hot breathy roar turn to a whisper above the top of his head.

His arms were shaking.

His eyes were closed.

He was still alive.

He backed away from the belly of the bear, letting go of the pole as the bear fell off to one side.

He was covered in a thick, cold sweat.

There was no other way.

CHAPTER 16

In the moments that followed the death of the bear, routine took over, ways the Boy had known his whole life.

Bleed the animal.

Don't think about how close you came to her claws.

The knife at his back was out as he stood over the carcass, finding the jugular, his good hand shaking, and then a quick flick and blood was running out onto the granite of the Sierra Nevada.

Don't remember her hot breath on top of your head when there was little you could do but go forward with the pole.

Next he made a cut into the chest. Working from the breastbone up to the jaw, he cut through flesh and muscle. When the cut was made he took out his tomahawk, adjusted his grip once as he raised it above his head and then slammed it down onto the breastbone several times. Soon he was removing the organs. Heart, lungs, esophagus, bladder, intestines, and rectum.

My hands are shaking, Sergeant.

It's just the cold, Boy. Just the cold. Keep on workin'.

It is cold out and getting colder, which will be good for the meat, but I still have much work to do.

Walking stiffly, he descended the mountain and returned to camp. He gathered his gear and when that was done, he began to coax Horse to get up one more time.

Horse seemed stunned that the Boy would even consider such a thing, but before long, whispering and leading, patting and coaxing, the Boy had him up and on his legs.

"I'll carry everything, you just follow me. We're going someplace warm."

Late afternoon turned to winter evening as he led Horse up onto the mountain. Halfway up, as they worked side to side across the gray granite ledges, snow began to fall, and by the time they'd reached the top, the Boy was almost dragging Horse. Never once did he curse at the animal, knowing that he was already asking too much of his only friend. And for his part, Horse seemed to suffer through the climb as though death and the hardships that must come with it are inevitable.

At the top, the Boy dropped Horse's lead and began to collect what little firewood he could find. Soon there was a small fire inside the cave. He led Horse into the cave, expecting more protest than the snort Horse gave at the scent of the bear.

The fire cast flickering shadows along the inside of the cave and though there was a small vault, the cave was neither vast nor deep.

It'll be easier to keep warm, Boy. That's good.

The Boy put his blanket over Horse, who'd begun to tremble. He fed Horse from a sack of wild oats he kept for the times when there was nothing at hand to crop.

Horse chewed a bit and then seemed to lose interest.

That's not good.

The Boy left the sack open before Horse and returned to the carcass of the bear.

Snow fell in thick drifts across the ledge as the wind began to whip along the mountainside.

'It has to be done now,' the Boy thought to himself.

But I'll need wood. The fire has to be kept going.

In the dark he descended the mountain, working quickly among the howling pines to find as much dead wood as possible. Every time he stopped to look for wood in the thin light of the last of the day, he felt his weak side stiffen.

When he'd collected a large bundle of dead wood, he tied it with leather straps and climbed the mountain once again, almost crawling under the weight, as the scream of the howling winter night bit at his frozen ears.

I am so tired. I feel all the excitement and fear of the fight with the bear leaving me.

Nearing the ledge of the cave, he thought, 'I could go to sleep now.'

And for a long moment, on all fours, the bundle of wood crushing down upon his back, he stared long and hard at the rock beneath his numb fingers, thinking only of sleep.

Back in the cave he fed the wood that wasn't too wet to the fire, watching the smoke escape through some unseen fissure in the roof of the cave. He held his cracked and bleeding fingers next to the flames.

You'll need that skin, Boy.

The Boy knew what that meant.

He'd known and planned what he must do next without ever thinking it or saying that he would do it. But if he was to have the skin of the bear, then what needed to be done would need to be done soon.

The bear was too heavy to drag off the ledge, back here into the cave near the fire.

That'd be the easy way, Boy. Never take the easy way.

He held up a handful of oats to Horse. Horse sniffed at them but refused to eat as he turned his long head back to the fire.

Okay, you rest for now.

Outside the storm blasted past the ledge. Everything was white and gray and dark beyond, all at once.

When he found the snow-covered bear, he began the work of removing the skin.

He completed the cut up onto the bear's chest. He cut the legs and then began to skin the bear from the paws up. His strength began to fail as he worked the great hide off its back, but when he came to the head, he made the final cut and returned to the cave to warm himself again. He took a handful of the oats, watching Horse's sleeping eyes flutter, and ate them, chewing them into a paste and swallowing.

Returning to the wind and the night, he dragged the skin into the cave and laid it out on the floor.

I can work here for a while and be warm by the fire.

But he knew if the meat froze on the carcass he would never get it off the bone.

For a long time after that, he crouched over the bear, cutting strips of meat. When he'd gotten all the usable meat he washed it in the snow and took it back into the cave. He spitted two steaks and laid them on the fire.

Into the cold once again, he cracked open the bear's skull for the brains and took those inside, placing them near the skin.

For the rest of the night he worked with his tomahawk, scraping the skin of flesh and fat and blood. When all of it was removed, he stepped outside, carrying the waste to the edge of the cliff and dropping it over the side.

The storm had stopped.

It was startlingly cold out. His breath came in great vaporous clouds that hung for a moment over the chasm and the ice-swollen river below and were gone in the next. The stars were close at hand. Below, the river tumbled as sluggish chunks of ice floated in the moonlight.

He washed his hands in snow, feeling both a stinging and numbness on his raw flesh.

He stood watching the night.

Clouds, white and luminous, moved against the soft blue of the moonlit night. Below, the river and the valley were swaying trees and shining shadows of sparkling granite. 'I am alive,' he thought. 'And this is the most beautiful night of my life.'

Dawn light fell across the ledge outside the cave. The Boy looked up from the skin he'd worked on through the night. The light was golden, turning the stone ledge outside the cave from iron gray to blue.

He felt tired as he returned to the skin once more, rubbing the brains of the bear into the hide.

"This is all I can do to cure it," he said aloud in his tiredness, as if someone had been asking what he was doing. As if Sergeant Presley had been talking to him through the night. But now, in the light of morning it all seemed a dream, a dream of a night in which he worked at the remains of a bear.

But I have not slept.

"There is too much to do," he said aloud.

You done everything, Boy. Now sleep.

The Boy lay down next to the fire and slept.

CHAPTER 17

In the days that followed:

He rubbed ash from the fire into the hide of the bear.

He smoked meat in dried strips.

He swept the cave with pine branches.

He had to lead Horse down the mountain to drink from the river at least once a day. He could think of no method to bring Horse enough water.

Winter fell across the mountains like a thick blanket of ice.

The Boy constructed a thatched door to block the entrance to the cave.

At night he stared at the wall and the moving shadows in the firelight.

By the time he'd collected firewood, watered Horse, and foraged enough food, the daylight was waning and he felt tired.

In the night he enjoyed listening to the fire and watching the shadows on the cave wall.

Winter had come to stay, and it seemed, on frost-laced mornings and nights of driving sleet, that it had always been this way and might continue without end.

CHAPTER 18

One night, as the wind howled through the high pines, he took Sergeant Presley's bundle out of his pack.

He stared at it for a long moment, listening to the wind and trying to remember that autumn morning when he'd found it next to the body.

Take the map and go west, Boy. Find the Army. Tell them who I was. Tell them there's nothing left.

In the bundle was a good shirt Sergeant Presley had found and liked to wear in the evening after they had bathed in a stream or creek and made an early camp. That was the only time Sergeant Presley would wear the good shirt he'd found behind the backseat of a pickup truck they'd searched in the woods of North Carolina.

Red flannel.

This my red flannel shirt, Boy. Shore is comfortable.

The shirt would be there.

The map. Sergeant Presley's knife. The shirt.

He undid the leather thong on the bundle and tied it about his wrist.

The soft cloth bundle opened and out came the shirt, and within were the knife and the map. And there was a leather thong attached to a long gray feather, white at the tip, its spine broken.

He laid the knife on his whetstone.

He laid the map on another stone, one he ate on by the fire. He left the broken feather and its thong in the bundle.

He held the shirt up and smelled Sergeant Presley in a draft coming off the fire.

He took off his vest and put on the shirt.

It was comfortable. Soft. The softest thing he'd ever felt. And warm.

He sat by the fire.

When he took up the map, he stared at it. He had seen the map many times, but always when it was laid out, Sergeant Presley was making a note or muttering to himself.

The Boy unfolded it, laying it on the ground. It was large. It was both hard and smooth. In the light it reflected a dull shine.

He stared at the markings.

Above Reno he read:

CHINESE PARATROOPERS. DUG IN. BATTALION STRENGTH.

Over Salt Lake City, in the state of Utah, he read:

GONE

Over Pocatello, in the state of Idaho, he read:

REFUGEE CAMP FIVE YEARS AFTER. OVERRUN BY SLAVERS.

Above this, across the whole of the northwestern states, was a red circle with the words "WHITE SUPREMACISTS" written in the center.

Across Omaha in big letters was the word "PLAGUE," and then a small red face with X's for eyes. There were red-faced "X eyes" listed over place names all the way to Louisville, in the state of Kentucky.

At Washington, D.C., he found an arrow that led into the middle of the ocean. Words were written in Sergeant Presley's precise hand.

MADE IT TO D.C. IT'S ALL GONE. BUNKER PROBABLY HIT EARLY IN THE WAR. NO REMNANTS OF GOV'T AT THIS LOCATION. TOOK ME TWENTY-EIGHT YEARS TO MAKE IT HERE.

On the back of the map the Boy found names.

CPT DANFORTH, KIA CHINESE SNIPER IN SACRAMENTO

SFC HAN, KIA CHINESE SNIPER IN SACRAMENTO

CPL MALICK, KIA RENO

SPC TWOOMEY, KIA RENO

PFC UNGER, MIA, RENO

PFC CHO, MIA RENO

PV2 WILLIAMS, KIA RENO

And…

LOLA

There was no mention of Escondido's "Auburn" on the map. The Boy traced the highway marked 80 as it crossed the mountain range and then fell into Sacramento in the State of California. After that, the road ran straight to Oakland. Written over Oakland, the Boy found I CORPS. Across the bay in San Francisco, circled in red, he saw the word CHINESE.

He stared at the broken feather and experienced the fleeting sensation of a memory. Which one, he could not tell.

CHAPTER 19

Horse had not died.

Winter broke and the Boy could hear ice crack in the river below. It was still cold.

The Boy led Horse to the bottom of the small mountain, down its icy ledges, watching Horse to make sure he didn't slip. There was only one close call, near the bottom. In the silence that followed the recovery, Horse seemed angry at his own inability and cantered off into the forest, snorting and thrashing his tail.

The Boy let him go, knowing Horse needed to forget the incident as much as the animal wanted the Boy to never remember it.

He was embarrassed, thought the Boy, keeping even the look of such a thought to himself.

For the rest of the morning they rode the snowy forest carefully. In the early afternoon, they crossed the river and came upon the great curve of the highway that climbed upward toward the pass. For a while the Boy left Horse to himself, letting him crop what little there was to find.

This is good. We need to be back on this road again. Even if just for a few moments of sunshine. It feels good to have the road under my feet and Horse's hooves. We have been too long away from the road.

He wandered back to their old camp.

Against the cliff wall, the Boy found the drawing of Sergeant Presley near the snow-covered remains of Escondido's charred lodge.

That evening back at the cave, as both he and Horse drowsily watched the fire, he took a piece of charcoal and shaved it lightly with his knife.

He considered the wall of the cave and saw no face or image in the flickering light. And yet he wanted to draw something.

He thought of the bear and quickly dismissed the thought. There were nights when he awakened in the dark and the bear was chasing him across the forest floor, and no matter how hard he urged his withered leg to move, it would not. Usually he awoke just before the bear caught him, but there were nights when he didn't, and in those nightmare moments, he could feel the bear's hot embrace, and the terror seemed a thing that would swallow him whole.

So he did not need a reminder of the bear.

He drew the mane first. The mane of the Big Lion. The male. That was what he remembered most in the times when he thought back to the night the lions surrounded him.

Next he added the eyes, the eyes that had seemed so cool and yet communicative, and then the teeth and the body, and the shadows that were his females. He drew the female who had watched the big male. She had been at his side, still watching him. They were together.

When the Boy was finished he lay on his back, watching the portrait of the lions, remembering them this way and forgetting the skins and the blood of that hot day.

On the cold morning when they finally left the cave the Boy was wearing the skin of the bear over his back and down his left side. The withered side.

This way others won't be able to see where I am weak.

That's camouflage, Boy, camouflage.

They rode out past the bubbling river and up the slope, onto the rising highway.

It was a cold day, and the wind came straight down the old highway, but the skies above were blue. Soon they left the familiar, and each new curve in the road was a strange and almost alien world of chopped granite, high forests, and cold, deep mountain lakes.

'Winter can only last so long, and life in the cave would have made me weak,' the Boy thought.

Horse can no longer survive on what little grass I can dig out from underneath the snow. For me, the bear meat is long gone and even the fish from the stream seem harder to catch because there are so few now.

For most of that day they rode high into the mountains, and in the evening they camped under the remains of a broken bridge.

The fire was weak and the air was cold enough to make him think maybe they'd left the cave too soon, but Horse seemed stronger in the evening than when they first began the day's journey.

It was good for him to work so hard today.

The Boy slept, waking throughout the night at each new sound beyond the firelight.

In the morning they came upon a pole covered in the skulls of animals and garlands of acorns, a marker set in the dirt by the broken road.

You know what that means, Boy. Someone's land.

High above he could see the pass that leads down into the foothills beyond. Beyond the pass, the city of Sacramento and finally on to the bay and I Corps.

I could ride hard and bypass the people who live here.

It was later, as they rode steadily up the broken grade, that the Boy realized they were being followed. Across the valley he saw movement. But when he stopped to look he saw nothing. Still, he knew they were watching him.

There was little left of the bent highway that once crossed over the pass. What had not been covered in rockslide had fallen away into a dark forest below. The years of hard winter had taken their toll on the old highway.

Men came out from the forest floor. They made their way to the foot of the trail the Boy was leading Horse down. Horse, sniffing the wind, gave a snort, and when the Boy looked behind, he saw more men coming out along their back trail, high above them on rocky granite ledges. They carried bows, a weapon he couldn't use because of his withered left hand.

The men were dressed for hunting: skins and bows. They were dark skinned, but every so often he saw fair skin among them.

Near the bottom of the trail he mounted Horse and adjusted the bearskin across his left side.

At that moment he thought it would be nice to have a piece of steel from an old machine he could hold onto with his left hand beneath the skin. A beaten highway sign with a leather strap perhaps.

He took hold of the tomahawk with his strong right hand, letting it hang loosely along his muscled thigh.

The men were mostly short and bandy legged.

All were covered in wide, dark tattoos that swirled like the horns of a bull on their bare skin.

A leader, long hair falling against the dark sweeping horns that coursed and writhed in ink across his considerable arms and torso, stepped forward and raised his hand.

Was this a warning or an order?

Be ready, Boy, you got speed with Horse, but arrows move just as fast. Maybe even faster.

In the end, he faced a semicircle of hunters and knew there were more behind him.

It'll show weakness if you turn your back to check, Boy. It's an interrogation. They just want to ask questions.

"*Wasa llamo?*" shouted their leader.

The Boy remained staring at them.

In the years of travel he had heard many languages. Sergeant Presley had taught him to speak English, though the Boy remembered that what his people spoke was different and yet the same.

English, Boy. English! Sergeant Presley had barked at him in the first years. One day, without remembering when, specifically, the Boy noticed Sergeant Presley never barked again. That lost language he had once spoken was yet one more thing the Boy could not remember about his people, just as he could not remember when he had first seen the feather in Sergeant Presley's bundle and what, if any, was its meaning.

Who am I?

Focus, Boy. All that's for another time. That's who you were. Live past today and you might find out who you are.

"*Wasa llamo?*" barked their leader again.

The Possum Hunters had used *llamo* to mean "name." He had learned enough of their language to get by during their year among them, enough when playing with their children.

The men jabbered among themselves, rapidly, like birds. It was too fast but the Boy caught words that may have once been English; words the Possum Hunters had also used, others that sounded completely different.

"*Wasa llamo?*" roared their leader.

Boy is what they called you, he heard Sergeant Presley say.

I have always just been Boy. It was enough.

And yet the broken feather from the bundle had once meant something to him.

"*WASA LLAMO!*" screamed the leader, unsheathing a curved hunting knife. It gleamed in the afternoon light of the bright sky. It was an old thing, a weapon from Before.

The leader turned to his troops, muttering something. The semicircle withdrew. It was just the leader now, facing the Boy.

The Boy tried to remember the words of the Possum Hunters. Words he could use to identify himself.

What was friend?

What was Boy?

How would he describe himself?

He remembered the children being warned to be careful of the bears that prowled the deep woods. "*Oso,*" he'd heard their mothers calling. Beware the *oso*. And the Possum Hunters, the men, had called themselves *cazadores*.

"Oso Cazadore," said the Boy in the quiet of the high mountain pass.

Silence followed.

The Boy watched the troop exchange glances, muttering, pointing at the bearskin.

The leader, his face like a dark cloud, shouted a long stream of words at the Boy, their meanings lost.

Until the last word.

The Boy heard the last word clearly.

"Chinese!"

As though it were an accusation.

An indictment.

Then the leader shouted it again in the still silence and pointed over his shoulder toward the west.

"Oso Cazadore," said the Boy again.

The leader laughed, spitting angrily as he did so.

Another string of words most of which the Boy did not understand and finally the word the children of the Possum Hunters had used when calling each other liars.

Pick the biggest one, Boy. When you're surrounded, pick the biggest one and take him out. It'll make the rest think twice.

The leader was the biggest.

The Boy dismounted.

Horse could take care of himself.

The Boy pointed toward the leader with his tomahawk.

The leader crouched low, drawing the blade between them, waving it back and forth.

Holding the tomahawk back, ready to strike, the Boy circled to the right, feeling his left leg drag as it always did after he had ridden Horse for long periods of time.

Get to work, lazy leg! Be ready.

The leader came in at once, feinting toward the Boy's midsection and at the same time dancing backward to circle.

The Boy moved his tomahawk forward, acting as though he might strike where the leader should have been. Sensing this, the leader flipped the knife and caught it in his grip, ready to slam it down on the unprotected back he knew would be exposed if the Boy struck with his full force at the feint. Instead the Boy shifted backward, willing the weak leg to move quickly. Once he was planted, he raised the checked tomahawk once more and slammed it down through the wrist of the leader as the man tried to regain his balance from stabbing through thin air.

What the Boy lacked in power and strength in his left side was made up for in the powerful right arm that had done all the heavy work of his hard life. Like a machine from Before, the triceps and biceps drove the axe down through skin and bone and skin again within the moment that the eye shifts its gaze.

The leader planted his feet, intending to reverse the knife with just an adjustment of grip and then swing wickedly to disembowel his opponent. He'd do it again as he'd done many times before.

But his hand was gone.

His mouth, once pulling for air like a great bellows, now hung open and slack. The leader dropped to his knees, his other hand moving to the spouting bloody stump.

For a brief moment, he stared at his hand as though this was something the leader had just imagined and not something that had really happened. His eyes, his world, gray at the edges of his vision, remained on the severed hand.

And then he was gone from this world as the tomahawk slammed into his skull with a dull crunch.

There was a clarity that came to the Boy in the moment after combat, a knowledge the Boy had that all his days would be as such: days of bone, blood, and struggle. The blue sky and winters would come and go, but all his days would be of such struggles.

Finally, in the last moment of such thinking, he wondered, what did cities ever know that he never would? Their mysteries would be beyond him. Without Sergeant Presley he would become like one of these savage men the Sergeant had warned him of. And one day, like the body of the man in the dirt and rock at his feet, such would be his end.

CHAPTER 20

In the blue water of the high mountain lake lay the rusting hulk of the bat-winged bomber from Before.

Bee Two, Boy.

The early education of the Boy by Sergeant Presley had included the identification of war machines and weapons past.

Stealth tech, Boy.

The bomber lay halfway in the crystal blue of the lake and partway onto the sandy beach of the small mountain village.

The village of the Rock Star's People, they called themselves in their weird mix of languages.

The Rock Star's People.

They're little better than savages, Boy. Stone age. Look at 'em with their bows and skins. Speakin' a little Mex, occasional English, and a whole lotta gibberish. Livin' out here in the sticks 'cause they're probably still afraid of the cities. At least they're smart enough for that. But other than huntin' and gatherin' and these huts, it makes you wonder what they've been up to for the last forty years. But I'll betchu' they got enemies, Boy. Betchu' that for sure.

Never get involved, Boy, because some stories have been going on long before you showed up. You don't know their beginnings, and you might not like their endings.

Yes, you would say that also, Sergeant. And yet, here I am. There was little choice for me in the matter.

With the death of the hunters' leader, the moments that followed the fight had seemed uncertain. The odds, thought the Boy as the leader lay dying, were slim that he would have time to get back on Horse and ride away from the circling hunters. As the moments passed, the Boy could hear pebbles trickling down the ledge behind him, knowing the bow hunters were surrounding him.

The Boy lowered his head, letting his peripheral vision do the work.

The enemy will come at you from where you can't see him. So look there, Boy!

But in the next moment the hunters lay down their weapons.

The conversation that followed was stilted, but from what the Boy gleaned over the course of the next three days' march, the hunters were inviting him to their village.

"Oso Cazadore," they repeated reverently and even approached to touch the skin of the bear.

Oso Cazadore.

Now, high in the mountains, at the edge of the water, the Boy stared at the final resting place of the Bee Two Bomber.

In the three days he'd traveled with the hunters they'd kept to themselves, disappearing in ones and twos to run ahead of the main group, returning late in the night. They'd ascended a high, winding course up through steep pine forests, across white granite ledges, through snow-fields ringed by the teeth of the mountains.

In that time the Boy learned they were the Rock Star's People and little beyond that.

In that time he heard the voice of Sergeant Presley's many warnings, teachings he was taught and which he'd intended to fully obey.

Except for one.

I will go into the cities.

I will find out what is in them.

A woven door of thatched pine branches swung upward from the bulbous top of the ancient bomber resting on the lakeshore.

And here you are, Boy, gettin' involved. I got involved once and ended up a slave for two years.

The Rock Star was what the Boy expected her to be. From the stories he'd heard. Stories not told by Sergeant Presley, but in the campfires of the Cotter family and even the Possum Hunters.

Old.

Gray hair like strands of moss.

A rolling gait as she crossed the fuselage and descended the pillars of stones that had been laid at the bomber's nose.

The small, deep-set eyes burned as she approached him. When she smiled, the teeth, what few there were, were crooked, with ancient metal bands.

"Come down from that animal," she commanded.

She spoke the same English as Sergeant Presley.

If I get down from Horse, the whole village will attack me. And yet, what choice do I have? What choice have I had all along, Sergeant?

Here you are, Boy.

Here I am.

The Boy dismounted.

She approached and reached out to touch the bear-skin the Boy kept wrapped about himself.

He had found a place for Sergeant Presley's knife.

Inside, behind the skin, waiting in his withered hand.

His good hand hung near the tomahawk. The care-freeness of its disposition was merely an illusion. In a moment it could cut a wide arc about him. In a moment he'd cut free of the rush and be up on Horse and away from this place.

So you think, Boy. If only it were so easy to get un-involved from things. If only, Boy.

"Bear Killer." She stepped back, cocking her head to one side and up at him. "That's what the children call you. Is it true? You kill a bear?"

After a moment he nodded.

"You're big and tall. Taller than most. But weak on that side." She pointed toward his left. "I can tell. I know things. I keep the bombs." She jerked her thumb back toward the water and the lurking bomber.

"Bear Killer." She snorted.

'If it comes,' thought the Boy, 'it comes now.' His hand drifts toward the haft of the tomahawk.

"Welcome to our village, Bear Killer. You've rid us of an idiot for a chief. I thank you for that." She turned back to the village and babbled in their patois. Then she left, rolling side to side until she reached the pillars, the pine-branch hatch, and disappeared once more inside the half-submerged bomber.

The Boy watched her until she was gone and wondered if indeed there were bombs, the big ones, nuclear, still lying within the plane. Waiting.

Impossible, Boy. We used 'em all up killing the world.

Rain fell in the afternoon, and that night the villagers, under clear skies, spitted a deer and gathered to watch it roast in the cold night.

A young man whose name was Jason led him to a hut made of rocks and pine. It belonged to the chief — to the man who died at the Boy's feet.

After three days of listening to the Rock Star's People, the Boy could at least communicate with them in small matters. But the communication was slow and halting.

Jason said that for killing the chief, the hut and all that was in it were Bear Killer's.

There was little more than a fire pit and a dirt floor.

Horse was fed apples by the children of the village and, as was his custom, patiently endured.

Later, the venison roasted, and the village watched both him and the meat and the darkness beyond their flames. There were far more women and children than men, and even the Boy knew the meaning of such countings.

When the venison was ready, they cut a thick slice from underneath the spine and offered it, dripping and steaming, to the Boy.

When the meal ended, the Rock Star was there among them. She had been watching him for a long time. She entered the circle, standing near the fire, wrapping skins and clothing from Before about her. She was faded and worn in dress, hair, and skin. But her eyes were full of thought and planning, of command and fire.

She told a story.

The Boy followed the tale as best he could and when he seemed lost altogether, she stopped to translate it for him back into English.

"I'm from Before, Bear Killer. I spoke the proper English like I was taught in school and all that."

The story she told involved a group of young people pursued through the forest by a madman with a chain saw full of evil spirits. One by one, the madman catches the younglings as they flee into what they believe is an abandoned house — the house where the madman lives with other madmen. In the end there is only one youngling left. A girl, strong and beautiful, desired by all the now dead younglings. Through magic and cunning she defeats the madmen, except for the one who'd found the younglings initially. The brave girl shoots bolts of power from her hands and the Mad Man of all Mad Men, as she calls him, falls backward over a balcony in the house from the Before.

"And when she run over to the railing to see his dead body lying in the tall grass, he is gone," the Rock Star translated to the Boy. Then, casting a weather eye into the darkness beyond their fire, the Rock Star whispered, "That madman still walks these mountains, still desires me, still takes younglings when it comes into his mind."

The Rock Star's People clutched their wide-eyed young. The men drew closer to the fire, to their wives, eyeing the night and the mountains that surrounded their lake.

"But he won't come here, children."

She paused, eyes resting on the assembly. She turned toward the mountains as if seeing his lumbering form wandering the silent halls of the forest dark even then.

"He won't come here, children. For I am that girl who was."

She turned and stalked off into the night.

The relief among the villagers was tangible.

In groups they returned to their huts, and for a long time the Boy stared into the fire, watching its coals.

CHAPTER 21

"Walk with me."

The command was simple, direct. The Boy saw her silhouette in the door to his hut by the half-light of early morning.

Outside, the Boy was wrapped in his bearskin and the sky was little more than cold iron. The village was quiet, as small wavelets drove against the sandy shore, slapping at the side of the old bomber.

When they were at the far end of the beach, nearing a series of slate gray rocks that fell into the waters of the lake, the Rock Star turned to him.

"I don't know you. I suspect, though, you're a man without a tribe." She let the sentence hang.

The Boy remained silent.

Good. Let people assume things, Boy.

"But you were passing to the west when the hunters found you," continued the Rock Star.

She paused to consider that for a moment.

"I imagine you want to continue west. But you can't. Ain't nothing there but Chinese now. You keep up that old highway and you'll come to a big Chinese settlement in the foothills the other side of the pass."

She picked up stones, flat and slate blue from the beach.

"Bad for you if you were thinking that was good. Chinese been trying to clear out the tribes. They took on one or two in the last few years and won pretty easily. They got the Hillmen working for them. But the Hillmen weren't never no real tribe. And the tribes the Chinese wiped out were little more'n scavengers anyway."

She seemed to want to throw a stone into the water, but the act of skipping it seemed something she knew was beyond her ability and strength.

"Now they — the Chinese, that is — have gone and stirred up a nest of hornets."

The Rock Star looked at the Boy directly, staring hard up into his face, searching for something.

"That man you killed in fair challenge was my war leader. He was an idiot, but as they say, he was my idiot. In the next day, we got to start out despite this last winter storm that's workin' itself up to be something. The tribes, far down the range, almost even to the old Three Ninety-five, are gathering. A big war leader is readyin' hisself to lay a smackdown on the Chinamen."

She took a deep breath.

"The headman called for me and mine to come. Wants my power."

She turned back to the lake. Whitecaps were forming beyond the bay.

"I've danced with the dark one in the dead of night. My power has watched over this people since the Before. My power will slaughter the Chinamen. My power has stood against zombies and vampires and all the serial killers of the Before. I was a powerful rock star in them days."

She dropped the stones back onto the beach.

"So if you're a spy, you know our plans. No good it'll do you, though. So you'll ride with us and know my hunters carry the poison. My poison is powerful. But my poison is not for you, see. My poison is for your horse. Ah, I see Bear Killer. I know'd the horse is a friend to you. So, you don't step to my call to fetch and be my war leader, it's the horse that gets it."

She sighed heavily in the wind.

"That's the way it be. Now take my arm and walk me back to the village, Bear Killer. And of a morning here shortly, we'll ride to the hidden valley and rave with the tribes at the great lodge. And when the tribes go to lay a smackdown on the Chinamen, you'll be my war leader and then you'll see my power. I'm keeper of them bombs, never forget that. I'll send the world back into darkness as I done the first time."

She held out her arm.

After a moment, the Boy took it.

The wind came up and his ears burned. But not from the cold.

That's right, Boy. I said involved.

CHAPTER 22

That night the Rock Star told the story of a great ship she had once sailed on that crossed the unseen ocean to a country far away. She told of fine dresses she wore and an evil prince who wanted to marry her. Instead, she chose a young poor boy, fair and bold, for her lover. But the evil prince murdered the poor boy.

The wind and the night closed about their small circle of fire next to the lake in the mountains, as the first hints of rain began to slap against the water and the sand. The Rock Star rose above the circle, seeming imperious. Seeming grand. Seeming once the young woman of the story.

"And I called an ice mountain out of the sea to come and attack the ship and slay the evil princeling. When my monster'd finished, that great ship slid beneath the waves with a titanic crash, like ice breaking off the high glaciers. Only I alone escaped in a boat, and every one of them fancies, all of 'em, drowned beneath the icy waters of that ocean, 'cept for me, and me alone."

In the morning when the Boy awoke, the hunters were packing, making a somber noise within the quiet village of the high mountain lake.

Jason pushed aside the blanket at the entrance to the old chief's hut.

"We *vamnato*," Jason mumbled fearfully in his pidgin language to the Boy, telling him it was time to leave.

The Boy gathered his things into his pack and went out to Horse.

Whispering and patting the animal, he promised to take care of them both.

"Do you trust me?" he whispered to Horse.

Horse regarded him, then snorted slightly and turned away to watch some new thing that might be more interesting.

Soon the hunters, carrying the Rock Star on a pallet, were waving goodbye to the tight-jawed women and crying children.

Following, the Boy rode Horse, his bearskin flapping in the strong wind that came off the lake.

Spring's a comin', Boy. Look sharp.

The company of hunters, with their skins and spears and bones of small animals knocking together in the wind whipping past their carried totems, skirted the lake along an old winding highway heading south. Soon they climbed up through a trail that led alongside high waterfalls, and when they crested the pass, they saw a long line of mountains falling away to the south.

Finding old crumbling roads when they could and keeping mostly south, the company trekked along the face of the high mountains, sometimes weaving down into the foothills, never daring to approach the valley floor.

The day was long gone to late winter cold when they stopped in a stand of pines alongside a mountain highway. The withered side of the Boy was stiff and aching. He got down from Horse and walked away from their forming camp. When the Boy looked behind him, he could see at least one of the hunters trailing, as if gathering firewood.

I'll be patient. When the time comes, and it will, I'll make a run, Sergeant.

There was no response from the voice of Sergeant Presley.

And yet there is something exciting about all of this, Sergeant. If these people are against the Chinese, then wouldn't that be good intel for I Corps and the Army?

The Boy didn't dare bring out the map secreted inside the pouch he'd made within the bear cloak. From his memory of it, he knew they were skirting south through the mountains. On the western side of their progress lay the long valley and many of the great cities of the past along the coast beyond. San Francisco, Los Angeles, and far San Diego, all in the State of California.

I should complete the mission. Find I Corps like you said, Sergeant.

Later, in the guttering light of the campfire, the Rock Star told of a night when the dead had walked the earth, coming out of their graves to clutch at her. She had hidden in a great palace of wonders she called the Fashion Hill Place Mall. The zombies, a relentless army of crawling undead, surrounded her and a band of other survivors. Using her great fire-spitting powers, she kept the other survivors safe against the relentless dead. But in the end, the survivors had each died as a result of their own folly.

There was Pete who tried to make a run for the parking lot, done to death by a horde of zombies he didn't see.

There was Fawn, who wouldn't share the sweet treats of the food court, pulled into an ice cave by a corpse who wasn't all dead.

There was Mark, who tried to have his way with the Rock Star, who was then a wild young girl with red hair. Mark was thrown from the top of the parking structure into a sea of the once human.

"And one day I flew away in a machine from the Before. Right off the roof of the mall. Rescued by myself because they wouldn't listen to me. Didn't have to be that way. But it was."

The days that followed were a long, slow crawl across the face of the mountains beneath the alpine tree line. High above them, snow clung to the tallest peaks, and still at the base of the trees they found piles of the stuff hiding in the permanent shade.

CHAPTER 23

On the last night, the night before the long climb up into the high valley, the Boy woke. Against the wide dark blue sky of frosty night, the wind swept clouds swiftly across the night. The dark shadow of Horse stirred for a moment.

For the thousandth time the Boy thought now might be the time to leave.

He did not hear the voice of Sergeant Presley.

Maybe I have gone too far down a road I should've never traveled. Maybe the voice of Sergeant Presley has finished with me.

Maybe I have gone too far.

The fire was low and the Boy saw the Rock Star, mouth open, staring into the glowing embers.

For a while he lay still, but his weak side was stiff and cold.

How much of the night was left?

He drank cold water from his bag and limped over to the fire to warm his cursed weak side.

All around, the hunters slept. The Boy knew two or three were watching him, watching with the poison on nearby and ready arrows.

The hunters had kept their distance over much of this cold trek across the western face of the Sierras.

Poison.

The Rock Star began to speak.

She did not look at the Boy.

She stared into the flames after he added a log and sparks rose on the night wind.

"I was a girl — little more than — on the day it all went down."

She swallowed. Her old face was hollow and dry like an empty water skin drained by time.

"I was a survivor though, even before all of the war that come. A survivor in a wasteland of malls and perfect families. My mother worked all the time. Worked so much I never saw her. We communicated by notes left on a little table in our tiny kitchen. One year I left the same note over and over and she never noticed."

The Boy rubbed his weak calf, working the heat of his good hand into the thin muscle.

"I lived at the mall. I was there when it opened, and there was many a time I was the last out the door at closing. Frank. Frank let me out. Told me to go on home.

"When it all went to hell, we ran. We ran for the mountains. I was in the San Gabriel Foothills when one of them bombs went off south of Los Angeles. We were climbing on our hands and knees. I saw a flash light up everything ahead of me. And then a few seconds later, a hot rush of dry wind.

"We kept on moving, farther and farther up into the mountains.

"All these tribes, all these people of the mountains, I knew 'em all in those first days when we ran from the cities. They was just survivors then, running as fast as they could while the bombs kept falling. I think about that sometimes. I kept looking for my mom in each new group we come across. But it was always someone different to be found. I can see the Mexican woman with the twin boys standing by the body of her husband as we all walked past them on the trail. I can see those boys' faces in all of them tribes folk down near Sonora. We traded some of our women years back with them when theirs kept making weak babies, worse than what you were born with. I see the bearded guy who got shot for his food in the back of a station wagon that had broke down. I see his face now and again in some of the men and children of the Psychos. He must've had kin that run off once we took to his stuff. But we hadn't eaten in three days. So, it was to be expected. What I'm sayin' — and I'm thinkin' about it all the more now as we come up to that rave — is, I'll be seein' all these people again. Except it's not them. It's their children and grands and great-grands. Strangers I passed, sitting among the fires of the refugee camps waiting for help that never came. Dark, muddy rain comin' down on us. Eatin' soup. Radio's gone. No one knows anything and the things people say don't mean anything to me. I was young and my world was limited to music and movies, or a boy I thought I loved and would run away with and we'd be together. We'd be a real family.

"All of us survivors thought we might make it in the first few weeks after the bombs. But the big winter that come taught us the error of our ways. What little survived that winter — two years long it was — what survived would be burned away in forest fires, taken by raiders, or plain just wore out.

"I was just a girl. I knew movies. I did whatever it took to survive."

The dark sky above the orange glow of the fire turned a soft morning blue.

"I'm a rock star. I'm the bomb keeper. I've loved the grim reaper." The Rock Star's voice was strong but passionless, as if these lines were played for the thousandth time too many and to no one in particular.

"Words of power, Bear Killer, dontchu forget about me. Don't forget I know them words. I've carried them from the Before. Carried them from a television inside my heart. From that fairy palace mall.

"Words of power."

CHAPTER 24

In the Hidden Valley, the Boy found the tribes.

He found what happened forty years after all the bombs fell.

He found savagery.

There were big men, cut and scarred, tattooed in ash. There were thin, misshapen men bearing the marks of exposure to the weapons of Before. There were warriors wearing the patchwork armor of ancient road signs beaten to form breastplates. Some wore the skins of wolves, some the skins of other animals and even humans. Here and there were human heads, held aloft, candles burning in their empty eye sockets.

There were the Psychos, who wore the skins of the lions that prowled the eastern desert. Teeth hung in great looping necklaces about their thick, raw, and sunburned necks. They dragged dull-eyed women behind them by heavy chains with little effort.

You watch yourself with them, Boy. You can tell from the cuts and branding and even the homemade tattoos, that bunch is strong and they dig pain. Forget their Mohawks, it's the necklaces made outta teeth. Anyone weaker than them ends up on that necklace.

And then there were the Death Knights, who wore battered Stop signs over their chests, mile markers on their arms, and wide-brimmed hats of leather from which the oily feathers of crows dangled in long woven cords.

They like to rule, Boy. They probably got a king or a warlord even. They're workin' some sort of rudimentary feudal system. My guess is you don't wear the crow feathers and armor, then you ain't to be considered. You fight one of 'em, you'll fight the whole bunch.

There were the Park People, who wore skins and carried long beaten scythes. They were tall and lean. One or two had red hair, but who knows the why of such genetics among their mostly brown skins? They cast long, silent looks from almond-shaped eyes, warning all to keep a good distance from them, as they drank the blood of a now silent pig from the battered cups they carried at their hips.

Koreans, Boy. Come up out of Los Angeles during the war is my guess. There was a lot of 'em there before. Probably held together based on that. If looks could kill, everybody'd be dead as far as they're concerned.

They and many others were the strange tribes of the Sierra Nevada, which runs the length of the eastern border of what the map calls the State of California. They had lost touch with what most call Before or the Before. Those things were not coming back, and among the youngest, were not even imagined.

What was lost was now simply gone forever.

These tribes held tightly to trail and track, hunt and prey, winter and summer. Friend and enemy.

They gathered in screaming laughter and thrumming chant before a great pile called the Lodge. Poles erupted from the riot of mud- and even blood-covered warriors. The poles were adorned with skulls and strings of nuts or pine boughs indicating camp and people, honor and disgrace. On one was a patchwork flag of one red stripe, one white stripe, one star on a field of blue. On another, hubcaps banged and clattered as they were twisted this way and that, making a singsong chime of bang and rattle. Others, strange and varied, wave and leap up and down across the forest floor of the high valley that lies beneath the stony granite mountains.

These tribes gathered before the large pile of stones and timber that formed a wall between them and the Lodge, a castle from the Before.

The people of the Hidden Valley had fought these many years against fire and other tribes to keep it to themselves.

But the whispers and tales of growing Chinese power, encroaching up into the native lands of the Sierra Nevada, were being told in the gutter speak of all the tribes. Whole tribes wiped out. Women murdered. Babies stolen in the night.

Now, messengers had gone out and they were gathering. Gathering against the coming storm. Gathering against the Chinese.

The Boy as Bear Killer sat astride Horse wrapped in his dark bearskin, the shining tomahawk at his belt. Beneath him the Rock Star's People milled about with their bows, proud to have a mounted warrior who had killed a bear counted as one of their own.

All around them, stretching far off into the smoky, dusky forest floor at twilight, were the Park People and the Death Knights and the Psychos and all the other tribes. Their number was beyond his counting except for him to know that this was larger than any gathering of mankind he had ever seen. When he imagined the size of Sergeant Presley's I Corps, it was never as numerous as on this night.

And in the distance, at the extent of his vision, other tribes were streaming forward, surging into the hot, clamoring mass at the foot of the pine log pile.

The leaders of all these tribes, including the Rock Star, have gone beyond the ramshackle wall of stone and pine, penetrating the maze of timberworks — seemingly haphazard but designed with defense and killing in mind — and disappear into the Lodge.

Hours later, just after nightfall, the leaders returned to the top of the wall. A tall man led them out onto the high wall of the Lodge, above which the waiting tribes could see the steep roof of the castle, which was once a rustic tourist resort.

The man was tall and rangy. He wore blue jeans and a long dark coat.

Clothing from Before.

His sharp jaw and blowing hair gave him a wolf's appearance. But even from among the milling mass of warriors, it was the blue eyes the Boy noted: clear, sparkling, glinting with thoughts of some plan.

The leaders of all the tribes formed a line, linked hands, and raised them high above their varied heads and hair. And at the center of the line, the tall man, the wolf-like man, the man in the clothing from Before, stood joined to all the other leaders. He raised his sharp jaw skyward and howled up into the trees and the night above.

This is the one you got to watch, Boy. This one's no join-er, and he ain't no leader. He's a taker. A ruin-er, and he's walked alone more often than not. Be careful, Boy. Real careful.

The tribes below and beyond the wall roared, punctuating their approval with whoops and screams.

The drumbeats began to roll across the forest floor of the valley, echoing off the distant mountains, lost in the crash of the high waterfall over which flaming logs tumbled into plumes of steam.

The Chinese would be defeated.

Night fell and campfires beyond the Boy's counting sprang up across the valley floor. The chattering of languages, one as seemingly alien as the next, murmured across the distances between the camps.

The Rock Star's People formed their camp, unsure what to do in her absence.

But then the bloated skin of fermented drink arrived, carried on a pole between two large warriors — black wolf skins and ash-covered faces, machetes made from the guts of old machines in great scabbards at their backs — and the Rock Star's People found their purpose.

All the tribes were drinking.

Now. Tonight is your night to escape, Boy.

It is good to hear your voice, Sergeant.

The Boy mounted Horse and began to ride the twilight camps. He smiled at those he suspected kept poison on their bows and when they smiled back, the smile was sloppy, happy, lugubrious, as if there was a friendship formed in all those cold miles between the mountain lake and this friendly place.

The Boy checked the great pile of stone and fallen timber that was the Lodge and saw only two torches guttering blackly at the gate. He rode to a nearby fire. Here there were men and women warriors, long spears, and woven hair like muddy ropes. They smiled after their guttural greeting failed to find meaning in the Boy's ears. They seemed to wish him well, and one woman even cast a hungry eye upon him. When he sensed the bearers of the poison arrows coming from the campfire of the Rock Star's People, shadowing him in the early dark, he rode back to their fire as if to reassure them.

The noise was getting louder across the valley floor as fires grew in leaps and explosions, sending sparks high into the star-filled night.

Soon, Boy. Real soon.

He got down from Horse and took a drink from the bloated skin.

The hunters cheered at what they perceived to be a long draft by the Boy beneath the uncorked stream of the drinking skin.

They smiled and chattered at him, forgetting he understood very little of what they spoke. He laughed and took a bigger drink and they all roared their approval.

We are all mighty hunters around the campfire.

Yes, that is something Sergeant Presley might have said, though I can never remember having heard him say anything like it. All the same, it seems like something he would have said.

When the night seemed alive with revelry and recklessness, the Boy lay down in the dark, not the least bit taken by drink.

Someone screamed. The pain of a wound was evident.

In the moments after, the mood was much more somber.

The Boy waited.

You are always stiff, my left side, especially when I have been lying on the ground for some time.

Now you must do your part.

The Boy rose and returned to Horse.

He laid his hand atop the long equine nose, looking into those forever uncaring brown eyes. The Boy raised his index finger to his lips as he led Horse away from the sleeping hunters.

They had almost faded into the shadows of tall trees beneath a starry night above, when a voice spoke softly to him.

"Nice night for a ride, Boyo."

The voice was a whisper.

The voice was the shadow of a grave.

In the dark a man came close, and though the Boy smelled the stranger, he did not hear him break the forest floor as he walked toward the Boy and Horse.

He's good. This one's got skills. Watch out, Boy.

"Come with me."

Beyond a moment's hesitation, the Boy led Horse after the stranger, following the lanky figure through the shifting shadows of the night forest.

The Boy slipped the fingers of his good hand to his tomahawk, hovering above the haft.

When the shot is clear I'll take it. I'll put it right between his shoulder blades.

The stranger moved fast, like some dark liquid seeking the path of least resistance, relentless as he slipped the tall pines back to the brick-a-brac wall that surrounded the Lodge.

They emerged onto the wide dirt porch of the ramshackle castle.

Two men walked from the shadows beyond the gate and the stranger, maintaining his loping, soundless stride, directed them to take charge of Horse.

The stranger turned to face the Boy as the ash-faced guards moved to obey.

By the light of the torches at the gate, the stranger is a drooping mustache and sad eyes that stared coldly back at the Boy.

"There's something you should see inside."

When the Boy didn't move, the stranger said, "C'mon," and dropped his eyes to the Boy's grip on the tomahawk. "It's good from now on. You can trust me."

The Boy followed the sad-eyed stranger through the break in the wall of rotten pine logs and earthworks surrounding the once grand and unknown building of Before turned collapsing fairy-tale castle now more than anything else.

After a few dog-leg turns within the wall, they arrived in a weedy courtyard at the entrance to the Lodge. Smoke-stained stones rose up to a sagging roof as windows gaped like open and jagged wounds.

The Boy spelled a sign above the entrance.

A-w-a-h-n-e-e L-o-d-g-e.

A wagon and a team of horses waited near two once grand doors.

Ash-faced guards worked in teams carrying bodies out from the dilapidated castle to the back of the wagon.

The Boy stood with the sad-faced stranger as the last body was thrown into the waiting transport.

When the last body was thrown with an unimpressive thump onto the other bodies in the back of the wagon, the sad-faced stranger led the Boy to the wagon, and before a tarp was pulled and tied, he showed the Boy the leaders of the tribes.

Underneath rictus grins, foaming mouths, and upward-staring eyes, a head of hoary gray hair rested above that same openmouthed, wide-eyed stare the Boy had seen at the beginning of this day, as the two of them had sat by the fire before dawn and she'd told him the story of her life as a young girl on the day the bombs fell.

The Boy listened for the voice of Sergeant Presley.

I understand what you meant, Sergeant. I understand "involved," now.

The stranger let the tarp fall, covering the horrified faces and contorted bodies.

"Now," said the sad-faced stranger. "MacRaven wants to meet a Bear Killer."

CHAPTER 25

"You really kill that bear you're wearing, boy?" asked MacRaven.

The sad-faced stranger had led the Boy through the rotting pile of wood that was once a tourist lodge to a grand ballroom of warped planks, cobwebs, and guttering candles for an audience with MacRaven.

Everywhere, there was dust and broken glass and damage. In the big room, moonlight glared through broken panes of glass set in large windows. By greasy candlelight, a banquet long laid out and thoroughly done to death revealed the carcasses of roasted animals and bones strewn with abandon. The hunger the occupants of the wagon must have possessed during the last moments of their final meal was evident.

At the far end of the room Mac Raven sat in a straight-backed chair. Among the shadows his ashen-faced warriors busied themselves in unseen tasks. There was blood on the floor and the sad-faced stranger told the Boy not to slip in it. The tone was friendly.

"I guess you must have killed that bear," continued the boom of MacRaven's voice from across the hall. " 'Cause if you didn't then you woulda said you did."

MacRaven, lean and rangy, rose from his chair in the thin light of timid candles.

"So I guess you did."

The wolfish man walked forward across the rotting boards of the floor.

"There aren't many that ride the horse these days. That bunch outside would just as soon eat your horse as ride it into battle. All twenty thousand plus of 'em, if Raleigh can count rightly."

MacRaven stopped before the Boy.

He was younger than Sergeant Presley was. Less than forty.

"I'm trying to build up some cavalry but it's not on this year's list of things to get done. Instead I've got a few who can ride. Maybe next year. Know what I mean?"

The Boy had no idea what he meant.

"I'll be direct. You're not with that bunch you came in with, nor any of those other tribes out there. That's as plain as day. So I don't know if you're a 'merc' or just passing through, but the truth of it is, I could use you. If you want work, I can give you that. If you want a way to go, well then I think I have something you might be interested in. An offer you should consider."

MacRaven walked back to his chair and picked up a hanging gun belt. He buckled it around his waist, one large revolver hanging low against his thigh.

"You don't want in, fine. Ride on."

Whatever you say, Boy, don't say that. He ain't strappin' on that gun for nothing. It means something, even if he don't know what it means, it means something bad. Though I 'spect he knows exactly what he means. Watch yourself, Boy, this one's a killer.

"So, you in, kid?" asked MacRaven.

The Boy nodded.

"What's that?"

"I'm in."

"Just like that. Hell, I didn't know if you even spoke the English until just now. Don't matter, I speak most of their languages anyway. That you speak the English recommends you altogether. Fine, you're in."

MacRaven swiped a drinking cup from off a table near the chair he'd been sitting in. He raised it to his lips. The tension in the room rose immediately. The Boy could sense the sad-faced man at his side about to burst into action. But then he stopped.

"That's right. This is poison." MacRaven chuckled.

He put the cup down.

"That wouldn't do now, would it, Raleigh?"

Raleigh muttered a tired, "No."

"This Army marches tomorrow," began MacRaven. "In four days' time we'll be at the gates of the Chinese outpost at Auburn. Those bodies in the wagon need to be inside the walls, with the Chinese. Raleigh and the other riders are going on ahead. You'll join them and make this part of my plan happen. *Excellente?*"

The Boy nodded.

In the night you ride and are not alone, though you should be, right, Sergeant?

The Boy thought of this atop Horse, riding the old Highway Forty-nine north, in the midst of other riders little more than different shades of darkness on this long night. The mountain road twisted and wound, and at dawn the company stopped for a few hours. Shadows were revealed in the dawn light that followed and the Boy saw the riders for who they were.

They were men. Mere men. And yet, in every one of them was the look of a hard man.

He's a hard one, Boy. Steer clear.

The Boy remembered Sergeant Presley's warning from villages and settlements they'd passed through in their seemingly endless — at the time — wanderings, when they'd come upon such a man.

A "hard one" was that mean-faced giant who carried the long board tipped with rusty nails, who'd watched the trade going on at the big river.

He'd had trouble in his eyes.

Trouble in his heart.

But they'd only found that out later, after they'd come upon the corpse of one of the salvagers who'd made a good haul out in the ruins of Little Rock, in the State of Arkansas. Then they knew the mean-faced giant had also had trouble in mind.

Each of these shadowy riders, in their own way, was that man.

Hard men.

Weapons. Spears, axes, metal poles studded with glass and nails. Swords. Machetes worn over the back like MacRaven's ashen-faced warriors. Whips.

Men who made their daily living dealing in the suffering trade.

In the shifting light of a cool and windy morning near a bridge along the crumbling mountain highway, the hard men seemed tired, and as if the leader of their company led in all things, the droopy-eyed and sad-faced Raleigh yawned as he approached the Boy.

"You take first watch with Dunn. When the sun's straight overhead, swap out with Vaclav." He pointed to a thick man with coal-black eyes and a beard to match. Vaclav carried an axe. Uncountable notches ran up the long haft.

The sun rose high over the trees and for a while Dunn took the far end of the bridge while the Boy watched over the sleeping riders.

If I go now, these men will catch me.

That's a fact, Boy. Now's no good.

I know too much of what they're about. They can't let me go.

But they don't even know you want to leave, Boy. They're testing you to see if you'll become one of them. Mainly 'cause of Horse. No doubt one of them, probably that Raleigh character, is watching everything you do. So whatever you do, Boy, don't pull out that map.

At times, the voice seemed as if Sergeant Presley was really talking to the Boy. Other times the Boy knew it was his own voice and just something he wanted to hear him say.

It felt good not to think and instead just listen to the noise of the river under the bridge.

He remembered winter and the cave above the rapids.

I should have drawn more.

I never should have left.

Go west, Boy. Get to the Army.

The Boy thought of the marks on the map.

Chinese paratroopers in Reno.

This MacRaven has an army. I Corps will want to know about this and the Chinese in this place called Auburn. Should I try to get away soon, Sergeant?

Now's not the time, Boy. They'll be all over you like white on rice.

Sergeant Presley would've said that.

In time Dunn crossed the bridge, sauntering lazily with a long piece of green grass sticking out the side of his mouth, back toward where the Boy stood guard.

Dunn was an average man: old canvas pants; dusty, worn boots; a hide jacket. In his sandy blond hair the Boy could see the gray beginning to show beneath his ancient Stetson hat.

"Dunn," said Dunn, extending a thick and calloused hand.

The Boy remained silent and then after a moment took Dunn's hand.

"Bear Killer, huh?" Dunn chuckled in the quiet morning, the noise of the river distant, almost fading as the heat of the day increased.

After a moment…

"Might as well be, as opposed to anything else, right?" Dunn paused to spit chewed grass off the side of the bridge. "Times are strange anyway. Names might as well be too."

"I never said my name was Bear Killer. That's just what the Rock Star's People called me."

The Boy saw a flash of anger rise up like an August storm and slip through Dunn's easygoing cowpoke facade.

Dunn turned and regarded the far end of the bridge, as if counting off moments to himself.

"That's one explanation. I'll buy it today for the sake of being friendly." He turned back to the Boy. The August storm had passed.

"And I'll give you this one for free," continued Dunn, his tone easygoing, his manner quiet. "How you want to spend it's up to you. Okay?"

The Boy nodded.

"Fine then. You ride hard and watch our backs. We'll watch yours. Don't question the work. There's no such thing these days as dishonorable work. Whatever the work is, someone's paying to have a job done and a job done is the way we do it."

After a moment the Boy said, "I can live with that."

Dunn watched the Boy for a long moment.

"There ain't nothin' left anymore. So sometimes work is something that's just got to be, regardless. We could use a kid like you. But you're gonna find some of the things we do might not sit right with you."

Dunn paused.

"If you're gonna ride with us then you might need to let go of some of those sensibilities."

Dunn nodded to himself, as if checking a list of things that needed to be said and finding all points crossed off.

"That's for free, kid. Next one'll cost ya."

Dunn smiled, then ambled over to another of the Hard Men to wake him for his shift.

When Vaclav awoke, black fury and a knife came out at once.

As if expecting someone else, Vaclav was ready.

But in that same summer-storm moment, the dark and swarthy Vaclav got up from the dust, then nodded to the Boy.

Hard men, Boy. Each and every one of 'em. You watch yourself.

I will, Sergeant. I will.

CHAPTER 26

The Chinese Patrol, or what was left of it, waited on their knees in the pasture as the Hard Men watched their interrogation.

Only their leader stood. He was standing in front of a stump, a day's ride from the outpost at Auburn.

Vaclav and the Boy worked with shovels in the big pit the Chinese prisoners had been forced to dig. It needed to be deeper, so Raleigh told Vaclav, and with a maximum of spitting and curses Vaclav grabbed a shovel and threw another at the Boy.

"New guy digs too," he spat.

They worked in the pit while Raleigh screamed in Chinese at the patrol leader.

Krauthammer, another of the Hard Men, who the Boy knew by the brief introduction of post-battle observation to be a searcher of pockets and a cutter of fingers for rings that don't slide off so easily. He had the patrol leader's pack out on the grass of the pasture and was going through it, tossing its contents carelessly out for all to see.

Dunn stood by the stump, one dusty boot resting upon it. He was chewing on another blade of grass.

Earlier, when Vaclav was up riding point, he'd spotted the Chinese patrol.

Leaving the wagon full of bodies in the road, the Hard Men pulled back into the forest after staking the wagon's horses and locking the brake.

"You're with me, kid," said Raleigh. "You too, Dunn. Rest of you circle around down by the river and come up along the road behind them. Once we attack, come on up and give us a hand."

No one said anything. They'd done this before.

Back among the trees, the hot afternoon faded in the cool green shadows of the woods.

"Chinese are killers, kid," whispered Raleigh. "You're too young to remember, but they killed this country. Now we're gonna take America back."

Dunn laughed dryly.

Raleigh rolled his eyes.

The battle was short.

When the Chinese came walking up the road, they fanned out once they spotted the wagon full of dead bodies. A few of them moved forward to inspect it.

A moment before they reached the back of the wagon, Dunn whispered, "I don't see no guns."

"They wouldn't have 'em this far out, Dunn. Too afraid of losing 'em." Raleigh's voice reminded the Boy of a rusty screen door.

Good, don't think about the fight until you have to, Boy. You don't know nothin' about it till it starts up, so no use gettin' worked up before it begins.

The Chinese carried long poles, spear-tipped ends.

Dunn charged out of the foliage, his horse snorting breathily as he beat the croup hard with a small cord.

The Chinese recoiled as first Dunn broke the brush, then Raleigh, and finally the Boy.

Don't think about it, Boy.

He knew Sergeant Presley meant more than just the fight. If for a moment he'd harbored the idea of riding away during the confusion of this battle, he knew they'd forget the Chinese and come straight after him.

I know too much.

They closed with the Chinese and the Boy chopped down on one of the patrol with his tomahawk then wheeled Horse about to swing into the face of an enemy shifting for a better position.

So these are the Chinese, Sergeant.

My whole life has been filled with the knowledge of them as enemies, as monsters, as destroyers. I have seen them play the devil in all the villages and salvager camps we passed through on our way across this country. But you taught me they weren't the only cause of America's destruction, Sergeant. You said they only came after, trying to carve away a little bit of what was left for themselves. I've never seen them as the devils so many have. You fought them for ten years in San Francisco, Sergeant Presley, but you taught me they weren't our worst enemy.

We destroyed ourselves, Boy.

You taught me that.

Now it was parry, thrust, and chaos as the Chinese oriented themselves to the attack of the Boy and Dunn and Raleigh. Some fell, bleeding and screaming and crying, but their leader organized the rest quickly and it seemed, at least to the surviving Chinese, as though they had turned back the main assault.

In moments, the other Hard Men were up out of the woods and all over the Chinese patrol.

A few hours later the Boy found himself in the pit, digging out its edges.

Above him Raleigh was still screaming in Chinese.

"Got it," said Krauthammer and held up paper. Then he held up a stick. After that, he pulled a bottle of dark liquid out of the pack.

"Put that one down first." Raleigh pointed toward one of the Chinese waiting on his knees.

Like sudden lightning, Dunn grabbed the Chinese and forced his head down onto the stump. Another of the Hard Men whipped a leather noose about the struggling head and pulled, stretching the brown neck taut as Dunn pulled the struggling body back.

"Vaclav," called Raleigh.

"What?" screamed Vaclav from the bottom of the pit.

"Can I use your axe?"

"Sure, why the hell not." Vaclav followed this with curses and muttering and finally, more spitting.

Raleigh took up the axe, and as all the Chinese started to chatter, he brought it down swiftly on the stretched neck of the chosen victim.

And then they chose another.

And another.

Raleigh turned to the leader and spoke.

The Chinese soldier nodded and held out his hand.

Krauthammer put the paper down and dipped the stick in the bottle of dark liquid.

Raleigh dictated and the leader began to copy.

When it was done Raleigh held up the paper, squinting as he read.

"Right. Kill the rest of 'em," he said, satisfied with what was on the page.

"Get to work, you!" muttered Vaclav through clenched teeth at the Boy, who had watched all of this.

They finished the trench while sounds that rose above those of spade and dirt pierced the hot afternoon of the pasture.

They buried the Chinese and took to the road once more.

CHAPTER 27

"Them bodies are smelling," said Vaclav.

They had been for some time.

"Tough. We need 'em to get through the gates, smell or no smell," replied Raleigh. "Only way them Chinese are gonna let us in, is if they think we're bounty hunters. These are the bounty."

The Hard Men, as the Boy thought of them, were held up in a ravine south of Auburn.

They were waiting for MacRaven.

"Those Chinese up in the outpost are gonna smell 'em out here first. Then where will we be?" continued Vaclav.

"Shut it," replied Raleigh. They sat in silence, the wagon at the center of the perimeter, each man up on an edge of the sloping ravine, waiting.

When MacRaven did arrive, he was alone. His ashen-faced warriors absent.

For a while MacRaven and Raleigh talked in whispers a little way up the ravine, away from the wagon. Then Raleigh summoned the Boy. "Get over here, kid," he whispered.

MacRaven rested a warm hand on the Boy's shoulder.

Don't show him you don't trust him, Boy. Don't even flinch in the slightest.

"Raleigh tells me you done good in the ambush. All right then, I got a new mission for you. If you're in? Good," said MacRaven without waiting. He was dressed in the mishmash battle armor of the tribes. His breast-plate was an old road sign covered in hide. His shoulders were padded and reinforced with bent hubcaps. He wore a skirt of metal chain across his pants. His smile, like some hungry beast's, encompassed more than just the Boy, as if the whole world were a meal, waiting to be taken in and devoured between his long teeth.

In time, Raleigh and the Boy were on the wagon and on the old road into Auburn.

A foul odor rose from under the hide tarp as the last of the afternoon washed out the brown-and-yellow land-scape.

"We do this right and there'll be rifles aplenty for all of us," said Raleigh as he drove the team forward, away from the other Hard Men.

As the wagon full of bodies bumped its way along the track, the Boy watched Horse recede, his lead trailing to a stake, Vaclav smiling at him as they drove up the ravine and out onto the main road leading down to the gates of Auburn.

"Chinese got a rifle factory somewhere and the chief thinks it's here. So we got to do this right," said Raleigh between clicks and chucks of encouragement to the wag-on team.

Raleigh told the Boy that MacRaven's plan was to take the bodies into Auburn and be paid a standing bounty, the Chinese offer on all warring tribes that were not Hillmen. Then, when the main assault of MacRaven's forces began at first light in the morning, their mission — Raleigh and the Boy's — was to string the bodies up and make it look as though their leaders had been executed by the Chinese.

"MacRaven'll have total control of all the tribes at that point." Raleigh gave a brief but sad smile. "At least for the rest of the summer. Then we go west and take San Francisco."

In the quiet, only the creak of the wagon could be heard beyond the clop of the team.

"Have you ever been to San Francisco?" asked the Boy.

"Nah. We came from up north, working in what used to be Canada. We rode together for years until MacRaven. Then, well, he was the man with the plan, know what I mean?"

"And what's the plan?"

Raleigh cast a glance at the Boy over his drooping handlebar mustache.

Overplayed it, Boy.

They rode on in silence.

But the voice of Sergeant Presley was there and the Boy thought about what he heard in it.

The mission for you, Boy, is still the same. Find I Corps. Give them the map. Whatever's about to happen here ain't your concern.

But they're going on to San Francisco. If the Army still exists there, then MacRaven and the tribes are going to come at the Army from behind.

This army won't be any match for I Corps, Boy. We had guns, tanks, helicopters. We'd chew this bunch up and spit 'em out.

He remembered the day Sergeant Presley had said that. They were hiding in the rocks, watching a village outside the dead lands of Oklahoma City — a village of salvagers being overrun by streaming bands of wild lunatics. The savagery had been brutal. They'd ridden three days just to get clear of that mess.

He remembered Sergeant Presley, his breath ragged in the cool night of that ride.

We had guns, tanks, helicopters. We'd chew this bunch up and spit 'em out.

But Sergeant Presley's gun had run out of ammo long before he'd ever met the Boy.

They'd seen the wrecks of countless war machines in their travels across the country.

They'd seen the burned hulls of melted tanks.

Downed and twisted helicopters.

Jets scattered across wide fields, only the wings and tail sections remaining to tell nothing of what had happened.

Even guns used as clubs by lunatics who didn't know any better.

He thought of the tribes on the march even now, closing the distance to this Chinese outpost.

Just like that village of salvagers outside Oklahoma City, Boy.

Sergeant, If I Corps had been fighting the Chinese all those years ago, over two hundred miles to the west, how do the Chinese have a settlement here?

I don't know, Boy. Stick to the mission.

I heard you say that many times, all the times I ever asked you what happened to those tanks and helicopters and jets we passed. Each time you said the same thing.

I don't know, Boy. Stick to the mission.

We don't know nothin' and orders is orders, Boy. You find I Corps and report. Tell 'em...

And yet there was the Chinese outpost, two hundred miles east of Oakland.

And there was Horse.

And there was drawing on cave walls.

And there is the mystery of what will become of me after I deliver the map.

Who will I be then?

And this voice was his alone.

CHAPTER 28

The Chinese officer was wearing the spun clothing of the soldiers. The pants and well-made boots. The long crimson jacket. The helmet. The officer carried a sword. The Chinese troops that met their wagon in front of the gate pointed rifles, long like Escondido's, at Raleigh and the Boy and the wagon full of corpses from atop the cut-log palisades.

What remained of an old overpass straddled the Eighty and served as the gateway to the Chinese colony of Auburn. High walls of cut forest pine screened the outpost along the southern side of the highway, surrounding the old historic district of the city from Before. Out of the center of the outpost, a domed county courthouse rose above the walls, and what lay within was beyond the Boy to see and to know.

Raleigh explained to the Chinese officers the character of the bodies and the Boy could not follow their wide-ranging discussion because it was in Chinese.

In time, more Chinese, older, fatter, dressed similarly to the officer, came out from behind the gate — even a few civilians. The Boy remained in the wagon.

All of his gear was gone.

His tomahawk.

His knife.

His bearskin cloak.

"If they see you're weak, they won't think much of us," Raleigh said when he'd told the Boy to leave his gear with Horse and the other Hard Men.

So he'd left his bearskin and weapons and Horse.

"You can trust us," said a smiling Dunn as he patted a jittery Horse, as if to reassure and unable to, all at once.

Raleigh turned back to the Boy in the middle of the conversation with the Chinese.

"They might make us sleep out here tonight."

That would be bad for the plan.

"I told 'em, ain't no way I was giving them the bodies without them paying me my bounty," said Raleigh, more for show, as if they might just be gone in the morning.

I don't know how this plays out for me, either way, Sergeant.

Be ready, Boy.

The Boy affected disinterest, which he knew was what Raleigh wanted him to show — that he was stupid and nothing to be afraid of.

The Boy stared off at the high wall and was surprised to see Escondido watching him.

When Raleigh turned back to the heated negotiation, the Boy looked up again at Escondido and barely passed one finger in front of his lip, almost as if he hadn't, but for anyone looking for such a message, the meaning was clear.

A moment later, the officers were retreating into the gate and Raleigh was climbing back aboard with a groan and a sly smile only the Boy could see.

"We're in," he whispered through the side of his mouth.

"They want a good look at them bodies. Chinese love their intel. Figure they'll know who's in charge this week and who they can bribe or play off against someone else next week. Won't matter much after tomorrow morning anyhow."

They drove through the gates and down the highway a bit before being directed up onto an off-ramp and into the center of the town.

They passed buildings.

A man worked at a forge, beating metal.

A shopkeeper with a patchwork lion skin in his front window nodded. Women crossed the street and entered the shop, talking loudly.

As they descended into the center of town from the highway, the soft glow of lights behind shop windows and houses came to life, blooming in the cool of the early spring evening.

A gang of children dashed down a side street, screaming in the twilight as they laughed and ran.

The Boy smelled spicy food.

But the hunger that had always been with him was dulled by what he saw.

The Chinese lived side by side with the people of other races. There were whites, browns, blacks, and Chinese.

The town murmured with life.

Like a city once must have.

The Boy thought of MacRaven's lunatic army of savage tribes moving through the thick forest east of the outpost.

He thought of MacRaven in armor.

He thought of the skeletons that were once cities.

He thought of Sergeant Presley's word. "Involved."

He waited for Sergeant Presley to tell him what to do now.

But he sensed the voice, like himself, had been silenced by the unfolding of life within the pine walls of this outpost.

Civilization.

Like Before.

Am I involved now?

And then…

Who am I?

CHAPTER 29

"They say they'll pay the bounty in the morning, which is fine for our purposes," said Raleigh as he chucked and clicked the wagon team to follow the Chinese guide up to the paddock.

They were being directed to the "Old School," which was a wide field where they could camp for the night.

"MacRaven will start the attack at dawn. The Chinese will be real busy right about then, so we can get these bodies strung up in peace. After that, maybe we can join the fight."

Raleigh looked at the Boy for a long moment, then, as if answering some unspoken question, he sighed.

"All right, I'll tell you the plan. Once they breach the walls with MacRaven's Space Crossbow, you'll need to link up with the chief and lead him up here so the tribes can find the bodies all strung up like they got executed by the Chinese. Dunn'll come up with our horses and gear. Then we can join the cleanup and start looting."

Real careful now, Boy. You done all the work to gain his trust. Now, don't overplay it.

The Boy waited.

"I don't get it," said the Boy.

"Why do we have to string these bodies up? Seems like the point's made if the tribes find 'em slaughtered already. They'll think the Chinese did it anyways."

Raleigh sighed. There was a moment of things weighed. Scales balancing.

"To the tribes one and all, dyin' in battle is one thing. But strung up for crimes is another. They'll be so angry and ready for all the Chinese blood they can spill, they won't even realize they're leaderless and under Mac's total control."

As an afterthought, as Raleigh turned to back the wagon, he added, "Brilliant, when you think about it."

"My guess is," continued Raleigh. "The Chinese will make their last stand down at that old courthouse. That's probably where the work will take place. I bet that's where the Chinese keep the guns and women, and that's where we'll want to get to, quick-like, once this tricky corpse business is done. First to fight, first to find, eh?"

Raleigh seemed happy, as if a fine breakfast had been announced for the morning and it would be something to look forward to throughout the long night.

They set to making a fire and then feeding the horses from the plentiful hay pile left on the Old School field.

In the early dark, they watched the fire as Raleigh heated strips of dried venison.

"I like it warmed even if it has been dried," he mumbled.

The meat was tough.

They ate in silence.

They'll slaughter these people, Boy. You know it and I know it.

You said, Don't get involved, Sergeant.

I know.

These are Chinese.

I know, Boy. And they're people too. Remember those salvagers outside Oklahoma City? Savages just like MacRaven's army murdered those people. Are you gonna let that happen here, again, to people like your friend Escondido?

"Watcha thinking so hard about?" asked Raleigh from the other side of the fire. Evening shadows made his sad brown eyes even gloomier as they stared out from his long face above the drooping mustache.

I know, Sergeant.

"Meat's tough," said the Boy.

"Good for the teeth," mumbled Raleigh through a mouthful. "Unless you got bad teeth. You got bad teeth?"

The Boy nodded.

You know what you've got to do, Boy.

I know, Sergeant.

"Can I see your knife?" asked the Boy.

Raleigh stood and pulled it from his belt. He handed it pommel first to the Boy and sat back down.

Raleigh was biting into the venison once more when a thought occurred to him.

In that moment of chewing, thinking about warfare and food and rifles, Raleigh understood he'd made a mistake. But he was tired and it had been a very long life. He had, he knew, no one to blame but himself. He had always known this.

The Boy was standing.

The Boy's arm was back.

What the Boy lacked on one side, withered and bony, he had on the other — a powerful machine, just like

MacRaven's Space Crossbow thought Raleigh. I have no one to blame but myself.

His teeth close on their final chew.

The Boy hurls the knife straight into Raleigh's chest.

All the air was driven from Raleigh at once as he fell backward from the impact. The darkness was already consuming him and the Boy. Raleigh thought, as he felt that one powerful hand about his throat, the Boy was like an animal.

The Boy was up from the body. Raleigh, eyes bulging, stared sightlessly up into the stars and the night beyond.

By dawn they'll be all over these walls, Boy. Whatchu gonna do now?

He'd heard that question from Sergeant Presley before, many times in fact. *Whatchu gonna do now?*

I can find Escondido, Sergeant.

Then what?

Tell him what I know.

Then what?

I… it's up to them after that.

That's right, Boy. Do all you can do. Then let it go.

The Boy walked back toward the ancient courthouse down in the center of the outpost. Warm yellow light shone within the windows he passed.

Ahead he saw a Chinese guard at the intersection of two curving streets.

"Escondido?" he asked.

The guard mumbled in Chinese and shone a lantern into the Boy's face.

"Escondido?"

The guard's slurred Chinese seemed angry, and for a moment the Boy realized how much of his plan hinged on simply being understood. But after a pause the guard began to walk, lighting the way for the Boy and insisting he follow along. A moment later they turned down a side street and up a lane, almost reaching the outer pine-log wall.

The guard climbed the steps to an old shack and banged loudly on a thin door.

The racket and voice within belonged to Escondido.

When the old hunter opened the door, he hit the guard with a stream of Chinese, then, seeing the Boy he stopped. His tone was softer as he sent the guard off into the night.

The guard retreated down the steps and was down the winding lane, back toward the center of the outpost, his lantern bobbing in the darkness.

"Never thought I'd see you alive. What happened to your horse?"

"No time. There's an army of tribes out to the east. They're going to attack at dawn."

Escondido reacted quickly.

He only asked questions that mattered. Strength. Numbers. Proof.

He didn't waste time on disbelief.

'I guess,' thought the Boy as he followed after the old hunter, 'when you've lived through the end of the world once, you're more ready to believe when it happens the next time.'

Shortly, they were standing on the steps of the old courthouse, their faces shining in the soft glow coming from within the old building. Chinese soldiers were speaking with Escondido. Every so often messengers left and returned. More and more of the soldiers were mustering in the old parking lot beneath the courthouse. As for the conversation, the Boy understood little of it.

Escondido turned away as the Chinese conferred among themselves.

"They believe you, all right. That patrol is well overdue. They seen your friend's body and they've put two and two together. The question for them now is, what're they gonna do? Yang, the garrison commander, wants to send the civilians and the Hillmen out tonight. He's only got forty soldiers, but he thinks he can hold the courthouse."

And how much is this, Boy? asked Sergeant Presley long ago.

Five.

And this? He holds up all ten fingers.

Ten.

And if each one of these fingers represents the total of all my fingers?

One hundred.

Good, Boy. Next you'll make me take off my moccasins. But we'll save that for another time.

There were far more tribesmen than one hundred. Far more than forty.

"If they go, do you want to go with 'em?" asked Escondido.

The Boy shook his head.

"I'm half tempted to run myself." Then, "The Hillmen are sending messengers out to their villages. That might even things up a bit. All right, you'll fight with me. I'll be on the eastern wall. You can reload my rifles. You know how to do that?"

The Boy shook his head.

"Well, we got all night to learn."

CHAPTER 30

"Feels like spring," whispered Escondido in the cool darkness as the two of them sat beneath the ramparts along the wall. It was morning, just before sunrise.

Below the wall, in the fields and forest beyond, all was a soft gray.

The Boy smelled a breeze thick with the scent of the field. And on it, he knew, he could taste the waiting tribes out there in the darkness.

"Be a long summer," muttered Escondido, his old eyes squinting at the far horizon. "But what do I know."

The Boy checked Raleigh's knife. It was stuck into the soft wood of the parapet.

Escondido had taught him how to break the rifle, pull out the expended cartridge, load another of the massive bullets into the breech, exchange rifles with Escondido. Repeat. They had more than a hundred cartridges. But not many more.

Escondido wiped angrily at his nose.

"I can smell 'em comin' up the ravine. If we fall back, or you see the Chinese start to leave, head down to the courthouse in the center of town. They'll make their stand there. That's if I'm kilt, understand?"

The sun washed the field in gold, and out of the low-lying mist, arrows like birds began to race up toward the parapets. Loud knocks indicated the arrows ramming themselves into the wooden walls just on the other side of their heads. Someone screamed farther down along the wall. There was a sudden rush of the slurring Chinese, spoken in anger and maybe fear.

Escondido popped his head over the wall, keeping his rifle erect.

He shouted a string of Chinese directed at the others along the wall.

Then he sat down with his back to the parapet.

"They're using them arrows to keep our heads down. There's thousands of 'em crossing the fields with ladders and poles now." He took three short breaths, then, "Here we go!" Escondido popped his head over the wall, this time sighting down the rifle, and a second later the world erupted in thunder and blue smoke.

As the echoing crack of the rifle faded across the forest, the tribes began to whoop and scream below, breaking the morning quiet.

Escondido backed down behind the wall, handed the spent rifle to the Boy, and grabbed the other from the Boy's frozen fingers.

The Boy had been told all his life about the legendary capacity of a gun to strike back at an enemy. But he had never seen one fired. He was never told of its blue stinging smoke and sudden thunder.

Three breaths as Escondido raised the rifle back over the wall. He targeted some unseen running, screaming tribesmen. A brief click as he pulled the trigger, and again the explosion.

They exchanged rifles. Unloaded and smoking, hot to the touch — for the other rifle, now loaded and waiting to be fired again.

Repeat.

"There's thousands of 'em," stated Escondido again.

Three breaths.

The explosion.

Repeat.

"They're coming up the walls, it'll be knife work shortly."

The explosion.

Repeat.

"Duck!"

The sudden whistle of flocks of arrows flinging themselves from far away to close at hand, then the thick-sounding *chocks* as the cloud of missiles slammed down into the walls and old buildings within the outpost.

The Boy grabbed Raleigh's knife when he heard the ladders fall into place on the other side of the pine logs. He put it in his mouth before he took the expended rifle and started the unloading trick he'd been taught.

Explosion.

"Be a long hot summer," muttered Escondido.

Repeat.

The Boy finished reloading and waited to exchange rifles.

When nothing happened he looked up.

Escondido was slumped over the wall, almost falling facedown. The Boy pulled him back behind the parapet.

A bolt had gone straight up through his jaw and into his brain. His eyes were shut tight in death.

The Boy heard feet scrabbling for purchase on the other side.

All along the wall, lunatic tribesmen jabbered, screamed, and spurted blood as they hacked away at the mostly dying Chinese.

The Boy, still holding the rifle, grabbed the sack of cartridges and tumbled off the platform, checking his landing with a roll.

He raced down a lane, his limping lope carrying him away from the bubbling surge of madmen now atop the wall and spilling over into the outpost. Chinese and Hillmen raced pell-mell for the old courthouse. Snipers from its highest windows below the old dome were shooting down into the streets.

The Boy was making good speed while watching the courthouse. He saw one of the snipers draw a bead on him and fire at the place where he should have been. Instead he crashed through the front door of a shack. Inside he found linens and pots and pans. There was even food in glass jars.

'Go to ground,' he thought, and wondered if this was the voice of Sergeant Presley. There was too much going on for him to tell.

Get behind the first wave of attackers, Boy. They'll go for the courthouse.

He remembers Raleigh telling him to meet MacRaven at the front gate so that he could lead the tribes to the planned horror of their murdered leaders.

Outside, Mohawked tribesmen were streaming down the streets with axes and blood-curdling screams. Bullets, fired from the courthouse, smacked and ricocheted into the cracked and broken streets.

When the first wave passed by the store, the Boy darted across the street and into an alley. He followed the alley and a few others as he worked his way back to the gate that sat astride old Highway Eighty.

He smelled smoke and burning wood.

Women were screaming.

Ahead, above the rooftops, where the gate should be, he saw an explosion of gray smoke and splintering wood.

The gunfire from the courthouse was increasing.

Breaking glass both close and far away.

Screams.

Whatchu gonna do now, Boy?

I've got to get Horse.

At the gate, the ashen-faced warriors were leaping over the collapsed remains of the entrance to hack with their machetes at the stunned Chinese riflemen mustering in the median of the old highway.

Through the smoke, MacRaven and a collection of warriors from the tribes of the Sierra Nevada were picking their way through the rubble. MacRaven turned, waving his machete, and behind him a vanguard of ashen-faced warriors pushed a wagon forward through the shattered remains of the gate. Atop the wagon rested a large gleaming metal crossbow.

The Boy crossed the open sward of grass to the on-ramp, waving at MacRaven.

MacRaven led the tribesmen toward the Boy as he pointed for the giant crossbow to be set up on the median of the highway.

"Have you found them?" roared MacRaven, his performance of concerned commander utterly believable.

The Boy nodded, unsure what to do next. He looked to the gate, hoping Horse would come through at any moment as more and more ashen-faced warriors poured through the breach.

MacRaven led the Boy away from the others as if to receive the planned bad news of their leaders' demise.

"Speak to me like you're telling me something horrible," he whispered once they were some distance from the others.

The Boy couldn't think of what to say.

"Just move your mouth."

He opened and closed his mouth as MacRaven nodded. Then, "Where did Raleigh put the bodies?"

The Boy pointed toward the Old School.

"On the field, up there."

"All right, in just a moment you're going to lead us up there. But first I want to watch my space crossbow take out their courthouse."

MacRaven turned back to the crossbow crew and raised his arm, then brought it down toward the dome of the courthouse.

A singing twang sent a six-foot iron shaft speeding from the gleaming crossbow into the cupola of the courthouse. Brick and debris shot out the other side of the building as rubble crashed down onto the lower levels and finally the steps leading to the parking lot.

"Great, huh?" said MacRaven, turning to the Boy. "It's from Before. It was designed to go up into space and shoot down asteroids so smart men could bring soil samples back to earth. I found it inside an old research plant down east of L.A. Place called JPL, whatever that means. Doesn't sound like a word, but maybe it was in another language I ain't learned yet. From what I could tell, they were gonna send it up into space before the war. Good thing they didn't, huh?"

The Boy heard a little electric motor whining as the drawstring re-cocked the crossbow. Three men levered another iron bolt off the floor of the wagon and placed it onto the weapon.

"I'll conquer the world with it," said MacRaven in armor amid the smoke and bullets. "Just wait."

The catapult fired again and the massive bolt disappeared into the main body of the courthouse. Its effects were devastating.

CHAPTER 31

The main group of MacRaven's entourage was twenty feet behind the Boy as he led them up along time ravaged streets toward the Old School and the field where MacRaven expected they would find the strung-up corpses of their leaders.

Instead, MacRaven will find the body of his most trusted man and a wagon full of corpses, Sergeant. A wagon many will have already seen back in the Hidden Valley.

You know how it is, Boy. Whatchu gonna do now? 'Cause you ain't got much time to do it in.

The blood was everywhere along their trek through the lanes of the outpost: in pools, splashed against the sides of houses, painting shattered glass.

The gunfire from the courthouse came in waves, and each wave seemed diminished from the one previous. The waves were punctuated by the giant crossbow's singing note and the audible whistle of the great bolt through the atmosphere and then its sudden crash.

Ahead of the Boy, at a bend in the lane, a woman lay in the street, naked and dead. An infant wailed from the porch of the shack she lay in front of.

Around the bend, three Chinese guards were riddled with arrows. They stared sightlessly at the Boy, MacRaven, and the wild entourage of tribespeople, who grew quieter with each found body.

The air was still cool, reminding the Boy that it was just after dawn.

The Boy looked behind and saw MacRaven staring intently at him.

The dead did not bother MacRaven.

Whatchu gonna do now?

I've got a knife and a rifle.

It ain't much, Boy.

The low concrete that abutted the sports field of the once school was all that remained and protected the Boy from the truth that was soon to be revealed.

Warriors were still climbing the walls toward the north.

But these warriors were different.

They wore clothes like the Chinese.

They carried large axes.

They uttered *whoop whoops* as they flooded toward MacRaven's group.

In a moment, it would be the hot work of thrust and slash.

MacRaven's entourage formed up quickly to stand against the sudden waves of Hillmen climbing the walls to counter-attack.

MacRaven fell behind the warriors of the tribes now eager to get their fair share of trophies. He signaled the Boy to come to him.

"Get back to the gate and find whoever you can and get them up here. It's a counter-attack!" A moment later,

MacRaven pulled a dead tribesman aside and thrust a Hillman through with his machete.

"Go!"

Now's your chance Boy. You get just the one.

I know.

The Boy ran back to the gate.

Black smoke climbed in thick pillars from the southern portion of the outpost, forming an inky backdrop to the crumbling courthouse. There were only a few Chinese snipers left in what remained of the old building.

At the gate, ashen-faced warriors were gathering to watch the crossbow's work while a captain marshaled them for the final attack on the last of the courthouse's defenders.

Dunn rode through the gate on his dark gray mare. He saw the Boy and waved his hat as he galloped the distance between them.

"Where's MacRaven?"

The Boy pointed toward the top of the outpost.

"Where's my horse and gear?"

Dunn smiled. "What, dontcha trust us, Bear Killer?"

The anger behind the Boy's stare checked Dunn.

"Nice rifle." Dunn's eyes were ice cold.

The Boy looked down at the rifle. He had completely forgotten about it.

"Give it here," demanded Dunn.

"Where's my horse?" said the Boy through clenched teeth.

For a moment Dunn's hand fell to his machete. But then he heard a far-off volley of rifle fire and this meant something to him.

"Hell, keep it. Vaclav's coming up with Raleigh's horse and yours also, I suspect. Where'd you say the chief was?"

The Boy stared for a long moment, then pointed toward the field.

Dunn kicked his mount and tore off across the grass of the on-ramp. The crossbow sang again and now the ashen-faced warriors were marching in formation toward the courthouse.

Won't be long now before things get sorted out. You better get while the gettin's good, Boy.

He trotted through the broken timbers of the gate, smashed by the iron bar flung from the space crossbow.

The rising highway to the east was flooded with carts and wagon teams. Wild-eyed women and scrawny children who had followed the army of tribes watched the fort with hunger. On the other side of the highway, buildings from Before lay fallow and fallen amidst a pine forest that had overrun that section of town.

Vaclav led Horse and Raleigh's mount down alongside the grass-covered highway. The other horses were wild with fear from the smoke and gunfire as Vaclav cursed and spit, trying to keep them under control.

When he saw the Boy he yelled, "Take your stupid animal already."

The Boy limped forward and took hold of Horse. The bearskin was tied across Horse's back and he found his tomahawk inside the saddle pack. A moment later he was up and whispering as he patted the long neck of his friend.

"What's going on in there?" said Vaclav, looking at the rifle with the coal-black version of Dunn's hungry blue eyes.

The Boy was just about to lie when they both heard shouting at the gate as Dunn came thundering through on his mare, knocking back two ashen-faced guards. He screamed something at Vaclav.

If the meaning isn't clear it shortly will be, Boy.

"What's he saying?" asked Vaclav.

Dunn waved his machete, still shouting as he drove his horse hard up the old highway.

Whatchu gonna do now, Boy?

Vaclav will be busy with the extra mount. Dunn, on the other hand…

The Boy raised the rifle and sighted down the barrel. The rifle was too long to steady with just his one good arm, which he needed the hand of to pull the trigger.

Horse has never heard a rifle before. Be ready, Boy. Horse might not like it.

He raised his withered left arm and set the rifle on the flat of his thin arm.

"What're you doing?" Vaclav screamed.

Is it loaded, Boy?

Dunn's eyes were wide with fear and hate as he raced to close the distance between them.

Horse danced to the right, turning away.

I've never fired a gun before, Sergeant.

Ain't nothin' but a thang.

Explosion.

The bullet rips into Dunn's mount and Dunn goes down hard, face-first on the grassy slope.

The Boy urged Horse forward and they were off across the broken and grassy highway, down an overgrown embankment, and into the ruins and the forest beyond.

CHAPTER 32

The Boy had passed by the overgrown ruins of places almost familiar many times before. There had always been in him that desire to understand such places, to investigate them. But in this moment of shouting men behind him, and soon the inevitable dogs, he knew there was no time for the usual consideration of things past.

Green grass sprouted through the split asphalt of a wide avenue, the remains of an old road led up through the ruins that the Boy suspected was the other half of the Auburn that existed before the bombs. At the top of the rise, looking back toward the smoky pillars climbing over the outpost, the Boy saw the remnants of the Hard Men coming for him. Other men, ferocious lunatics, followed behind Raleigh's riders with bellowing hounds at the ends of thick straps of leather.

Escape and evade, Boy, we done it a million times. If they're bringing dogs, then distance is what you need. Out of sight, those dogs will start to slow down when they start searchin' for your trail. Then you can confuse 'em.

The Boy patted Horse and knew that an outright race would put him beyond the dogs. But the Hard Men on their horses would spot his trail and the following would be easier.

He turned and started through the overgrown brush and tangle of a collapsed bridge that once crossed the road.

I'll keep moving west, Sergeant.

He rode Horse hard for a time, working his way down a wooded ridge and following a twisting maze of dense brush and warped trees along falling ridges and a steep slope that will eventually lead into the river delta around Sacramento.

By noon he had lost the Hard Men, but his progress had been slow. Way off, back up on the ridge, he heard dogs baying, moaning as if in pain.

If they catch me, will those dogs stop their noise, satisfied at what will happen next?

Sometimes I wonder if there is any good left in this world.

He thought of the bodies and carnage of Auburn.

At sunset, he pulled out the map from its hidden place in the bearskin. Sacramento was far ahead to the west.

Behind him, he could smell woody smoke in the fading light and he wondered if it was from Auburn or the campfires of his pursuers.

It was good to be alone again.

Is that the way of my life, Sergeant? My way through this world? Alone?

But there was no answer.

Why should there be an answer, Sergeant? When you were alive we never talked about those things. We talked of food and survival, and sometimes I just listened to your stories about the way things were Before. And sometimes also, why they had to end.

You take everything with you, Boy.

Yes.

He looked at what forty years of wild, unchecked growth had made of the terrain. It was a wall through which nothing could pass undetected.

The Old Highway is maybe a mile off to my right. I'll have a better chance of evading them there.

They could be searching the road for you, Boy.

If I put as much distance tonight between myself and the hounds, by morning I'll have a better chance.

He remembered Sergeant Presley's hatred of "chance."

If all you got is a chance, Boy, you ain't got jack!

It's all I have now, Sergeant.

He rode the highway at a trot. The night was cool and mist rose from the lowlands on both sides of the highway. Cars and trucks, forever frozen in rusty dereliction, littered the road and made him wonder, as they always did, of the stories behind and within them.

You'll never know, Boy. I could make up a story for you like I used to. You could tell yourself a lie. But what good would it do, even if you could know how things ended for those people?

Sometimes the Boy heard himself asking, *What has happened here?* Sometimes the cars were jammed together, as though frozen in a single moment of waiting. Sometimes they were overturned. Sometimes they were parked by the side of the road, every door open, every window broken. What was within was gone, even down to the seats. All that was left was rusting metal and an untold story he would never hear.

He looked at the cars scattered along the highway.

It is beyond me to ever know why such things have been left the way they are.

And yet I want to know.

He rode on, long after the sliver of a moon had completed its descent. It was dark and damp and cold. In the misty gloom he saw standing water in the surrounding fields and broken buildings.

The water looked like a rug.

Before long, he had ridden in close to the skeletal towers of the old state capitol in Sacramento. He heard frogs everywhere and even the highway was submerged. He came to a bridge that had long since fallen into the muck of the dark river below and he could go no farther.

It is too dark to find a way around, Sergeant.

He looked behind him and saw nothing in the misty night.

The frogs will warn me if anyone comes along.

Sorry — he pats Horse — we can't have fire tonight.

He draped his blanket over his friend and rolled up in his bearskin at the side of the bridge, far out along it, almost to the edge of the broken span over the swamp below.

In the milky light of morning he surveyed the bridge. There was no way to the other side. The city, twisted, bent, and broken, lay all about him, submerged in the cold water of the wide river.

The course of the river must have changed in the years since the bombs.

Or because of the bombs.

He led Horse down an off-ramp and they waded through the watery streets of a long-gone city. Windows, regularly spaced, gaped and screamed in silent horror as they passed.

My whole life I've wanted to explore such places. But there is nothing here now.

Is this why Sergeant Presley said no? Because there is nothing left of the things that were once here?

At noon the murk had mostly burned off and they — Horse and the Boy — had crossed over to the far side of the river on an old rail bridge that still stood. The Eighty continued west on the other side of a field.

The Boy looked back at the dead city.

I could wander you for years and what could you give me back?

Could you show me who I might have been?

And why is that so important to me?

He tries for a moment to imagine what it must have looked like — looked like with people in it. People from Before.

That night, beyond the city, after a day filled with long silences punctuated by the last lonely birds of winter, he camped next to a wall whose purpose he didn't understand. Why it lay next to the old highway or who built it and for what he did not know.

He ate three small rabbits that he took with the rifle in the afternoon and set wild corn in front of Horse.

The world is filled with wild corn and you want nothing more, Horse. Life must be pretty good for you.

He thought of the five rounds he'd fired to take the three rabbits.

Two had been wasted.

Yes. But if I am to use the rifle I must practice with it. I must be sure of it when I need it.

He reached into his bag and took out the charcoal. He shaved it with his knife and looked at the wall.

He drew a great bridge in long, sketchy strokes that ran the length of the wall. Then he drew the skyline of the hoary city sinking into the swampy river. Below, near the gritty pavement of the old highway, he filled in the moonlit water, reflecting the shadows of the city back up at itself.

The night was bitterly cold and even the fingers of his good hand ached like those on his bad side. Later he returned to the fire and warmed himself, looking at the mural.

Was that it?

It seemed as though there should be something more.

He thought of drawing Horse. Or himself. Or even MacRaven.

But nothing seemed right.

Lying on his side drifting toward sleep, facing the hot fire, the cold at his neck, he saw the city come to life.

And he lived there.

And there was a day…

The best day ever.

He awoke to the orange light of the coals in the deep of night and saw the shadowy city rendered on the wall. He could not remember what was so good about the dream of the day in that city before the bombs. Only that it was the best, and worth having, and that he had been cheated, as though a valuable piece of salvage had been stolen from beneath him while he slept.

It seems as though there should be something more to the picture on the wall, he thought again, remembering the dream.

And as he fell back to sleep he heard, *I bet the people who lived in that city thought so too, Boy. I bet they did.*

CHAPTER 33

In the days that followed, the Boy rode in quiet along the muddy river that reminded him so much of the big one back east, and the Possum Hunters and Sergeant Presley, when he had been young.

He felt old.

The days passed and towns on the map either didn't exist or lay buried beneath wild grass and corn.

He passed a convoy of military vehicles forever parked in the median of the great windswept highway.

He smelled the salt of the ocean on a sudden shifting breeze.

It smelled of Texas.

But cleaner.

He passed rusting vehicles lying swaddled in the reeds that shot up out of the mucky fields and stood for a long time considering the wreck of an Apache helicopter, held longingly by a clutch of thorny rosebushes.

He climbed a high pass and saw long iron spikes cast to the ground, all in one direction, as if thrown by the hand of a giant. Large windmill blades lay buried in the dirt and grass.

In the town beyond, he saw the charred remains of buildings reaching up to the gray sky.

The wind and the clouds march east, lashing the buckled highway with spring rain. At the end of the day, the Boy felt as though much more had been required of him than just movement. He was exhausted.

On the day he reached the bay, the weather turned warm. At least, if he stood in the center of the road at full noon and turned his face toward the bright sun, the day felt warm. In the shade of bridges and crumbling buildings, the cold had always been and always would be, just like the rusty destruction he found there along the bay's edge.

He saw the bay from a high hill and on the far side of its blue water, he saw the great pile of rubble that was San Francisco, in the State of California. Only a few tall buildings remained standing. The rest lay buried in the piles of concrete and twisted rebar he could see even from this distance.

Ain't never been nuked, Boy. Chinese wouldn't do it. Needed a deep water port on the West Coast. Seattle, San Diego, and of course LA were all long gone. We fought for that pile of rubble for ten years.

The Boy could hear the campfire stories of the great battles and "ops" of the San Francisco of Sergeant Presley.

On Market Street we lost all our armor, Boy.

And…

I was the last one off the roof of the Ferry Building. Close one that day, Boy.

And…

I saw the TransAmerica Building go down after a Jay Thirty-three went in about halfway up. Dust for days after that one, Boy.

And...

The Army will be down along the East Bay. Headquarters in an old college library. That's where you'll find I Corps, Boy.

Tell them I made it all the way.

Tell them there was no one left.

Tell them who I was, Boy.

And...

You take everything with you.

CHAPTER 34

I'm glade you died, Sergeant.

You thought they would still be here — waiting for you.

The wreckage of military equipment littered the highway that wound its way along the green-grass slopes of the East Bay. Broken concrete pads and burnt black fingers of framing erupted through tall wind-driven grass.

You crossed the whole country and lost all your friends, Sergeant. The general, even. Someone named Lola, who you never told me about. All of them.

The Boy passed a convoy of supply trucks, melted and blackened forty years ago.

"Five tons," said the Boy as the morning wind off the bay beat at his long hair, whipping his face and shoulders.

Farther along, the tail rotor of a helicopter lay across the buckling highway.

Apache, maybe.

The KIAs and the MIAs and all the people you imagined were still here, waiting for you to come back — they're all gone.

Later, as Horse nosed the tall grass, the Boy walked around three helicopter transports long since landed in the southbound lanes. They were rusty and dark, stripped of everything.

"Black Hawks," he mumbled, sitting in a pilot's seat, wondering at how one flew them through the air like a bird, which was impossible for him to picture.

Climbing up through the concrete buttresses that remained of Fort Oakland, he came to the tanks.

Blackened. Burnt. Abandoned. High up on the hill he could see the ragged remains of canvas tents and the flower blossoms of spiked artillery pieces.

Sergeant, your dream of finding them here couldn't have survived this.

He led Horse up the hill through the long grass and around the craters and foxholes long since covered in a waving sea of soft green and yellow.

When he reached the spiked artillery pieces now resting forever in permanent bloom, he could see the remains of the Army, of I Corps, below. All the way to the shores of the sparkling bay's eastern edge he could see burnt tanks, melted Humvees, helicopters that would never fly, a fighter jet erupting from the rubble of the few houses that remained along the bay.

I followed you through the rain and the snow and along all those long moonlit nights while you told me about this place. The people. What we would find. Who you were.

And.

Who I might be.

He stood among the tent posts on top of the hill.

Of the Army he'd waited his whole life to meet, only ragged strips of canvas remained, fluttering in the breeze.

Off to the right, down along a ridgeline, he could see a field of white crosses. The graves were open and the crosses lay canted at angles.

I'm glad you died with your dream of this place, Sergeant, because…

… this would have killed you.

All the way.

Tell them who I was, Boy.

Tell who, Sergeant?

And who am I now, Sergeant Presley? Now that you are gone and the dream that you promised me is dead, who am I now?

But there was no answer.

CHAPTER 35

He smelled smoke.

The smoke of meat came to him on the wind of the next day, in the morning, before light.

At first light, he scanned the horizon and saw, across the bay, the columns of rising smoke. He checked the map. Sausalito.

He'd spent the day before combing the wreckage of the Army. There was nothing to be had. Everything that was left had burned long ago. When he went to the cemetery below the ridge, he found bones in the bottom of each open grave. Nothing more.

Maybe there is someone, maybe even I Corps, over there on the other side of the bay, Sergeant?

But there was no answer.

Someone was there.

Later he rode out to the north, crossing large sections of muddy bay where ancient supertankers rested on their sides. Occasionally he passed large craters.

At the northern edge of the bay, mudflats gave way to the tall brown grass of the estuaries. A long thin bridge, low to the water, stretched off toward the west.

A heron, white and tall, stood still, not watching the Boy.

The bridge may only go so far.

After a small break and time spent looking at the map, he decided to try and cross the bridge.

You would ask me why I was in such a hurry to get to the other side, Sergeant. You would say, *Whatchu in a hurry about, Boy?*

I would say, "I want to know what's in Sausalito."

Then you would say, *You always did.*

That is what you would say.

But the voice didn't say anything.

The Boy had not heard the voice since the open graves and the tattered canvas.

The ride out into the marshes made the Boy feel lonely — lonelier than he'd ever felt in all his life. Other than the heron he'd seen at the eastern side of the thin bridge, he saw no other life.

'That is why I feel so alone, because there is no other living thing,' he thought. He'll speak to me again.

In the afternoon, the wind stopped and fog rolled in across the bay. Faster than he would have ever expected, the fog surrounded him and he could see little beyond the thin road ahead.

Only Horse's hooves on the old highway broke the silence.

He expected some bird to call out to another bird, but there was nothing. No one to call to, even if it were just another bird.

It was then that he began to think the bridge might never end — that he would ride forever through the fog.

And what about food? I can't go off in those marshes to hunt. I would be stuck. And Horse, what of him if I have to run?

Stop. You would tell me to stop, Sergeant.

The road will end. And if not, I will turn back and go the long way around the bay.

The thought of having to ride back through the eerie stillness at night did little to comfort him, and for a long time he rode on until at last the bridge began to rise back onto dry land.

See, I had nothing to be afraid of, right, Sergeant?

CHAPTER 36

They worked in the small bay. They were tall and brown skinned like the Chinese of Auburn.

The day had turned cold and gray.

For a long time the Boy stood with Horse, watching them from the dusty road. In time they became aware of him and began to gesture to one another regarding him. Still, they continued to work with their long rakes, sweeping beneath the cold dark water of the bay. Out in the deep water beyond, whitecaps were beginning to form.

I thought I might find the Army here, Sergeant.

His voice had gone now. It had left him in the fog of the bridge over the marsh.

No, it was before that. It was when he saw the open graves and the bones within.

Maybe the knowledge of what happened to I Corps finally killed you, Sergeant. Killed you in a way death could not. Killed the mission you left me to finish.

In time they came in from the water, rolling down their pant legs and donning leather-skinned long jackets trimmed with sheep's wool. A man, older than most, but not the oldest he'd seen, waded out through the tall grass to the road and climbed the embankment to where the Boy sat atop Horse.

Standing in front of the Boy, he said something in Chinese.

He repeated it.

The Boy shook his head.

The man was weathered like the sides of their clapboard shacks.

The Weathered Man stared off toward the bay for a long time. His face was tight and brown, his cheeks red like apples. He watched the dry brown and gray shacks of their farm.

'He is wondering what to do with me,' thought the Boy.

The Weathered Man turned and walked down the embankment, and as an afterthought waved his hand at the Boy, as if he should come along with him.

There was a fire pit outside a long weathered barn that reached out into the gray waters of the bay. The rakes were stacked neatly against the side of the old building.

The Weathered Man drove a stake into the ground for Horse and returned shortly with hay. He laid it down in front of Horse and reached up to caress the long nose, muttering softly in Chinese once more.

He pointed toward a worn long table near the water's edge and the fire for the Boy to sit at.

A giant blackened grill was placed over the fire and then piles of green wet seaweed atop the grill. Salty, white smoke rose up in billows. The rest of the people worked at cleaning small, flat stones they'd brought in wide baskets up from the waters of the bay.

Rough clay plates and cups were set out. There was fresh hot bread and a stone crock of creamy butter, another of red sauce, and another of a pungent dark liquid that smelled of fish and salt.

The wind rose up off the bay in breezy gusts. The Boy's left side was stiff, and he massaged what he could to work life back into the thin muscles of that side.

More of the Chinese appeared, coming from inland, setting down rakes and hoes to go down to the bay and wash their hands in the stinging cold water.

More round loaves of crusty bread were set out, as the flat stones that had been brought up from the bay went onto the grill.

'They eat stones?' thought the Boy, who had seen many different people eat many strange things.

The Weathered Man watched the fire dully, his eyes far away as he stood over the grill with a short rake, moving the stones about.

Shortly, the stones came off the grill and were thrown onto the long flat table. More stones were laid upon the grill and the Chinese sat down, each grabbing at a stone and prying off a hidden lid. Then they raised their stones to their mouths and slurped. They threw the stones into a basket and each of them reached for the next stone, this time adding either the red sauce or the dark liquid smelling of fish and salt, or even the creamy butter, and in some cases a bit of one or the other, and for a few, all three.

The Weathered Man sat down on the bench next to the Boy and looked at him and then the stones. The Weathered Man took one, cracked the lid and slurped, watching the Boy.

The Boy reached out and took one. He peeled back the lid with difficulty, as his withered hand was required to hold the stone. Inside he found the oyster, gray and steaming, swimming in liquid. He ate it, feeling it slide into his mouth and then explode in warm saltiness as he chewed its meat. He looked into the shell where the oyster had once been and found a pearl-colored base swirling white and gray.

It was the most beautiful thing he had ever seen in his short and very hard life.

They ate more oysters and bread. A few talked. The Boy tried the red sauce. It burned slowly and made him sweat at even the few drops he'd added to the oyster using a knife-shaped tool kept in the stone crock.

'It's too hot,' he thought of the sauce.

Afterward, as the heat faded, he liked the taste it left in his mouth. It reminded him of the wild peppers they'd found in the South along the salty marshes of the State of Louisiana.

He tried the dark liquid. It had a salty, deep, satisfying flavor that was almost overripe. But when combined with the yellow butter and the heat of the cooked oyster, it was like eating a good cut of meat taken from a fresh kill, tender and young.

Of their talk he understood nothing. In time, the looks that had been cast his way ceased, as if they had assigned him a place in their world — as if he had always been there and would remain there.

The last batch of oysters was laid out and finished with almost the same zeal as the first.

Two women wearing gray clothes and bright headscarves, their faces tanned and apple cheeked, struggled together with a flat-iron-gray tub brought out from one of the clapboard shacks. The Boy heard a sound like the tinkling of bells, light and musical, as though whatever things were in the tub tapped back and forth against each other.

The tub was set down and the rest of the Chinese gathered around it, taking up bottles of every shape and size and twisting off the caps that sealed them. The bottles made a small popping hiss. They drank from the bottles, few the same color: some green, some brown, a few blues or almost clear. In the clear ones the Boy could see a pale yellow liquid, foaming near the top.

The bottles were from Before, but they had been filled with something from Now.

Later he would think of that sentence.

Especially the part about something from Now.

As if there had ever been such a thing.

The villagers drank in long pulls, then expelled a breathy, "Ahhh." There was much burping.

The Weathered Man, weathered like the clapboard shacks of the village, returned to the table, said something seemingly final in Chinese and handed a green bottle to the Boy.

The Boy took the bottle. He looked inside and could only see a few bubbles. He looked at the cap, which seemed pressed as if stamped onto the bottle. He looked at the Weathered Man.

The Weathered Man took the bottle and with a twist brought the cap off and handed it back to the Boy as foam rose out of its top. The Weathered Man drank from his bottle, watching the Boy, telling him with his eyes that the Boy should do the same.

The Boy closed his eyes and drank. Foam and suds raced up into his nose. But the drink was cold, ice cold. It tasted of the fields.

When he opened his eyes the Weathered Man was smiling at him, as if saying, "See," and then, "What do you think?" all at once.

A warm flush rose up in the Boy.

And he was not so cold.

And he was not so alone.

"Pee Gee Oh," said the Weathered Man, holding the bottle up.

"Pee Gee Oh," said the Boy, and drank again. The Weathered Man smiled and drank.

They each considered the bay, watching the white-caps roll and disappear across its waters. There was still daylight now as winter faded and spring appeared.

'The days were growing again,' thought the Boy.

He drank and looked at the little village by the bay. It was a collection of weathered clapboard buildings and steep roofs, growing out of the tall green grass among the curvy stunted trees whose limbs gathered in bunches like hats. All around him the Chinese talked seriously or laughed or whispered. Some played games with rectangles of stone.

He thought of their apple cheeks, bright red from the cold water and the wind.

He thought of their oysters hidden each day beneath the waters.

They were kind.

They were a village of kind people.

If he could mark things on the map he would spell this as the Village of Kind People Who Will Give You Food.

And Pee Gee Oh.

Whatever that was.

It was good.

He took the last drink from the bottle, feeling warm and fuzzy. He considered the hills to the east, on the other side of the bay, the lands there broken and bent, mired in destruction and overrun by the swollen rivers he'd crossed.

He thought of MacRaven and Dunn and all the tribes.

Those people, those Chinese, were like these.

And now they were dead.

He went to his saddlebag and took out his sack of charcoal. He looked around.

I need a place to draw. But the charcoal won't show on the sides of their shacks.

He found a patch of concrete back toward the road. Weeds and grass grew up through the broken spaces.

He made a small fire.

He drew the courthouse first.

He saw the Chinese watching him from afar, standing around their tables, enjoying the last of their Pee Gee Oh.

He drew the dome of the courthouse, sketching the part of the dome that had been sheared off by the giant crossbow bolt.

He could hear the singing twang as it launched.

He drew the streets as he remembered them, mainly the intersection where he'd seen the bodies riddled with arrows.

He heard the villagers muttering over him as he worked on all fours drawing the fire and the smoke and the carnage.

He heard them and forgot them all at once.

He drew the ramparts, the pine logs burning like the breath of evil monsters, as the tribes, feathered and in war paint, crawled over the spiked tops. He drew Escondido firing into something unseen.

He drew smoke.

He drew falling arrows.

He drew fire.

He drew the woman lying in the street, staring at the sky.

He could not draw the crying of the baby or all the other screams he seemed to remember now.

He stood back.

He could feel the weight of the Chinese watching him. He could hear their breath escaping through their open mouths.

Someone dropped a bottle and it exploded with a crash.

No one said a word.

There was one more thing.

He stooped to the drawing once more. His side was not stiff. He didn't feel anything here by the bay. He was there at the outpost, on that golden morning just after dawn.

The smell of burning pine.

The screams and bullets and smoke appearing in the windows of the old courthouse.

He was on the median of grass astride the great highway.

MacRaven told him: "I'll conquer the world."

MacRaven, his wolf's face smiling like a child's, his eyes shining. MacRaven, in armor, staring out at the Chinese.

The Boy stood, letting the last of the charcoal fall from his numb fingers.

And someone began to cry.

CHAPTER 37

They gave the Boy and Horse a shack to sleep in for the night. It was small and it lay next to the road and the ocean, its only furnishing a baked clay brazier with hot coals. The wind beat at the shack in the night, and once, when he stepped outside to urinate, he saw a clear night sky and the moon riding high over the bay. He saw the dark shapes of birds crossing the waters in the night toward the broken shadows of the ruins of San Francisco.

He was so tired and so comfortable from the meal and the Pee Gee Oh that he almost could not sleep.

But then he did.

Later the Boy was not sure if he was dreaming or awake when he heard the hooves of another horse disappear off into the night.

He awoke to the hands of the Weathered Man gently shaking him, giving him a cup of tea, beckoning him to come outside into the morning light.

The Boy wrapped himself in his bearskin and led Horse out into the gray mist, drinking the tea, his withered hand holding the lead. Horse would only go as far as the Boy went and when he stopped, so did Horse.

The Chinese soldiers wore the same uniform as their comrades in Auburn. They also wore cartridge belts about their waists and carried long rifles.

One of the soldiers turned from inspecting the concrete pad and the charcoal drawing.

Their leader, a bright-eyed thin man walked toward the Boy, speaking in Chinese. When he realized the Boy did not understand, he turned back to the others, speaking rapidly.

They mounted their horses and made signs that the Boy should come with them.

The Weathered Man nodded in agreement.

The troop of Chinese horse soldiers, along with the Boy and Horse, rode away from the village a short while leather, following the coast road. Just before the village was lost to a bend in the landscape, the Boy turned back to look upon it once more.

'I am always arriving and then leaving,' he thought.

What would it be like to stay?

I wish you would speak to me again, Sergeant Presley. That you would say, *Ain't nothin' but a thang.*

But the Boy knew it was only his own voice.

Knew it was what he wanted to hear.

Knew it was a lie he wanted to believe, which is the worst kind of lie we tell ourselves.

The Weathered Man was already out in the water with his rake.

He was working.

Long strokes through the water.

Only the rake betrayed the Weathered Man's presence in the water and the fog. Then the troop passed the bend on the coast road and the Weathered Man was gone.

The troop rode on through the quiet morning mist. From a small inlet they could see a great shroud of fog clutching at the ruins of San Francisco, across the bay.

I can go there now, Sergeant; if you will not stop me I will go there.

He hoped the voice would come. He hoped it would tell him, as it had all the other times before, that he must avoid such places.

But it didn't.

At a small farm, the troop leader dismounted and knocked at the door of a large spreading house. After words and more words, a small man, squinting and hobbling on bad feet, opened the door and came out. He peered at the Boy as if seeing him from across a great distance.

The leader spoke softly and then the small man walked forward, standing in front of the Boy.

"*Hey canna me?*" the small man said.

The Boy had no idea what this meant.

"*Whas goons runnna you?*"

The Boy shook his head to mean he didn't understand.

"*Betcha ken rednecks?*"

After the third failure the small man turned back to the troop leader and shook his head sadly. The leader laid his hand on the small man's shoulder and whispered something in his ear. Then he patted the old man and moved off to remount his horse.

They rode farther south and for a moment, the Boy thought they might be going to cross a massive bridge that spanned the entrance to the bay and landed in the ruins of San Francisco.

The Boy felt a surge of excitement.

The troop descended into a little cove that opened up onto the bay. A small city ran alongside the edge of the water and climbed up into the green heights overlooking Sausalito.

The edge of the bay was guarded by rock walls that ran upward over the green hills inland and down to the water's edge. Soldiers with guns watched from the high walls as the troop came down the road toward the gate and disappeared into a spreading shantytown that threw itself along the mudflats and out into the calm waters of the bay. In the shantytown there were many Chinese mixed with others like himself. Like the outpost at Auburn.

There were buildings where the smells of food came wafting heavily out onto the muddy lanes. They passed stores where he could see objects waiting in the dark beyond the front porch. He smelled fish. He smelled the oil of the rifles. He smelled the same smell of the fields that he'd tasted in the Pee Gee Oh.

Children and women came out and watched as the Boy was escorted through the winding maze of the shantytown that lay at the foot of the gates to the city beneath the green hills and along the edge of the bay. Soon a small crowd followed at a distance.

The troop came to a large gate of polished dark wood set in a smooth white wall. Tall buildings rose up in stone and timber on the other side. But only their tops could be seen.

The leader dismounted and indicated the Boy should wait. Then he disappeared through an opened crack in the gate.

When the leader returned there were many other Chinese soldiers with him now. There was chatter, voices bouncing and bubbling, but over all pervaded a sense of seriousness, even concern.

An older Chinese soldier, steely eyed and with an air of command, his iron-gray hair streaked with black, came forward in highly polished leather boots.

He barked in Chinese at the Boy.

The troop leader interceded.

The older Chinese soldier watched the Boy.

The troop leader, who'd been inspecting the drawing that morning at the village by the water, turned to the Boy and waved his hands at the ground.

He wants me to draw what I drew at the village where they eat stones.

The Boy went to his saddlebag and took out his bag of charcoal.

He took out a long piece and sharpened it with his knife.

He looked at the troop leader, letting the thought "Where should I draw?" form itself on his face.

For a moment the troop leader, intent and hopeful, didn't understand.

Then he raised his hand to his head. He looked around.

He led the Boy to the smooth wall that encompassed the gate.

The Boy tried to see the attack.

The old courthouse.

The bodies.

The horror.

He limped forward until he could feel the wall blocking out all the watching pairs of eyes.

He raised the charcoal to the wall and made the first line. A curving arc that represented the dome of the old courthouse from Before.

At once there was a gasp from the crowd.

The older soldier began to speak in definite and harsh tones to the troop leader. But the troop leader gave a quick reply and silence returned.

The Boy looked back at the troop leader.

The Chinese soldier nodded.

The older soldier rolled his eyes toward the sky and then lowered them into a thin slit. Then, he too nodded at the Boy.

The Boy gave them war.

The Boy gave them the rain of arrows.

Fire and smoke.

The staring dead.

The Boy went big.

He showed the ashen-faced warriors, grim and determined as they worked their shining crossbow.

He showed them the Psychos in their Mohawks and tattoos, their axes held aloft, reminding him even as he worked of winter trees in morning's first light.

He showed them MacRaven in armor.

When he stepped back, he heard his foot make a sandy scraping sound as he dragged it across the flagstones of the pavement. It was the only other sound he'd heard besides his charcoal *scratch-scratch-scratching* against the high wall.

He turned.

He saw horror in their eyes.

They had known those people.

A woman wept. She was Chinese. She was pregnant.

The Boy thought of the Chinese snipers in the courthouse windows.

Soldiers and fathers in the same moment.

The older soldier walked forward.

His hand traced the broken dome.

He turned to the Boy and raised a hand pointing east, pointing over the bay, over the green hills and the river beyond, and the city it had swallowed and the fields and into the foothills and to the place of the drawing.

The Boy nodded.

He had destroyed their world more completely than MacRaven's shining crossbow ever would.

"Name?"

The voice came from the side of the crowd, from near the open crack in the gate. It gurgled, as though erupting up through a sea of mud.

The Boy turned.

"Rank?" It was an old Chinese man. Fat. Tall. Bent. His gray hair was slicked back over his large liver-spotted and peeling head. He wore the old Red Chinese army uniform from Before. The Boy had once seen the tattered scraps of such a uniform. Sergeant Presley had shown him one they'd found inside a downed transport, crashed in a field outside Galveston.

You told me it was the uniform of a Chinese general, Sergeant.

For a moment the Boy had almost heard the voice of Sergeant Presley. It reminded him of hearing someone call out for a child at dusk, telling them to come home finally.

The Boy remembered that day. It had been cold. They'd huddled inside the creaking wreckage of the big transport crashed long ago in the plain of waving grass.

You told me, Sergeant, that they were Chinese airborne. You told me they tried to drop them all across North America after we nuked the Middle East. You told me they were all in on it, but they got scattered, shot down. Jumped by our few remaining fighters. Pockets of Chinese airborne everywhere. Even made a good defense in Reno. The map said so.

You told me that, Sergeant, and now I need you to tell me what to do.

"Serial number?" barked the old Chinese general, wearing the same type uniform Sergeant Presley had shown him on that day they spent hiding in the wreckage.

Another uniform the same as this one.

Another Chinese general.

The Boy croaked, "I don't…" It had been a long time since he'd spoken aloud.

"I speak… American," said the old man, the Chinese general. He rolled forward on a crooked cane.

He probably was once very strong, but now he moved worse than the Boy.

"I am General Song. I defeated the American Army."

The Boy lowered his eyes to the sandstone pavement.

I am glad… and then he was about to think, 'that you are dead, Sergeant Presley.'

But he stopped.

Behind the Chinese general stood a girl. She was young. His age. Chinese.

She was beautiful.

And…

She looked at him.

Without horror.

Without fear.

Without pity.

She was beautiful.

CHAPTER 38

He wanted to see her again.

He wanted to be left alone by all these Chinese.

He wanted to be left alone so that he might draw her.

He wanted to draw the way she had looked at him.

All about him, the Chinese were in an uproar.

Suddenly there was activity and work. Riders were dispatched to the east. A woman gave Horse an apple. The Chinese general and the girl disappeared behind the massive gate, the old soldier casting his steely gaze back upon the Boy.

She stood before the Boy, even though she was gone now.

She looked at him.

The troop leader led him to a shack by the water of the bay. The troop leader tied Horse to a hitching post nearby and pointed toward the shack.

Stay.

The Boy went inside. It had a table, a chair, and a cooking pit. Stairs led to a loft with a pallet and blankets. Out the back door was a small dock and the bay beyond where tiny slender boats bobbed in the windy afternoon.

Toward evening he smelled fire. Then food cooking.

The troop leader returned with a plate of chicken, chilies, and garlic. There was a small wooden basket full of rice.

They both ate at the table.

The sun was setting when the troop leader went out for a moment and returned with a bundle of clothing. He draped the pieces over the chair.

Overalls made of wool.

A rubber trench coat with a high collar.

Rubber boots.

A hooded gas mask.

He took out a slip of paper.

"Please," he began to read haltingly from the paper, "put... these... on... and... come... with... me."

The Boy brought Horse inside the shack. The troop leader gave a pained look, then seemed to accept this. He left and returned with hay, setting it down in front of Horse.

The Boy nodded to himself and began to dress in the items.

He had seen them before.

Sergeant Presley had worn similar gear when he'd entered the ruins of Washington, in the District of Columbia.

The clothing made him feel warm, and within moments to the point of suffocation.

When the Boy came to the mask he donned it, unsure if he had done it properly, trying to remember how Sergeant Presley had worn it. The patrol leader went behind the Boy and pulled the straps of the mask tightly, jerking them almost. Then he patted the Boy's shoulder.

The Boy looked out through the steamy eye holes.

He could hear his own breathing.

He tucked his withered left arm into the pocket of the trench coat and made to take up his tomahawk but the leader shook his head.

The Boy placed the tomahawk on the small wooden table.

Then they left, stepping outside into the twilight of early evening. From behind the soft-lit windows of the shantytown, the Boy could hear, muffled by the hood of the gas mask, the low murmur of voices.

Someone cackled.

There was distant laughter.

Someone played long whining notes on a lone violin, then repeated them.

Dogs barked.

They arrived at the shining wooden gate. Two sentries stood aside as the massive portal swung open.

Beyond the gate they found a long, empty street. Large houses with stone exteriors, polished wood trim, and sloping rooftops lined the street, which looked out onto a park and the open bay beyond. At the end of the street the water of the bay glimmered softly in the night behind a low wall. Torches guttered before each house along the quiet street.

Through the mask the Boy could smell the heavy scent of jasmine. A smell that reminded him of Sergeant Presley and their days passing through the South.

He thought of the map.

It was still in its secret pouch inside the bearskin.

He thought of his tomahawk and said to himself, "Might not get it back," as though Sergeant Presley were warning him. But still, it was just his own voice.

They stopped at an old building from Before. It rested on the far side of the road, standing on pillars that rose up out of the lapping waves. The Chinese soldiers, and others more finely dressed than the dwellers of the shantytown, were gathered about its steps. A hush fell over the small crowd as the troop leader with the Boy in tow, approached.

Inside, great glass windows opened up onto a view of the wide bay and the shadowy city lying in ruins beyond its waters.

There was the Chinese general.

The Old Soldier.

A group of Chinese, dressed in soft clothing that caught the flickering light of candles, stood at the far end of the room.

They held fans over their mouths.

They watched the Boy with sideways glances, murmuring to one another.

The girl was there too.

She watched him from the farthest corner. She watched him from just behind the Chinese general.

The Boy sat on a stool in the center of the room, as he was directed, then the Chinese general came forward, standing halfway between the Boy and the audience.

"I am General Song. Do you remember that we met earlier? Outside the gate."

The Boy nodded.

The general smiled. Pleased. As if his greatest fear had been that the Boy might have forgotten their earlier meeting.

"Our governing council" — the general stopped and indicated those who stood behind him, pressed against the far wall, fans covering their mouths — "would like to ask you a few more questions, if that is possible."

"I thought you were their leader," said the Boy.

The general smiled.

"I am no longer... I am now merely a scholar who knows a little more of the past than most because of my military service, and only because I lived through it."

"I will answer what questions I can," said the Boy.

"Has our outpost, the one you drew — has it been destroyed?"

The Boy remained silent.

"The place you drew. Did anyone survive?"

The Boy spoke through the mask, his voice muffled. The insides of the mask were slick with sweat and heat. Mist clung to the lenses.

"I didn't understand you. Could you please say that again? I'll come closer," said the Chinese general, and when he did he asked the same question again.

"I don't know," replied the Boy. "I doubt that anyone who remained there could have lasted much longer."

The Chinese general turned back toward the audience at the far end of the room and spoke in their language. The people in the audience murmured among themselves and then someone spoke above the others. The Chinese general turned back to the Boy.

"And how is it that you survived?"

"I escaped."

And thus a pattern formed. The general spoke in Chinese. The audience murmured. Someone spoke. The general asked a new question.

"Where did you come from?"

"The east."

"Who are your people?"

"I don't have any."

"How far east?"

"A place that was once called Washington Dee Cee."

"What is there now?"

"A swamp."

"Who destroyed the outpost, I mean the place that you drew?"

"A man named MacRaven. He has an army of tribes."

"How big?"

"More than you have in all the soldiers I have seen who carry your rifles."

"The characters on your rifle indicate it was given to a man who was a known skin trader. What has become of this man and how did you acquire his rifle?"

"He rescued me from lions in the high desert beyond Reno. We fought together on the walls of your outpost. He did not survive and I took his rifle when I escaped."

"Will this MacRaven the barbarian come here?"

"I don't know." Then, "If I were you I would plan for him to. He seemed that sort of man."

"How do we know you are not part of this MacRaven's barbarian army and that you yourself didn't kill the owner of the rifle and come here as a spy or a saboteur?"

"I know 'spy.' I am not that. The other word I do not understand."

"A destroyer. A terrorist."

"I am not a terrorist."

"And how do we know you are telling the truth?"

The Boy stopped for a moment. He was hot. Sweat was dripping down the inside of his mask. He moved to take off the mask and the Chinese general lunged forward with sudden vigor and command.

"Do not take that off! It is forbidden here for you to remove your mask."

The Boy could feel his audience pressing themselves farther away from him, toward the back of the room.

The Boy lowered his hands from the mask.

The general walked closer. "I am sorry," he said softly, his eyes speaking an unspoken message of friendliness. "They do not understand."

"And why," began the general again, "should we trust your account?"

The Boy stared for a long moment at the crowd surrounding him. When his eyes rested on the girl he forgot everything he'd intended to say.

He forgot…

… everything.

When he was reminded of the question by a gurgling cough from the Chinese general, he spoke.

"I don't know why you would trust me."

The audience murmured at the translation.

A discussion started.

"May I ask a question?" said the Boy.

Silence.

The general walked back toward the Boy.

"Ask."

"What has become of I Corps?"

The general did not translate.

His face fell.

His mouth opened.

His shoulders slumped.

He seemed suddenly older.

The general shook his head to himself as if finishing an argument he'd started long ago and lost many times since. Then he looked at the Boy.

"They are no more." And, "I know that for certain."

There was no pride in his voice. No triumph. No satisfaction.

But there was guilt.

There was shame.

"When I was young I thought it would be different," said the Chinese general very plainly. "I thought only of victory."

The general sighed heavily.

"I know differently now." He looked at the Boy, maybe beyond the Boy. "I am responsible."

"You were there?" asked the Boy. "At the end of I Corps?"

The general whispered, "Yes."

"If the man who brought me here," the Boy indicated the troop leader, "would return to my things and bring me the bearskin I wear… I have something for you."

Orders were given and the discussion among the Chinese renewed. All the while, the general watched the Boy and waited for the return of the requested bearskin.

I have given away all my intel, Sergeant. I know that is not what you taught me to do. But what good is it to anyone, now that all of you are dead?

There was no reply.

The bearskin arrived and the Boy laid it out and retrieved the map from inside the hidden pouch.

Sergeant, I'm doing this so that maybe they'll trust me. I'm doing this so they'll be ready for MacRaven when he comes. I remember what we both saw outside Oklahoma City.

The Boy stood.

He raised his right arm and saluted the Chinese general.

He held out the map.

Tell them who I was, Boy.

Tell them I made it all the way, never quit.

Tell them there's nothing left.

"There's nothing left," said the Boy.

CHAPTER 39

The night air felt cool and dried the sweat on the Boy's face as he was led back from the meeting beyond the gate. The wind had picked up from off the bay. It would be a long, cold night. The shantytown was quiet and only a single candle burned in the odd window they passed along its lanes.

In the shack it was warm from the heat given off by the brazier, its glow a dull orange. Inside, Horse raised a sleepy eye then returned to his rest and dreams. The troop leader left and came back with more hay. He said something in Chinese, a farewell perhaps, then closed the door to the shack behind him as he left.

The Boy took off the sweaty gear they had given him and went out the back door.

He walked to the end of the narrow two-plank dock and lowered himself into the freezing dark water of the bay.

It was cold.

Maybe the coldest water he'd ever felt.

He thought of the girl as he floated in the darkness.

Back inside the shack he put his clothes on and, as though he had known all along what he would do next, he took up the carved piece of charcoal once more.

He made a line. The outline of her hair. Long and straight. A curve over the top of her head.

Then another line for her delicate chin.

And a line falling away from the chin for her neck.

They'll see this.

He put the charcoal back in its pouch and sat by the glowing coals of the brazier, watching the simple lines he had drawn.

The lines were enough to remember her by.

In the morning it was the troop leader who appeared once more. They both took Horse out into the mist and walked him along the bay's edge, following a winding muddy street. Fishing boats lay motionless in the calm waters of the fog-shrouded bay.

They crossed into a ruined section of the shantytown.

Ruins from Before.

Buildings with chunks of concrete and whole sections missing. Buildings where the plaster facade had fallen away long ago. Buildings from which metal girders twisted wickedly upward. Buildings that had fallen into little more than piles from which rusty strands of rebar sprung like wild hair.

A work crew hovered over the ruins of a building, testing it with their crowbars and the occasional shovel. Other men moved piles of rubble in wheelbarrows.

They are removing the town that was here Before, Sergeant.

They came to a building. It was in better shape than most. Inside they found the Chinese general.

He hobbled forward, his big frame leaning heavily on a bent cane.

"I have studied the map you gave me." After a pause the general continued breathily, "Can you tell me about all those places? What is there now? That's what we wish to know. Our outpost was our farthest settlement. We cannot go south due to the nature of contamination in that area, so it seems we must know what lies to the east. If we could go over the map together, you might tell me a little bit about each place. If that would be acceptable to you?"

The Boy thought of the girl.

He thought of leaving this place.

He had left every place he had ever been.

He wondered if he might see her here.

If he left he would never see her again.

"Yes."

"Good," said the general and led him to a large desk. The map lay spread out across its expanse. The floor that surrounded the desk was a sea upon which books rose like sudden and angry waves. Leaning against the walls were all manner of things. Tools, ancient rifles from Before, many things the Boy had no name for.

"So we know you came through Reno. What were your experiences there?"

The Boy thought for a moment. How did one describe the fear of an unknown mad animal lying in wait in the dark? How did one describe that laughing terror and the single leering face seen as a shadow through dirty glass for even just the part of a moment?

"Reno is like a hole where an animal lives." He thought of the bear cave. "Where something that isn't human makes its home now."

The general laid his finger on the map over Reno.

"Colonel Juk was their commander. I have always wondered, over the years, what became of his unit and the men we sent there. Their last report told of being dug in and facing American armor coming out of the desert to the southeast."

The Boy watched the map and all the places Sergeant Presley had been.

"How is it like a wild animal in a cave?" asked the general.

The Boy thought for a moment. He approached a wall and moved aside a heavy machine gun, dusty and untouched. He cleared a space along the wall.

He took out his charcoal.

He began to draw.

He drew the blind window-eyes of a corpse that was once a city. In his mind the angles were somehow distorted and maniacal. The buildings took on a surreal aspect, as if sanity hadn't been a requirement for their architect. As if the years since, and the madmen within, had somehow turned the buildings "wrong." He drew the bridge they'd passed under. The Boy, Horse, and Escondido. It was an open mouth, full of smashed teeth. He drew a high window, a long window twisting to the side, almost bending away from the perspective of the viewer. A window among a hundred other lunatic windows in shadow. In it the Boy placed the shadow of a man seen for just a moment. With a few quick lines he began the face, the jaw, the hair, and before he could add more to those few scribbled, hesitant, unfinished lines, the lunatic seemed complete.

When the Boy turned back, the general, watching him, nodded.

The old soldier turned to the map, his finger still resting above the word "Reno."

"I understand."

After a moment of looking again at the map, the Chinese general cleared his throat.

"Tell me about Salt Lake City."

And then...

She entered, carrying a tray of teacups and a pot.

CHAPTER 40

At the end of the week General Song sat in his patched leather chair from Before. Shoulders slumped. Eyes wide. Staring.

On the walls that surrounded him were many charcoal markings formed into drawings.

At Des Moines, two figures, a small boy, eyes wide with terror, and a black man, his face an angry curse — heavy oversize packs on each of their backs — ran across a field of sickly grass. Above them, crows — all the crows in the world — swarmed, diving and attacking them. In the foreground, a crow swooped away from the boy and the man. The crow's eyes were two black oblongs of animal indifference. The wings seemed to rise in triumph. Its beak was open as if the *cawww!* that must come from it was a mighty roar. All the birds were rendered with such malevolence.

Beaks open.

Claws reaching.

Wings spreading.

One could almost hear a sonic sea of victory caws as each bird swooped and dived, wheeling overhead.

Herding their prey.

Carnivorous now.

Finally, after the end of the world and an ocean of wild, genetically powerful corn that had broken and overtaken the lands of middle America — surviving what civilization, mankind, had not, in Des Moines, Iowa — crows ruled the land.

Outside Madison, Wisconsin, powerful dogs with short necks like bulls and wide mouths full of canine teeth surged forward. Real hatred could be found in their snarling muzzles as opposed to the crows' mere soulless-ness. The black man leaned hard on a door. His face was twisted in rage, his eyes focused. Next to him was the Boy, long hair covering his face as it turns back toward the approaching pack of wild dogs. A long hallway trailed off to the horizon. Someplace abandoned. An old shopping center. They were trapped. The fierce dogs bounded toward them. In the lead dog, every muscle was perfectly and beautifully rendered like taut cables of charcoal-driven power. There is an urgency the viewer feels when looking at the black man, who must open the door if he and the Boy are to survive. It is the kind of picture one looks at then turns away from, praying that such a thing will never happen to them.

Or to their loved ones.

"Who is the black man?" he'd asked the Boy.

"Sergeant Lyman Julius Presley."

At Detroit, sailboats were piled high against a beach of black rocks and garbage. The sky was overcast and gray. The lake struck the shore hard, almost angrily. 'One could hear,' thought the general, 'the damaged spinnakers and tangled tackle clanging compulsively in the wind while occasional ancient spars groaned in torment.'

"Were you with Sergeant Presley when you made it to Detroit?"

"I was always with him."

"What is your earliest memory of him?"

"We were walking on the road. He was carrying all our things and I kept falling behind him because I was still little. He was singing one of his marching songs about Captain Jack and he said to me, 'Keep up, or I might leave you behind.' "

At Cincinnati there was a river. There were no buildings. No trees. Only a dark hill on the horizon. A road sign, unreadable, bent forever away from the place.

"Why did this Sergeant Presley keep going, even though all the evidence seemed to indicate that his country was destroyed?" asked the general.

The Boy simply looked at the picture and then, when the general felt as if the Boy would not answer, the Boy spoke.

"He told me one time that he couldn't quit. That to quit was to die. That he'd quit once, before I met him, and a lot of people got killed."

And.

"I've always thought that those people getting killed had something to do with where I came from."

At Pittsburgh was the American bomber. The nose and cockpit were in the foreground as the fuselage stretched away, cracked in the middle. The only wing visible lay collapsed. A car lay trapped under the nose. Rusting cars dotted the landscape of the freeway.

"How come you never asked Sergeant Presley about where you came from?" asked the general.

"I did and he told me that the past wasn't important anymore because it was just wreckage and junk and not worth going over. He told me that the only thing that was important now was the future."

"And yet he was still looking for his country under all this wreckage, like that of the bomber on the wall?"

Silence.

"He said America was more than just the things we'd seen: the rubble of the cities, the broken highways, the burned-up tanks. He said America was a good idea. And that as long as he was alive, the good that was in the idea was still alive."

At Baltimore, a shaven-headed man with malevolent eyes held a shovel. A twisted farmhouse, windows out of perspective, rose toward the ceiling of the room where the general sat. A woman, scrawny and underfed, looked at the ground with bruised and blackened eyes. She stood behind the malevolent man, in his shadow. In an orchard in the background, under a crescent moon, wild figures leapt about a fire as something man-like lay atop a grill, its legs splayed, its arms akimbo.

"Who are they?" he asked the Boy.

"They are the Cotter family and they're evil."

And there were other pictures…

The general leaned back in his chair.

This was what happened after war.

'I remember,' he thought. 'Before it all, before the bombs even, I remember walking down a boulevard in Beijing; the cherry blossoms were just beginning to fall. I remember the posters, and the songs about bravery and our country that we thought we loved so much. I remember I was very proud of my uniform and that when the time came I would earn its inherent respect. I remember thinking I would do anything for my country.'

We all thought that way.

Anything.

We had no idea.

We were wrong.

CHAPTER 41

The Boy had drawn a story wherever the Chinese general had placed his finger on Sergeant Presley's map. If the Boy had been there or knew something about the place, he had rendered it in charcoal across the walls of the general's study.

"One day," said the general, "we must go to these places and find what is left there. Not to conquer as our current leaders wish and which will only bring the wrath of the barbarians down on us as it has already. But we must go to these places in order that we might make something new. What you tell me in your drawings may one day make a difference to those that must go to these places on the wall."

And each day she had brought them tea in the afternoon.

And one day...

After she set the tea down and while the general stood close to the wall studying a picture of Little Rock, Arkansas, in which the Boy skinned a deer with trembling hands, the girl moved next to the Boy.

In the picture, the Boy was laying out the heart and liver on a crumbling table inside a large building, a library perhaps, by the look of the collapsed bookshelves. There was a river passing outside shattered and dirty windows. Among the collapsed shelves of books, the black man built a fire from fallen volumes. There was hunger on both of their faces.

The general said little once the picture was finished and as he studied it. He stood silently before it, consuming its every detail. Today, the girl did not leave as she usually did once she placed the tray of tea on the large and very old desk.

The Boy, because the day was cold and his withered side was stiff, reached for the tea, already inhaling its hot jasmine aroma. And she caught his hand just before he grasped the cup.

He looked into her eyes.

She squeezed his hand.

He was frozen.

His heart did not beat.

He was sweating.

And he squeezed back. Hard. Almost too hard.

"Jin," she whispered.

The general called her Jin. He had learned that much.

She squeezed his hand once more and took a cup of tea to the general.

After that, she left and did not look at him, as the general had turned from the picture and was now talking to the Boy. Words in the English. Words the Boy did not understand because he could not concentrate on anything other than the moment of her touch. His face felt as though it were on fire.

"Is there no place that survived in some part beyond a mere day-to-day existence?" asked the general.

The Boy was watching the girl named Jin, though she had already left the room.

"She is the only one who believes in my work," said the general, watching the Boy's eyes. "She is the only one who, like me, wants to know what happened out there. She is not afraid of it. She is not bothered by the harsh reality of these times like so many of our people, who simply wish to live behind their gates and keep themselves from the 'contamination' as they call it, of the world as it is now. They require only that their lives be beautiful and a reminder of a homeland that is gone. They willingly live a lie, simply because it is fragrant."

The general paused and sipped at the tea he had taken up in his two liver-spotted hands.

"Jin and I seek the truth because the truth holds its own beauty. In my opinion, it is the lies of our past that have brought about the current state of destruction. Late in my life, I vowed never to live another lie. My only sadness is that I made the vow after the world had been burned and poisoned by a rain of nuclear radiation."

The Boy watched the general.

"Sometimes I think she merely humors an old man," said the general, lost in the map again. "But she is a good granddaughter and I feel that she can look past the damage and the rubble and the warmongering of our collective past, both China and America, and find what was noble and beautiful about us."

He fell to mumbling when his eyes found some new, previously unconsidered mark on the map, "I was saying…"

That night the Boy lay on the floor of the shack near the brazier. It was exceptionally cold outside. His side ached. His hand was cramped and black from the charcoal he used to draw pictures on the walls of the general's study.

Horse stirred as the fire popped.

The Boy was watching the lines.

He was watching Jin.

Horse complains for a moment as if sensing an animal outside in the cold wind and the dark night.

There was a moment of quiet that threatened to go on forever.

And then...

There was a knock at the back door that led out to the two-plank dock.

The Boy opened the door.

Jin pressed her mouth into his and he could feel her cold, soft cheeks grow warm. Her slender body melted into his arms, alive and living within his grasp. He felt her arms about him, clutching at his shoulders. And for a moment one hand slipped down to his withered arm, caressing him there.

"I am Jin," she said haltingly. " I do not... speak American" — she said something in Chinese — "very well." Then, "But I am learning."

He closed the door and brought her to the fire. She stood warming herself while he got the bearskin and wrapped it around her.

"What is your... name?" she asked.

The Boy looked at her.

In the light from the glowing brazier, wrapped in the skin of the bear, she was even more beautiful. She looked at him expectantly, her eyes shining in the firelight.

"What do they call me? What do your people call me?"

"They call... you... the Messenger."

"Why?"

"You brought... the news of the barbarians. I do not want... I do not want to call... you the Messenger."

"Why?"

She kissed him again and again until their intensity threatened to consume them. Breathlessly she broke from his hungry embrace, panting, "It... cannot be."

Later, they sat staring into the fire, she reclining against him, the two of them almost sleeping, dreaming.

"Why?" asked the Boy.

She drew her fingers along his powerful arm.

He liked that.

Later she said, "You know that this is... not done?"

He held her hands, resting them on her belly.

"If you were my woman, then it would be all right."

"No, that can never... be."

"Why?"

She took up his withered hand. She turned to face him. Her dark eyes caught the firelight.

"I... can know... can tell. I can tell... you are brave. To me you are very... pretty... no... handsome. You are... clean. 'Whole' is the word? To me. But our leaders will not let those who live inside the gate... I do not like this word... it's... is their... but they say 'sully'... you know... to be unclean? With the barbarians."

She sighed deeply, her eyes searching the darkened rafters for the right words. For the story. For the explanation.

"Even before we came… to here. To this place, America. We were separate and apart from others. Mandarin and Cantonese. Government and peasant. Not the same, do you understand? But after the war… even more so, there were many… defects. Many of the survivors from other places… Americans… were like you."

He understood. She was perfectly formed. Perfectly beautiful, and he was not. It would be wrong of him to make her his woman. It would be wrong in this place.

"Even our people… were affected by the radiation from… bombs. But those children… how do you say…" She searched the room, her eyes casting about and finding nothing. "Never existed?"

The Boy nodded, understanding.

"They made them disappear. They made… rules, laws, I mean. No intermarrying with those who are sick… unclean. Now, they cannot even stand… to have them inside… the gate."

She watched his eyes, searching to find the wound her words, the truth, had caused him.

But he remained steady, his gaze never wavering from her deep brown eyes.

"To me you… it does not matter, you are whole, to me," she said again.

The Boy looked at her for a long time.

In his eyes she saw the question.

"Is that why I had to wear the suit beyond the gate?"

"Yes… they fear you will contaminate… them. They understand little and are afraid… much." Then, "It is not wise of them. They do not have… wisdom."

"Wisdom changes things. I knew a man who was very wise. But he is gone now… I need wisdom."

"We… all… do," she whispered.

An hour before dawn he led her to the dock. A slender boat, tied to the wooden planks, bobbed atop choppy wavelets.

As he helped her down into the tiny boat, he felt a sudden moment of terror, as if he were casting something valuable, something precious — his tomahawk, his best blanket, food even — down into a pit. Or an ocean. Or an abyss.

And I am hoping it will come back to me.

And.

She is more valuable than my tomahawk or a blanket or even food.

Why?

"Will you be safe?" he asked her.

Why was she valuable?

"Yes. I'll use the boat to… go around… the point and then come close to the wall. I know my way over… and our home is just… just on the other side."

He leaned down to untie the boat.

"When you stood…" she began, "in front of our leaders… in your mask… and at the wall… you were not afraid to tell them… the truth. They are… always… have been… afraid of truth." She looked at him. She shook her head slightly. "You are not afraid… of anything… even of the truth."

And.

"I also… am not afraid," she said finally and turned the boat toward open water.

She looked small and helpless in the boat and he watched as she paddled out and away from him, rounding the point and finally disappearing. He watched the water for a long time, until he almost felt frozen inside. Within the shack he lay down on the bearskin in front of the fire.

Why?

Because she saw me when she looked at me.

Without horror.

Without fear.

Without pity.

And because she did not look away when she let me see that she was beautiful.

Thinking he was still awake, he slept. When he awoke with a start, wondering what was real and what was not, he smelled jasmine.

CHAPTER 42

The Chinese were preparing for war.

Soldiers drilled with their long breech-loading rifles. Large cannon were dragged forward by teams of laborers to an outer wall that was being hastily thrown up to surround the shantytown and the inner city. Every day riders left, thundering off toward the east at all times.

When the Boy returned to the shack by the water after another day of drawing for the general, he saw a strange man waiting under a roof down the lane, staying out of the spring drizzle. He was Chinese. He was thin. He appeared to watch something far away, but the Boy could feel him watching the shack. Watching him. For the rest of that wet and rainy afternoon, when the Boy looked out the door of the shack, he could see the man waiting in the darkening light, "not watching."

Jin came to him again after midnight. She was soaked by the drizzle that slapped at the water of the bay.

"We must... exercise much caution," she said.

The Boy considered checking the street.

She held onto him tightly.

"I would give... myself to you," she whispered.

Blood thundered in his ears, beating hard in the silences between the soft rain on the roof and the hard slaps out on the water beyond the thin walls of the shack.

"But… it… cannot… be."

They sat by the fire, listening to it pop and crackle.

The Boy thought of the bear's cave where he and Horse had lived for the winter.

"Why?" he murmured.

Looking into his face, she reached forward and brushed away the dark hair that hung there.

"When my people came here… there was a great war. Our home, China, was destroyed. I am told that the first years were very, very difficult. Hard winter. Constant warfare. Famine. The children who were born… after these times… were not… good."

Jin lay her head on his chest.

"It does not matter to me." Then, "But if I am 'sullied'… then it will be… very bad… for me."

The rain had stopped outside. Dripping water could be heard, everywhere and at once, almost a pattern.

Almost music.

Almost as if one could count when the next drop would fall.

"Here," he said staring into the fire.

She looked at him and nodded.

"Here, in this place," he said angrily.

She nodded again.

"Yes. In this place… that is the way it must be," she said.

He thought more of the cave of the bear and all the other places he had been. Places that were not this city. Places that were not here.

She stayed too long that night.

Dawn light was breaking the top of the eastern hills. In blue shadows, standing on the dock, he held her tightly to himself.

"I must… go now," she stammered and yet still clung to his chest.

"There are other places than here," he said. "I would take you with me to those places."

You take everything with you.

In the small boat, in the pale light, her long alabaster hands were shaking as she began to row for the point.

She heard the first birds of morning.

Her hands were shaking.

When she turned back to him, he was just a shadow among shadows along the waterfront.

Her hands were shaking.

The heat of the day built quickly. There was the smell of fresh-cut wood and fires burning out beyond the earthworks. The thick scent of the fields and dark earth mixed, and when the Boy drank rainwater from a barrel it was cold and satisfying.

A cannon cracked.

A *whump* followed a second later.

"They are sighting the guns," said the general. He was looking at Sergeant Presley's map with a large and cracked magnifying glass.

"How close did you come to Galveston, down in Texas?"

The Boy walked toward the picture he had drawn. The picture of the Great Wall of Wreckage.

"No closer than fifty miles."

Sergeant, you said to me, on that day when we looked at the map together and the weather was so hot and the air was so thick, you said, *That's right, Boy. Never closer than fifty. Radiation.*

Your voice would be a comfort to me now, Sergeant.

The Boy had been waiting all day for it. He had been waiting for it since it ceased. Since the open graves and tattered canvas. But now, of all days, on this first hot day of the year, he needed to hear it.

I need to know what to do next, Sergeant.

I need wisdom.

"What did you find there besides what you have drawn in this picture?" asked the Chinese general.

Sergeant Presley, I'm going to take the girl and run.

"What do you mean?" the Boy replies.

I don't have a plan, Sergeant. I'll take her and ride fast and far away from here. Is that what I should do, Sergeant?

"Were there villages or people there?" asked the Chinese general.

The Boy thought of long winter nights in the bear cave. He also thought of MacRaven and his ashen-faced warriors moving through the forests and the foothills and the swamps, approaching the bay.

Where can we go and be safe, Sergeant?

"The people there were deformed," answered the Boy. "There was a warlord who ruled over everyone, but we never met him. The sick told us that he came and stole their children in the night and made them his soldiers. They said he ate people. They said he was a demon. They said his soldiers were demons now, no longer their children."

There's an army coming and they're probably looking for me, Sergeant.

"It sounds like a terrible place. Are they deformed like…?"

I would go back to the cave, but MacRaven…

"Like… me?"

Sergeant Presley, you always said north was too hard. If you weren't ready for winter it would kill you. If we have to run for a long time, there might not be time to prepare for the next winter.

"I am sorry… I meant no disrespect," said the general as he stared at the Boy.

West is the ocean, Sergeant. I don't know how to make a boat go.

"No. They were much worse off than me."

So that leaves south.

"I am sorry," mumbled the general, looking back to the map. "It sounds like a very dark place."

We'll go south, Sergeant.

"We barely escaped."

I know you would say, *Don't get involved. I always told you that.*

In his mind, Jin murmurs in the firelight.

But I love her, Sergeant.

The Chinese general put down the magnifying glass. He hobbled around the desk and came to stand beside the Boy.

"It is all my fault," said the general after a great sigh.

"I don't understand," said the Boy.

"The deformities. Your deformities." Pause. "They are my fault. I mean no disrespect to you. I am not like… the rest. I see nothing wrong with a man if his body is weak. Old age has taught me that bodies fail. Even if we are successful at not dying, and doing our best to stay healthy, bodies still fail. A body doesn't make a man strong or weak. It is the heart of a man or woman that makes them such."

My heart is strong for Jin.

You would ask me, Sergeant, *Is that enough?*

"You seem troubled. I hope I didn't…"

"No. What happened at the end? The end of the American army."

The general looked away to the sketches on the walls. He looked at the broken sailboats in Detroit, piled up like toys after a flood. The general could hear the clang of the spinnakers and the knock of the weather vanes in that long-ago winter wind.

He let go another great sigh.

"In the end there were few American soldiers left. There were few of us left, for that matter, also. That last year was little more than a long stalemate that preceded our final battle, if one wants to call such a day a battle. Our scouts thought there might be influenza sweeping through the American defenses above Oakland, so we decided to attack with everything we had left."

The general turned and hobbled back to his chair, sinking into ancient leather with a groan.

"I started the war as a lieutenant. In the end I was a brigadier general in command of forces. My superiors tasked me to lead a reconnaissance in force against the American positions. All such actions in the past had met with defeat. In fact they were little more than suicide missions. I thought it was my time to die. I said my goodbyes. I kissed my very pregnant wife and my son, my granddaughter Jin's father, and we set out in rafts lashed to the few amphibious vehicles left that still worked. It was quite a departure from the way we'd arrived ten years earlier, when we'd invaded the United States. Then we'd attacked with fighters, a carrier group, and an airborne invasion all along the western United States. Now I was being towed to my death in a leaky raft by a broken-down amphibious armored vehicle that belched dirty black smoke."

The general breathed deeply again, gathering himself and letting go of some past oath to secrecy that no longer held him.

"I kept waiting for the American artillery to open fire as we crossed the bay. But it didn't, and we made the beach, to our great surprise. No gunfire, no mortars. No fixed-bayonet charge. I ordered our mortar teams to set up. We advanced through the wreckage of the old city of Oakland, finding no one. When we came to the trenches at the bottom of the hill we found a ragged soldier, thin to the point of death. He was little more than the bones that held him up. He waved a white flag. From a distance he told us of the sickness. He said we should stay away.

"I withdrew and called my commanders. They told me to hit the camp with everything we had but to stay clear. We spent the day shelling it and shooting up into the heights. Shooting as though there was no end in sight to our supplies, after ten straight years of fighting in the streets amid the rubble of San Francisco."

It was quiet in the study. Warm sunshine made the air thick and heavy with the scent of flowers and dust.

"But that was not the end," muttered the general after a long pause.

"I was ordered to put on chemical armor and go up the hill by myself. It was a very hot day. Earthquake weather, like today. It is always that way on hot days that follow the cold. I trudged through the tall burning grass up to their headquarters. There was no one there, only graves and the dead, lying in their cots and trenches.

"What can one say of such things? The war was finally over."

CHAPTER 43

The knock at the back door of the shack in the quiet of the sleeping shantytown was deafening and the Boy willed it to be unheard in the night.

Her entering and embrace of him were one action.

"I had a..." — she uses a Chinese word he did not know — "a nightmare... in the afternoon as I slept." Then, "I thought that... you had gone away... and that I had lost you forever."

She held him and he could smell the jasmine in her long dark hair.

"You had gone away," she said breathlessly between kisses. "And I kept thinking... in the dream, that I must start looking for you. But there was always some house task to perform."

She buried her face in his chest as the Boy closed the back door.

"It was... horrible," she murmured and he could feel her tears.

"Come with me. We'll leave tomorrow," he whispered, and he thought of the man who had been watching the shack all day from the other side of the alley.

Is he out there in the dark?

Can he hear our whispers?

She held him tighter.

"I will protect you," he whispered.

"I will serve you," he whispered.

"I will love you," he whispered.

And with each murmuring she held him tighter and he could hear her whispering, "Yes," over and over and over.

Involved is involved, Sergeant.

She left after midnight.

From the dock she stepped into the small boat.

"I will meet you in the ruins outside the... western gate, toward the bridge. Look for the house where only the fireplace remains standing, like a... pointing finger. When the sun is directly overhead, I will meet you there."

The Boy tried to sleep.

When he did, he dreamed.

He and Sergeant Presley were running through the night. They were running from those dogs. They were always running.

"I've got to find Jin," he told Sergeant Presley. But in each moment there was some fresh terror in the old mall they ran through, the one with the corpses hanging over the central pool from the broken skylight above. The one with the dogs. The one with the bones.

"I've got to find Jin," he told Sergeant Presley, whose eyes were calm and cool even though the Boy remembered that they were both very frightened that day. It had frightened the Boy even more when he'd looked at Sergeant Presley, who was starting to slow down that last summer before he died in the autumn, and had seen the fear in those eyes, which had been angry but never afraid.

In the dream, in the nightmare, he lost her. He knew it, and the look in Sergeant Presley's calm dream-eyes told him that he was sad for the Boy. And it was something about that look that terrified the Boy more than anything else in the dream.

He awoke in the night.

"I will not lose her."

He felt emptiness in his words.

As if he were a child saying he would conquer the world.

The Boy saddled Horse that morning.

Soldiers passed in the alleyway, heading off to work along the growing wall.

He packed his things and led Horse into the lane. There was no sign of the watching man, only an old woman sweeping farther up the street.

Three cannon opened up with successive cracks and distant *whumps.*

He led Horse back toward the eastern wall, following the soldiers.

Great logs had been cut and lay stacked, waiting to be put in place along the wall.

They had no idea. They had no idea how big MacRaven's army was.

The Boy mounted Horse and rode past a sentry who said something he did not understand. He seemed to want to stop him, as if only because the Boy was a stranger, but he did not.

The Boy rode through the gate and into the trees, heading east.

They'll think I've gone to inform MacRaven.

You would ask me, *What's your plan, Boy?*

I will ride through the hills and circle back around and come out along the western wall. They'll send riders to head me off, thinking I'm going east. The Pacific is to the west and we don't know about north. That leaves only one way, Sergeant.

From a small hillock just above the ruins of Sausalito and the inner city, the Boy saw the shantytown below, spreading out next to the bay, and the earthworks being cut into the fields beyond. The Boy watched the alarm being raised. The sentry was talking wildly and waving toward the east. Soldiers were gathering.

From the hill, the Boy could see the big rusting bridge that cut across the sparkling water into the pile of gray rock that was once San Francisco.

I should have checked the bridge to make sure it was safe.

But you would say, *That's all right, Boy. Sometimes you got to improvise.*

He rode through the broken edges of the old town, casting his eyes about for the finger-pointing chimney.

If they have discovered our plan, then they will set a trap for me.

You would say, *Always be think'n, Boy.*

He found the pile of rubble that had collapsed around a lone red brick chimney pointing up into the hot blue sky.

She came out carrying a bundle. Her face was joy.

Her face was relief.

Her face was hope.

He helped her up onto Horse and she held him tightly.

This was the way it would always feel from now on. To feel her holding him as they rode. As they rode into the face of the world. Into cities and wherever they might wish to go.

All their days should be such.

"Hold, boy," came the gruff voice of the Chinese general. He hobbled as fast as he could down the cracked and broken street leading back to the inner city.

The sun was overhead and the day was hot.

"I know," cried the Chinese general. "I know it must be this way. At first I thought it might be a trick of my old age, that I was seeing things that weren't there. I thought I was beyond understanding the ways of the young when they are in love. But I sensed what passed between the two of you. Now you must leave and go as far away as you can. If our leaders know of your whereabouts, then they will send men after you."

Jin speaks rapidly in Chinese. The Boy could tell she was pleading.

"It's all right, granddaughter," said the Chinese general, her grandfather, breathlessly. "I understand. I don't need to forgive you…"

The Chinese general began to shake, wobbling back and forth. Horse reared and the Boy fought to bring him under control as Jin clung to his back. The rubble all about them began to shift in great piles.

As soon as the shaking had started, it stopped.

"It's just a tremor, boy," said the general. "But there will be more."

The Boy patted Horse, whose eyes were rolling and wild with fear.

The old general came closer, pulling the folded map from his uniform.

"I have one more question to ask, boy."

The Boy felt ashamed, as though he had stolen something from the general in spite of all the old soldier's kindness.

"But first, take this." The general held the folded map up with trembling, gnarled fingers. The Boy reached down and took it.

"And this."

The general held up a small sack.

"There are American dimes made of silver inside. Most traders will barter for them. You will need to know where you are, that's why I want the two of you to take the map. Where you have been is not important anymore. You will need to know where you are going now."

The Chinese general turned to Jin.

"You are precious to me. Your father and mother named you well. I shall think of all our walks together, always. You have been a faithful granddaughter, and beyond that, my friend."

There were great tears in his tired, rheumy eyes. They poured out onto the brown wrinkles of his fleshy face.

"It is I who must beg for forgiveness… from both of you," sobbed the general, fighting to maintain his soldierly bearing.

Jin speaks in Chinese again, crying this time.

"No," commanded the general. "I must. I must ask for forgiveness. I must ask you to forgive me and those of my generation for... for destroying the world. And you must forgive us, so that you can be free to make something new. I am sorry for what we did."

The general turned to the Boy, wiping at tears, his voice winning the fight for composure.

"And now answer my question. We will not survive the attack of the barbarians, will we?"

The Boy wheeled Horse, still skittish after the earthquake.

"I do not think so."

The general lowered his eyes, thinking.

"Go now. Do not look back, never return here. The world is yours now. Do better with it than we did."

The Boy felt Jin's hot tears on his bare shoulder.

"Go!" roared the general.

The Boy put his good foot into Horse's flank and they were off down the old road leading to the rusting bridge that was once called the Golden Gate.

It was very quiet out.

They rode into the forested hills above the bridge, dismounted and crawled forward to the edge of the ridge and watched the sentries below.

"There are more guards than usual," whispered Jin of the sentries who were watching the bridge.

"It might be because of the invasion. Or us, if word has gotten out."

They watched, hoping the extra guards would leave. The sun was high above.

"Tell me about the bridge. Is it safe?"

"It is… dangerous. But there is a marked way."

"What will we find on the other side? Are there people?"

"No, not in the city. There is only destruction there.
People go there… to salvage. There are small villages…
away to the south."

Horse cried, signaling the Boy.

The Boy loped back to Horse and saw the riders.
Chinese cavalry — gray uniforms and crimson sashes
— carrying their heavy rifles, twelve of them, following
Horse's trail up from the ruins of Sausalito.

CHAPTER 44

"Hold on tight." Then, "Tighter!" screams the Boy.

Horse was sliding downslope through the scree that abutted the shattered remains of the road leading to the bridge. The Boy held on for dear life as Jin clung to him.

The guards at the bridge raised their weapons to port arms, as if this act, as it had so many times before, would bend the offenders to their will.

You said, Sergeant, *Surprise the enemy and the battle might just be half won, Boy!*

Horse checks a fall and the Boy yanks him on to the road and straight toward the bridge.

The riders who had followed their trail, at the top of the hill above the bridge now, began to fire down upon them. Their shots were wild and the sentries at the bridge began to scatter, fearing they were being shot at by invaders. A wild shot hit the chest of one of the Chinese bridge guards with a loud thump, knocking him to the pavement.

Horse crashed past two guards and raced onto the bridge, straining hard for the distant far end.

Great iron cables ran skyward toward the suspension pylons, but other numerous cables that once were connected to the roadway had fallen onto the bridge or lay draped in great coils spilling over the edge. It even seemed to the Boy that the bridge hung lower on one side. A few ancient trucks, decrepit with crusted rust, littered the bridge at odd angles.

"Stay to the right… it's the safest side!" screamed Jin above the bullets, above the *clop-cloppity-clop-clop* of Horse's sprint along the old roadway of the bridge.

The gusty wind dragged at the Boy's long hair as he looked behind them to see riders and horses tumbling down the steep slope leading to the bridge.

I have a lead and a little time. That is good. But I'm riding into the unknown, and that is bad.

For a moment he felt the familiar fear that had chased him all his days. But the embrace of Jin, her thin arms about his chest, reminded him of wearing the bearskin in the dead of a winter storm.

At the end of this bridge, somewhere, there must be a cave like the bear cave for us.

Halfway across the bridge, the Boy could see the concrete piles of once-San Francisco. Huge jutting slabs of gray concrete rose up into small mountains, stacked at different protruding angles. Only a few emaciated buildings remained upright.

'The destruction is almost complete here,' thought the Boy, and in the moment he had this thought, his eyes, searching the rubble, watched as it began to slide in rising chalky yellow sheets of dust.

He blinked twice, assuming his eyes must be watering in the wind of the hard chase.

But now the road underneath them was shifting to the left, twisting, almost.

Cables above were waving back and forth. High and ahead, one ripped loose from the roadway and swung wildly across the bridge, sweeping a rusting wreck off the side and into the ocean below.

In San Francisco everything was shaking. Dust was rising everywhere. One of the tall buildings collapsed into itself and was replaced by plumes of thick brown dust billowing up into the bright noon sky.

Cables sang sickly in a high-pitched whine. The Boy could hear explosions as rusty metal bolts, gigantic, tore themselves away from their foundations on the bridge.

The shaking increased and the Boy drove Horse hard for the far side of the crossing.

It was only when they passed down the off-ramp and onto the other side of the bay, clearing the last of the sagging, shearing, crying, bending cables that the Boy breathed. He wheeled Horse about to check their pursuers and could see nothing of them.

The shaking had stopped and the air was filled with the sounds of birds calling and dogs barking.

The animal noise rose.

"Earthquake," whispered Jin, shaking. "A big… one."

The Boy turned Horse back to the once-city.

A moment later rending metal, groaning in chorus, sheared through the quiet.

When they turned back, Jin, Horse, and the Boy watched the Golden Gate Bridge twist and then crash into the ocean.

Later, they rode along the only avenue clear enough to pass through the city. It was a wide thoroughfare running along the waterfront. Every building was a pile of gray concrete and dusty redbrick. Pipes and rebar jutted from the wreckage like nerve endings caught forever in the act of sensory stimulus. What had not disintegrated into gigantic piles of rubble lay either heaped atop another building or forever fallen off at some odd angle.

"At least they cannot follow us now that the bridge is down," said the Boy.

"But they will," replied Jin.

They came upon the remains of a military defense. Artillery pieces lay scattered about, their long barrels blooming like sunflowers.

"Why will they follow?" asked the Boy.

"Because… they must," replied Jin.

The Boy chose a narrow avenue through the rubble that led into the heart of the once-city.

They climbed up where buildings had spilled themselves into one another and crossed streets littered with explosive sprays of redbrick thrown outward.

"They cannot let me go," said Jin. "Because they are afraid of mixing with… the…"

"The barbarians."

"Yes. The barbarians."

Shortly they entered an open space. Gothic cathedral arches rose out of the debris, as did splintered beams of wood in front of what was once a small park.

They watched and listened within the silence of the place as Horse turned to the wild grass that survived in the park.

They drank water from their skins to wash away the floating dust.

"It is dangerous to be here. The rubble could shift at any time," he said.

"Very. The old city… is a very dangerous place. We… will not want to be here for… long."

"What lies to the south?"

"I have only heard… there are ruined cities in the south. But many have burnt down or are little more than… ruins. There is a fishing village along the Pacific Ocean beyond a city that faced south into the sea and burnt down long ago. I… have been there once, when I was a girl."

"And beyond that?"

"The war… before the battles here… the big war was fought there. Many 'nukes' and… chemicals. The land is said to be poisoned and filled with monsters."

"Oh."

He brought her toward him and they kissed in the quiet and shattered remains of the square.

"Are you happy?" he asked.

"Yes."

"Even if we must go past the monsters?"

She kissed him again.

"Yes."

The rest of the day was long and hot. At times they had to walk Horse up long hills of dangerous rubble, picking their way through the broken rock and twisting rusted metal.

In the late afternoon the wind picked up and they could hear the sound of bones dully knocking against each other in a haphazard fashion.

"No one else lives here?" asked the Boy.

"There are dogs and ghosts. The dogs… are very wild."

Dusk was falling to gloom as they rode slowly down the long highway leading away from the city. In the darkness ahead the Boy saw a building standing off by itself. It was only two stories high. It was long and squat.

M-O-T-E… he spells.

Probably "motel."

He left Jin atop Horse in the parking lot as he checked the ruined place. All the doors had long since been torn off. He found the evidence of campfires in the bathtubs of most of the rooms.

Someone had stayed here for a time, but not for long. Now they were gone.

They took a room downstairs. The bed was little more than exposed coils and springs. He pushed it against the wall and tried to clear the floor of debris as best he could. There was a large hole in the wall leading to the next room. He led Horse through the doorway of that room and settled him for the night.

"I'll be back," he told Jin.

He was gone for some time, and when he returned he brought wood and placed it in the bathtub for a fire.

Once the fire was going he gave her the last of Horse's corn and they chewed it and drank cold water.

He watched her dark eyes staring into the fire.

"Are you happy still?"

She turned to him and smiled.

"So happy. So… free."

'Other women are not like you,' he thought as he watched her. 'Most — all the ones I have ever met in all the villages and places like the Cotter family's old dark house — are merely possessions to be had by whoever is strong enough to take and keep them. But you want to find out who you are and you will let no one own you. And I do not think anyone could keep you if you did not want to stay.'

"It will not be easy. But in time we will find a place and make it our own," he said.

"We will," she agreed softly.

He pushed the frame of the bed against the doorway of the room and draped a blanket across it. The Boy hoped this would help hold the heat of the fire in the room. About the hole in the wall between rooms he could do nothing. Their breath was now forming tiny puffs of moisture in the cold night air.

When he turned back from securing the doorway, he found Jin at the end of the room near the door to the bathroom, close to the fire.

She had wrapped herself only in the bearskin.

She beckoned him within.

CHAPTER 45

They rode south the next day, stopping early to make camp in an abandoned place that would hold for the night. There was fire. There was water. The Boy hunted during the day, using the rifle to take small game.

The night that followed was long and cold, and their embraces became deeper and more meaningful in the passing quiet.

Lying awake, she on his chest in deep sleep, the Boy thought.

He thought of all that he had to do and places they might go and be safe.

He thought of life, and though there was a new problem he could think of in each day ahead, he was glad.

To have these problems was to have her.

My life has never been this good.

And…

I never want it to be another way.

He slept and did not dream.

In the morning they crossed a small mountain ridge and saw the ocean stretching away to the south and west. The

Boy saw the overgrown ruins of a thin spreading town that must have once climbed up to the ridge.

But it had been consumed and little remained other than concrete pads and crumbling, blackened walls that poked through the coastal vegetation.

"The village is farther along the coast. I... doubt they will be looking for us there yet. We can purchase... food and other things. Where will we go after?"

He looked toward the south.

How far away is the city of Los Angeles? On the map it seems a long way off. If those who she says must follow us are afraid of the damage caused by radiation then maybe they will turn back if we head into the worst of it. Or at least make them think that we intend to.

"Into the poisoned lands," he said.

She was silent.

"Do not worry. I have faced monsters. Our bearskin was once one."

"But... why must we go there?" she said softly.

"You said that they must follow us?"

"Yes."

"Then we will go where they will not follow us."

CHAPTER 46

Shao Fan walked the road at night.

'It will be a good spring after such a hard winter,' he thought.

His hunters were spread out behind him, his trackers far ahead, looking for any sign of the fugitives.

We will not find them tonight.

It has been a long day. And yet you must be out and away from your home for another night.

Yes.

This day, for Shao Fan, had started just before dawn, out on Point Reyes, above the lighthouse. His trackers had been watching the lighthouse keeper and his family.

When the man left at dawn, they'd followed him along the coast and up to a little bay. Savages had been allowed to dwell there and sell the fish they took from those waters where the old Chinese aircraft carrier had been grounded in the shallows and surf.

They watched the lighthouse keeper. He entered an old building, perhaps once a seaside resort. Smoke came through the roof and Shao Fan and the hunters could smell bacon cooking.

Later, when the man came out, holding his tea, the little half-caste children racing out behind him onto the dewy grass in the golden light of mid morning, Shao Fan knew that the rumors about the lighthouse keeper were true.

The air had seemed thick with salt.

The children were tainted, so you know... you had to... do what must be done in such cases, thought Shao Fan.

Did I?

Now, on the night road far to the south of Point Reyes, on the other side of the bay, searching for the barbarian and the general's granddaughter, drawing his long, thick coat down across his lean frame, Shao Fan did not answer his own question.

That morning, when Shao Fan, followed by his crew, came out of the scrubby coastal pine, crossing the field onto the beach, the man, the lighthouse keeper, did not move. His handleless cup is held too high. As if, in that moment before one drinks his tea, he has decided that this day should be the measure by which all days are judged.

As if one could make such a request.

And then when the lighthouse keeper saw Shao Fan and his men, he knew the error of such thinking on the subject of days and their measure.

Today of all days, the lighthouse keeper must have thought, was the end of the measuring stick.

They'd drowned the children.

It was the law.

The birth defects that always come with the American barbarians, the survivors of our nuclear weapons, must not be allowed to continue. In time, they, their ways, their defects will disappear, and the world will be a better place.

Or so says the council.

The concubine was dispatched, swiftly, even as the lighthouse keeper's cry for mercy was drowned out by the thundering surf in the misty morning air.

There was no protocol for her demise. Only that it must be.

And then the march with the lighthouse keeper to the crossroads.

That also was the law.

And for that there was a protocol.

The salty cold of morning and crashing waves had faded in the hot steaming fields inland. Everything was golden.

It would be a good spring and a hot summer.

They'd hung the lighthouse keeper at the crossroads.

A warning.

Do not mix with the barbarians.

Shao Fan recalled the words he always thought of whenever the sentence was carried out.

Be careful who you fall in love with.

Shao Fan always remembered those words when the transgressor was pulled aloft by the rope and horse.

Be careful who you fall in love with.

And that was how the day had begun for Shao Fan and his hunters.

And the day ended and night fell as Shao Fan sought another who had broken the law.

The general's granddaughter.

He had crossed to the southern end of the bay by swift sail. His men, without their horses, walked the fields near the old highway leading inland. They waited in the sudden night breezes that swept the southern bay for the scent of campfires. But there were no camps to be found and no trails to be followed on this windy night.

'They have gone south across the mountains and into the ruins of Santa Cruz,' thought Shao Fan. 'We will not find them tonight.'

They will try for the village at Moss Landing.

He called for a halt and the men turned to their packs seeking food and hot tea.

We'll halt for an hour and march hard for Moss Landing through the night.

CHAPTER 47

The village lay on the far side of a muddy estuary. They passed long-gone fields that had lingered through a hard winter. A cemetery of wrecked boats wallowed near the entrance to the estuary.

They crossed a small road leading to a wide bridge.

The village was little more than a line of warehouses from Before, arranged along a narrow road running the length of the islet. An ancient and rusting large commercial fishing boat, now rigged with a mast and furled sail, had come into port to unload the night's catch. Villagers flocked to its side as the fish were unloaded in great netted bundles.

"Where do we go?" asked the Boy. He was leading Horse while Jin rode.

"Take us to that long hall there. We should be able to... purchase there. Remember... say nothing. Otherwise they will think you are more than just... my servant."

The Boy led them onto the street and they passed down its length until they reached the parking lot of an old warehouse. Fish were being trundled within by handcart.

The Boy helped Jin down from Horse. She adjusted her robe, ensuring the bag of silver coins was tucked within her sleeve.

Then they wandered the stalls.

There was little they needed to purchase beyond a large, wide wok made by a local blacksmith. At another stall she purchased oil and spices. Later they found a few more blankets of good quality and some rice. Finally they decided upon two large bags to carry their purchases.

The sun was high overhead when they exited the warehouse. They smelled frying oil and saw the villagers gathered around a large fire where a bubbling cauldron seethed and hissed. Strips of fish were being fried and quickly eaten.

A villager, jolly and smiling, waved them over.

The villagers talked with Jin in animated Chinese. The Boy held Horse and shortly Jin returned with a woven grass plate of fried fish and a small shell full of dark sauce.

The jolly villager smiled at them as they stood in the warm sunshine eating the fish, dipping it in the pungent, salty sauce.

"I do not… think… they care…"

"Care for what?"

"Care that we… we are together."

"We could stay and join their village?"

"No… that will never be possible. In time the leaders will send someone to look for me… they will find us here. And then it does not matter what the villagers care for. Still… all the same it is nice that they do not care. Maybe one day things will change."

The Boy said nothing.

If he had to mark this place on Sergeant Presley's map he would write, the Village of Happy People.

They mounted Horse and turned toward the south.

It was bright and hazy with mist.

"What lies that way is unknown," she said. "We are at… the edge."

Then, my whole life has been at the edge.

He turned to her.

She looked up at him. Her eyes shone darkly in the bright sunlight.

"I hope things change for… all people… one day. I hope they will have then the happiness we have now," he said.

"Me too."

They rode south onto a long beach where the surf thundered against the shore and white sandy cliffs rose above them.

In the afternoon, the sky turned gray and the wind was whipped with salt and water.

"A storm is coming on shore," she said.

In time, while there was still light in the sky, they came upon old wooden buildings surrounded by drifting dunes. The wood was gray with salt and sun and age. Bone-white fingers of driftwood poked through the sand.

"We'll camp here tonight."

CHAPTER 48

In the night, surrounded by the warm silence of the dunes, the Boy heard the breaking waves beyond their camp rolling hard onto the beach.

'We will continue straight into the south,' he thought. 'According to the map there was an old highway that ran along the coast there.'

He thought of the map in his mind. He saw Monterey south of where they were now, a place called Carmel and the old highway south to Los Angeles.

Everyone knew Los Angeles was destroyed. Sergeant Presley always said so.

On the map there was a large red X across Los Angeles.

They will not follow us there.

You would say, *You think so, Boy.*

And

Or do you hope so?

I am doing the best I can, Sergeant.

And

I know. I just got to ride ya, Boy. Make ya check yourself.

I know. You would say that to me. You would tell me to be both cautious and sure at once.

The breaking waves pounded the shore beyond the silence of the dunes.

If we could live here…

When he returned to their fire, Jin had reorganized their packs.

Sergeant Presley's lay open.

There was the knife.

The flannel shirt.

And the gray feather with the broken spine.

"I have… never seen a feather like this… before," she said, holding it up, inspecting it. "Where did it come from?"

The Boy knelt down beside her.

"I don't know."

"Boy" is what they called you. It's the only thing you responded to. So "Boy" it is.

But why then did you keep the feather, Sergeant? Why is its touch almost familiar? As though it meant something once… about me.

I remember being carried as we ran. There was yellow grass and a blue sky. Someone, a woman, was screaming.

And the feather.

And…

"I think it was once my name."

She stared at the feather.

Then she looked at the Boy.

She said nothing.

In the morning, the Boy smelled other horses coming out of the north.

They could have been anyone's horses. Even wild ones, roaming. He'd seen them before.

But he knew it was a lie even if the voice of Sergeant Presley didn't tell him so.

They'd be coming.

"Let's go."

Soon they were dressed and away from the bones of the old lodge sinking into the dunes. Horse threw up a great spray of sand as they kicked away from its ruin.

Farther down the beach there was no smell of horses. The Boy listened to the wind.

He heard no *jink* of harness and tack.

No cries of men calling to one another as they searched.

Behind him, the Boy saw the trail of Horse through the sand and grass and knew they were not hard to follow.

There was little left of the place once called Monterey, the skeletal remains of a few tall buildings, the foundations of many smaller buildings consumed by fire and forest. Massive green pines grew in wicked clumps up through the old roads and foundations.

They rode up a long hill of once-neighborhoods that were now little more than ancient charred wood overgrown by sea grass and pine. Just before starting down the other side, the Boy turned to scan their backtrail.

He saw the men on horses coming for them.

A line of riders picked their way along an old road. Ahead of them he saw individuals running back and forth across the fields and ruins, searching for their trail.

The Boy urged Horse and they rode hard over the small saddle of the mountain and down into a forest the map would name Carmel. Huge foundations of houses that once must have been little palaces dotted the sides of their track. The forest floor was littered with pine needles and thick brush.

'They will follow us easily,' thought the Boy.

Off to his right and down toward the rocky coast, he could see the remains of other ancient stone palaces crumbling into the sea.

Don't just run, think.

They're following you like dogs.

You would say that, Sergeant, wouldn't you?

We can't run. Horse might fall and then that would be the end of us.

I could start a fire to cover our trail.

Too damp from the storm.

Stay ahead of them for now and look for a place to lead them into a trap.

It's all I can do.

"Is everything... good?" asked Jin.

"Yes. We are good."

But he heard her worry. He thought of what traps he might make.

What do I have?

The tomahawk.

The rifle.

What remains of the parachute cord.

Two knives.

It's not much.

It is all I have.

'They know we are on their trail,' thought Shao Fan.

He rolled a cigarette and wished it was the weed he smoked at night, alone, in the dark.

I have been too many days at this.

You are an assassin.

There is no rest for the assassin.

No rest for the wicked.

He looked at the marks on the ground.

The horse had turned several times. They must have watched them come up the valley.

We will have to watch their trail for traps now. It is their only chance to escape us.

'Savages!' he thought, and spit bits of tobacco out onto the forest floor.

The afternoon was ending. Shadows long and blue surrounded his company.

How much longer can I push them? They are cold and hungry and if they miss a sign or the makings of a trap... then disaster.

He told them to make camp. They would sleep until morning and be fresh for the trail.

Besides, the savage and the girl are running into the poison lands where no one may go and live long. They are up against a wall. They will have to turn or stand and fight.

He thought of his lacquered box of weed. Since they are camping, he reasoned to himself.

"Be careful who you love," he mumbled and set to loading his pipe.

CHAPTER 49

The next day, Shao Fan watched the old house as his men entered it. The day was hot and the air smelled of pine and mustard.

Spring is upon us.

Think about this business, he chastised himself.

They'd risen early and the sleep had done them good. They'd picked up the trail of the fugitives in the first light of the cold and misty morning and followed them down into the hot valley.

They are heading for the coast road, Shao Fan told himself all along. Which seemed a good thing, at least as far as he, Shao Fan, was concerned. He could increase speed, now that their prey's options were narrowing between the sea and the mountains.

But in the dry and dusty ruins south of Carmel, the trail drew them to an old "mansion."

'Perhaps they were not aware of our pursuit after all and have stopped to enjoy rest and forbidden pleasure,' thought Shao Fan.

The two scouts, long knives in hand, crossed the open yard and entered the rotting house through two separate broken windows. The scouts thread the remaining shards of glass nicely and are in with barely a noise.

Well-trained men make work easy.

After a moment there was a creaking groan, too quickly followed by a thunderous crash. Plumes of ancient dust expelled themselves through the broken windows like smoke from the mouth of a corpse.

When the dust settled, the hunters and Shao Fan moved forward to find that the second floor had collapsed onto the two scouts within, crushing them.

'A trap,' thought Shao Fan.

Ahead, the mountains fell down to the sea, and in glimpses the Boy and Jin caught the silver remains of the coast highway winding away to the south in the afternoon sun.

Jin smiled at him when he turned to show her the road, and in his heart her doubts and fears disappeared.

They won't follow us much farther.

You would tell me, *You hope, Boy. You hope for that.*

I do.

The parachute cord is gone and my traps will be crude now. They will be wary, knowing I have skill with traps.

They don't know I am out of the parachute cord.

The Boy stopped occasionally to create bent limb traps spiked with sharpened stakes. He felt rushed as he worked and they were not his best. But each one would slow them down, and in time they would crawl, the more they were taught not to run.

The first trap took two scouts. Shao Fan was now down to just three scouts and the hunters.

An hour later, a limb snapped forward and blinded one of the three remaining scouts as stakes raked his eyes and face.

'The man will lose an eye,' thought Shao Fan.

I should let the hunters go and ride this savage down.

But how many will you lose?

And Shao Fan found that he did not care. He wanted to be finished with this, as he was finished every time they hauled the violator aloft while the noose tightened about the neck.

No screams.

Just the dance.

Finished.

I want every time to be the last time.

But they never learn…

… so there will be no end to it.

To think that my days will always be such…

And Shao Fan was too exhausted and too depressed, if he were to admit the truth, to finish the thought. He assigned the blinded scout to a hunter. The man will be tied to his horse to follow along after the hunting party.

They avoided the next two traps now that the scouts knew what to look for.

They moved much slower than Shao Fan would like, but they had to.

The Boy considered the old ruins that hung over the cliff near the sea. The coast road ran like a moving snake past them and on to the south.

The Boy wanted to take the coast road now. He wanted to ride hard to the south, and in time their pursuers would turn back, or so he thought.

And what if they didn't?

Then there would be just the road between the mountains and the sea. There would be no place to hide. Once they chose the coast road, their pursuers would ride them down and they would be left with very few options.

Ruined walls crumbled along a wide plateau that ended over the ocean in a rocky black cliff above waves that slopped in great troughs and wallops against the continent.

What traps do I have left?

How many have I taken in the traps and how many of our pursuers are left?

How many traps will I need to make until they lose the will to follow?

How many traps until they are too angry to stop?

If we ride the coast road, they'll follow and follow quickly. They'll know we can only go one direction and if they get close enough I won't be able to stop and make traps. So it is in their best interest to get close, to show me they are close.

They heard the surf boom distantly below the cliff as it smashed itself into the jagged rocks. It was late afternoon and the sun was falling toward the ocean.

The Boy and Jin walked the ruins, crossing through a crumbling lobby where a large and tattered canvas hung on the wall. In the sooty picture, windswept eucalyptus trees twisted in the nook of a hill as tall grass bent toward a horizon of blue skies and soft white clouds. And though the sea was not represented in the picture, the Boy knew it must be nearby.

Chairs and couches had long since been smashed for firewood. Beyond this there was a large swimming pool, cracked and empty. Dirty rainwater had collected in its depths. Wild palms had erupted through the crumbling pavement. Beyond all this was the main building, every window empty, every door missing. There were long, dark halls along which rotting hotel rooms, forever waiting to be occupied, stretched off into the darkness.

'We could make a stand here,' the Boy thought.

We will make our stand here.

Two knives.

One tomahawk.

One rifle.

Cartridges.

You take everything with you.

They wandered to the back of the ancient ruin, crossing long, dark hallways of disintegrating carpet and mildewing rooms. At the end of it all they came to a great room that overlooked the ocean. Out to sea, the water and waves raced off to the south.

"Wait here," he said to Jin.

"No. I want to come with you."

"I'll be fine. I just need to see what's above us."

"Then… so will I."

Above they found two more floors, the same as the first, clotted with rotting furniture along their long halls, and at the top a door led out onto the roof. The roof was littered with palm fronds by countless storms.

"We will fight them from here." Then, "Once they are all dead we will be free to go where we will."

Jin nodded. The wind pulled at her long hair.

"I… believe you."

In the hours that followed, they stripped electrical wire and cables from inside the walls. They found ancient metal fixtures, rusting and jagged.

There were no weapons.

No propane tanks that had not long since been gouged.

No firearms to find.

No knives to loot.

But still they made traps.

Traps where a floor might fall from above if a certain pillar was loosed by a taut cable disturbed in the debris.

Traps where boards fitted with jagged rusting metal might snap forward as a careless foot dragged electrical wiring along its path.

They blocked the entrances to the second floor so that the entire first floor would have to be traversed before ascending to the next floor. They did the same for the second and finally the third.

They were sweating hard and the Boy felt his strength fading as they hauled out ancient rotting furniture and stuffed it into the stairways, blocking off all avenues of approach other than the one the Boy had decided the pursuers must choose. After this, he turned to making barricades where he could shoot with his rifle down the long dark hallways as the enemy threaded the gauntlet of traps.

'I wish I had both arms,' he thought, the dark outside telling him night had fallen. Jin's face, shining in the light of their torch from the sweat of her exertions, came close to his.

"Now, I… am your… left." She touched the with-ered arm he had hidden and protected and cursed his whole life.

I must have said that out loud. I am very tired.

Together they built the last barriers.

It was late when they settled in the farthest room be-neath the roof. A once-grand suite. They had a small fire and Jin made rice in her wok. There were eggs also. And tea.

They made love. He held her close and she whispered over and over in his ear that she loved him.

That she loved Broken Feather.

Later, as she slept he thought of the feather in Sergeant Presley's pack.

She is my left arm now. My left side.

Me.

Broken Feather.

He slept for a while and when he awoke it was still deep night.

There was a little more to do.

Jin did not wake as he took his charcoal and a small torch. For the rest of the night he worked at the faces he sketched near the traps. Or sometimes along a mildewing wall where he would get a good shot from the barricades.

Something to distract them from his traps and hiding places.

It was just before dawn when he left to feed Horse. He gave Horse water and walked him down onto the beach. He whispered the things he always whispered to Horse. Things that made Horse feel good about himself.

Vainglorious things.

He staked Horse in the tree line beyond the beach to the south. There was a little water and grass. If they didn't make it, in time Horse would pull free. Be free.

He patted Horse one last time and looked deep into the eyes of his friend.

Trying to read his mind as he'd always tried to do.

Failing as he'd always failed.

He returned to their bed and lay down, taking everything in. Listening to the morning. The offshore wind, smelling of salt and fruit. They gray light turning to gold. The old place.

They were coming now.

In sleep Jin drew closer to him and murmured something in her dream.

"Now I am your left."

CHAPTER 50

The Boy watched them from a corner window on the third floor. He saw the hunters coming along the trail left by Horse. They scanned the stumps of chimneys and overgrown lots, wary that he might snipe at them from the tall grass beyond.

They'll come to this old place from Before.

He watched until they disappeared in front of what was once the lobby. The place of the dirty canvas picture.

Shao Fan called for a halt. The thick silence of the heat and loneliness of the place was broken by an offshore breeze, dull and sweet, sweeping through the high eucalyptus trees along the road.

He'll be inside. The savage and his traps.

He'll be watching us, even now.

Shao Fan knew there would be traps. But his men, his hunters, knew how the savage worked now. They'd be alert. They'd know what to look for.

So, they had to go in. All race transgressors must have their appointment at the crossroads.

Shao Fan signaled two men. The last two scouts.

They rode up to him and he whispered instructions. Moments later they were off to the south.

Shao Fan dismounted and signaled his remaining men to do the same.

They brought their breech loaders.

The Boy took his first shot as the hunters exited the main building. He shot from the corner window of the third floor looking down on nine men as they crossed the crumbling pavement near the cracked and broken swimming pool.

He rested his gun on a platform deep inside the shadows of the room.

The shot hammered through the silence and the men scrambled for cover.

Just one shot. Then move to a new position. Just like you taught me, Sergeant, even though you said there would never be a need because all the "ammo" was used up killin' ourselves. Still, I'd wanted to learn and you'd showed me.

I think it was a way for you to pass the time and teach me the only thing you'd ever known, and not think about the past.

He withdrew into the dusty shadows of the old room and heard them calling out to each other below. Beneath that, he could hear the dying man.

He found Jin at their camp on the third floor.

"They're here."

She nodded and said something in Chinese.

"I want you to go to the roof now. Block the door with the broken concrete I left there. Don't open it until you hear my voice."

She nodded and he led her to the access stairwell that climbed up to the roof. She turned back to him, the broken feather in her hand. From it dangled a small leather thong. Quickly she reached up and tied it into his long hair.

He watched her ascend the steps and push on the rusty door. Bright light filled the dingy gloom of the stairwell. She glanced back at him and he silently beckoned her to close the door, wishing she didn't have to. Wishing they could be free of this day.

If wishes were fishes, Boy, beggars would ride.

Yes, you said that also, Sergeant. You would say it to me now.

The Boy made his way down to the first floor, all the while avoiding his traps. He took up a position behind the first-floor barricade at the end of a long, dark hall. The other end led to the pool area.

They would come through the hall from there.

In his mind he traced their route. They would funnel into this corridor as they found the other corridors were blocked and trapped.

Take a shot and move to the second floor. Be disciplined in this.

He waited, hearing nothing.

Maybe a mouse moving along the rotten baseboard.

In time he saw a dark figure detach itself from the shadows at the far end of the hall. The light from the corridor outlined the silhouette of a man carrying a rifle at the ready.

The Boy transitioned the rifle across the sacking he had laid for a rest atop the barrier, letting the sight fall on the outline of the man down the hall.

He heard a crash from somewhere in another part of the building and then a man was screaming in Chinese.

The swing trap.

When he looked again, the shadowy figure at the end of the hall was gone.

Maybe he was on the floor and crawling forward?

The Boy waited and watched.

A low rumble and then a loud crash in another hall told the Boy someone found the collapsing-wall trap. He heard no scream or cry for help this time.

There wouldn't be. The wall should have fallen on the intruder's head. He was either unconscious or dead.

But I don't know that for sure.

There were nine and now three were down. That made six.

Maybe.

The shadow detached itself from the wall again and moved right into the sight at the end of the Boy's rifle.

Without even thinking the Boy fired, flinging the man backward and out of sight.

Blue gun smoke mixed with the dust and heavy heat.

Five.

On the second floor, the Boy moved fast and he knew they could hear him below.

Good. They'll think they have me trapped. Maybe they will become careless.

He thought of Jin on the roof.

The traps here on the second floor were deadfalls, sure to break a leg or pierce a man through with the stakes he would fall on below.

He took up his place behind the barricade at the far end of the second floor.

He listened, willing himself to slow his ragged breathing.

Almost there.

You would say, *You think so Boy? Or do you hope so?*

Both.

One of the Chinese climbed through an open window behind the Boy as he watched the dark corridor. The Boy didn't hear the intruder until the man softly brushed against something just as he hoisted his body through the window.

The Boy set his rifle down and whirled with his tomahawk out. The man climbing through the window rolled just as the Boy raised the axe and struck. The head of the tomahawk buried itself in rotting wood and crumbling drywall.

The man cried out in Chinese and an instant later, far off, as the Boy dragged the axe out of the wall, he could hear running feet at the far end of the second floor. The sound, hollow on the rotting wood and disintegrating carpet, beat out an urgent approaching staccato.

The man in the room had his knife out, waving it back and forth between the two of them. He was smaller than the Boy and there was fear in his eyes.

The Boy rushed him, slamming his body into the man. They fell to the ground slick with sweat as the Boy pinned the man's knife hand with the flat of his tomahawk, leaning hard into the Chinese with the bony, withered side of himself.

The man cursed, almost whining.

The pounding footsteps coming up the hall disappeared in a crashing wave of snapping boards as the floor fell out beneath them. There was a brief cry and a sickening bone-snapping sound, loud and clear.

The Boy slammed his head into the face of the man beneath him and a spray of blood erupted from the smashed face. Instinctively, hands moved to cover the broken nose.

The Boy rose, his tomahawk swinging back above his shoulder, then his head, and a second later slammed the axe down through the man's sternum. There was an *umpf* of escaping air and the sound of breaking bone.

He rose and returned to the barricade. Down the dark hallway a Chinese was looking into the dusty hole that was the floor. He could hear a man crying below.

"Three," muttered the Boy and fired at the man staring down into the hole.

"Two."

Shao Fan stood at the far end of the second floor.

Chang lay dead halfway down the hall.

His last hunter watched out the window.

I know he's here. They're both here, the savage and the girl. But how many more traps?

He heard a soft whistle from outside, above the crash of the sea. Shao Fan looked out the window onto the wild yard of lush overgrowth that bordered the cliff.

The two scouts waved, smiling, and between them was the transgressor Jin. She was bound and gagged, her eyes wide with terror and tears. She knew Shao Fan. Knew his business. Knew what must come next.

'Forget this savage,' thought Shao Fan, and ordered his man to withdraw. They lowered themselves through the window with the rope they always carried.

No sense in risking the traps we didn't find on the way in.

It was a good idea to send the scouts up the cliff and onto the roof from the beach. 'It has probably saved our lives,' thought Shao Fan as he started a fire in the second-floor hallway.

We'll burn this place down with the savage inside. Protocol indicates we can dispose of the savage in any way we choose.

Usually it was a savage female, which they preferred to drown. But just this once, since it was a wily male, the characters on the report could read, "Burned in a fire."

For a long time the Boy waited behind the third-floor barricade.

They're afraid to come up after us. Good, maybe they will go away now.

In time he smelled the smoke, and when he listened hard, he could hear the crackle of flames catching the old carpets and tattered drapes and broken furniture and dry wood.

Fire!

He raced back to the third-floor stairwell leading to the roof and rapped on it heavily.

"Jin, it's me!"

Nothing.

The smoke came in gray puffs up through the floor beneath his feet. The snapping crackle of the fire was growing.

We'll be caught if I don't get her down off the roof!

"Jin, open up it's me!"

He didn't ask again as he reared back and slammed into the rusty metal door. It banged open in a wide arc. In the bright sunlight the Boy turned around and around searching for Jin on the debris-cluttered rooftop. He raced to one edge as black smoke crawled up from the other side.

Below he could see Jin in the bottom of the empty pool. She was bound and gagged, her eyes pleading with him. She looked left and right trying to tell him something. A moment before he heard the report from the rifles, he saw the Chinese hiding in the worn-out bushes and in the shadows of the old lobby. All at once bullets thudded about him into the crumbling concrete of the building. The Boy fired and then flung himself to the rooftop as bullets raced off into the sky above.

Lying on the roof, the Boy broke the breech of the rifle, pulled out the spent shell, and pushed another into its place. He crawled several feet to a new position and popped up behind the parapet.

A shaven-headed Chinese was pulling Jin by her hair up the steps of the empty pool.

A bullet smacked into the concrete wall of the roof, sending shards up to cut the face of the Boy. Other Chinese were taking aim.

The Boy ducked back behind the cover of the wall.

I'll get one shot and I have to use you to aim, he said to his withered hand. So work!

He moved in a new direction along the wall and when he rose from behind it again, he saw the shaven-headed Chinese drag Jin across the inner courtyard and into the yawning entrance of that other building where the shredded picture from Before hung on the wall, the lobby. The remaining Chinese were retreating into the darkness. The Boy could see the tallest of them, their leader, hunching low, shouting orders angrily as they retreated.

The Boy raised the rifle, knowing there would be just this one shot before she disappeared.

But he could already feel his withered hand, shaking and weak, refusing to be used, refusing to steady the rifle.

Sweat poured into his eyes as drifting black smoke stung his nose.

He aimed for the back of the man as he dragged Jin into the darkness of the lobby.

The Boy fired, knowing he missed.

And Shaven-head and Jin disappeared into the darkness.

Only their leader, the tall, thin Chinese with the mustache, remained. He smiled at the Boy, then darted after Jin and the other hunters.

Black smoke was coming through cracks and rents in the roof. The Boy smelled melting plastic and acrid smoke. Heat came up at him in waves.

He searched the sides of the building for a way down, but already the flames were crawling up through most of the roof and out the windows below.

Think!

I am thinking!

He loped toward the far end of the roof, closest to the cliff's edge and the sea below. Below the roof, a balcony hung out over the cliff. The Boy lowered himself down onto the balcony and saw thick sheets of flame racing across the ceiling of the room connected to the balcony.

Below, the sea pounded the rocky coast. The water was a deep blue in places and in others it churned a foamy green. A stunted tree hanging off the cliff's edge swayed in gusty blasts of heat from the fire.

The Boy slung the rifle over his back. He climbed on top of the railing and leapt for the tree. Flailing with his good arm, he crashed into its branches and a moment later was sliding down the cliff toward the water below. He clawed for purchase and his good arm found a rock to grab onto.

He hung halfway down the cliff, breathing hard.

Above, black smoke rose into the sky.

It would be a steep climb back to the top. Almost impossible.

He was exhausted.

Below, he could hear the sea washing itself against the black rocks of the cliff.

If they come to look for me, there's not much I can do, and I'll be smashed to bits against the side of the rocks if I drop down into the ocean.

Above, the burning roof collapsed into the main structure with a groaning crash. Black, oily smoke billowed high into the sky and the flames seemed to roar above the ocean's strike against the coast.

The Boy hung there, waiting.

He heard nothing.

No voice.

I need you now, Sergeant.

I'm dead, Boy. Sorry about that. I tried my best.

In time, he worked his way down to the rocks below and followed them along the water's edge as the surf threatened to drag him into its turmoil. The sun was sinking into the ocean and all was purple and red fire.

When he made the beach, he was limping and no matter how strongly he told his withered side to move, it wouldn't. It was a lock that would not open. He found Horse and dropped the rifle, his fingers trembling as he drank what little water Horse left him.

When the dregs were finished, he mounted Horse and rode back to the fire.

The building from Before was little more than smoking timber. The Chinese were gone and there was no sign of Jin.

He searched for their trail but it takes time. There had been too much confusion in the dirt and the dust of their tracks.

When he found their trail he saw they were riding north, back toward the Village of Happy People.

CHAPTER 51

He rode through the night but the going was slow. It took all his skill to stay on their trail. They did not stop as he hoped they would.

How many hours ahead of me are they?

Tall coastal pines rose up in thick stands as he crossed a small ridge, their scent heavy in the dew-laden cold.

He thought of the amount of time he was trapped on the cliff.

It was almost evening when he'd made it back onto the beach.

When did it start?

The fog crossed the beaches and marshes as he rode, following their trail through the night and the sand.

The battle at the old place had started in the morning.

He continued on through the night, even when the fog was thick and cold about him. The bearskin had gone in the fire and only Horse's heaving body kept him warm.

I have been cold before.

He passed the shadowy remains of ancient palaces and almost lost their trail.

He found the tracks of their horses in the ash of some long-gone fire.

His eyelids were heavy.

'Fatigue settles over me like the bearskin would,' he thought.

He sucked the night wind into his nostrils, feeling the cold flood his brain as he rode out onto the coastal plain following tracks through the ether of fog and saw grass.

I have been tired before.

I have been here before.

You were with me, Sergeant.

He thought of Jin and rode through the swirling salt-laden mist as nightmares of what might happen to her tormented him.

At dawn, he saw the Village of Happy People lying across the still, black water of the channel. It was quiet. The trail of the hunters led the Boy here.

They had ridden hard and they were tired. They would have stopped to rest.

He rode across the old bridge.

There was no one out.

Mist shrouded the sunken boats lying in the dark water, and the beach beyond was lost to nothingness.

The Boy heard the creak of the wrecked boats shifting in their graves at the pull of the invisible tide.

The Boy heard the gentle groan of rope.

He rode forward.

Halfway down the street, she hung from the ancient cargo hook above the main dock.

Her arms at her sides.

Her long dark hair hiding her face.

She swung gently at the end of a rope in the shifting mists of dawn.

CHAPTER 52

He remembered later.

Later that afternoon. He remembered screaming. Running toward... and screaming.

Why wasn't I on Horse?

He couldn't imagine himself running.

He sat in the shadow of a dune. Dense fog had run across the bay and into the dunes. The dunes just like where they stayed that night after the village...

He remembered the sound of the rope. He remembered the villagers coming out. They were crying too. He screamed at them... like an animal. Like the bear. Like the lion.

They were crying like children.

They lay down in the street and wept, begging him for forgiveness in a language he didn't understand. Begging him to let them grieve for this horrible thing that had been done.

How can I ever sleep again?

It wasn't her anymore.

She was stiff and cold.

He held her, hearing the sound of his pain as if from far away.

Knowing it was he who made that sound.

Knowing that Sergeant Presley could not help him anymore.

Knowing that the world was cruel and made of stone.

Her grave was beneath the sand and the sea grass.

He watched the grave, and what was once the cold of a foggy afternoon and wan sunlight became night and fog.

He watched.

He watched.

He watched.

Who am I now?

He didn't sleep.

Revenge.

He saddled Horse and thought of his revenge.

Don't do this, Boy!

Why?

He hears the creak of the rope that…

That…

The "who" of his revenge was easier to think about than the "why." The "why" was too painful. Much too painful.

He saw the face of the leader who came to take her. He was the "who" of his revenge. The object of his revenge.

And in fact…

He saw Sausalito. Their little walled city. Their wall.

All of them behind that wall, they were the "who"…

Of his revenge.

This is how everything went wrong, Boy. Don't you see? Revenge. Hatred. Fire. Boy, there is no good end to this.

Revenge.

He left the fire burning near her grave.

He rode up through the sea grass to the old western road. The One.

He could see her fire burning in the fog.

Let it burn forever.

In the east the sky was light and the fog was turning white.

This ain't a way to go, Boy. Forget this and live. Live. That's all you got to do in this world now. Keep on livin' until humanity gets a chance to start again. You do this and you'll set it back. Hell, you might even break it altogether. The world can't take much more.

Revenge.

He turned and the fire near her grave was gone, swallowed. Lost to the fog.

Who am I now?

Revenge.

CHAPTER 53

It was night when he moved down among them and their camps at the southern end of the bay.

The Psychos and their bare chests. Their war paint and muddy hair. Blood and Mohawks.

The Boy had watched them from the low hills all day, their boats and rafts taking shape, wood and oil drums dragged in from the ruins.

They would attack tonight.

He had watched them for three days. The mood — their mood was grim, and in the last hours before night the fires started and the dances began.

They're working themselves up to attack, Sergeant.

Don't do this thing, Boy.

I have to.

No. You don't. You want to, but you don't have to, Boy. There's a difference.

He patted Horse.

There's enough grass and water from this stream. If I'm not back tomorrow you'll pull that stake up and go. Take yourself off somewhere high into the mountains. Find wild mustangs.

In the dark he walks down among them.

He was painted in blood. His own.

The long hair that once hung straight down over his left eye, the weak side, was gone, shaved. Only the wild strip of the Mohawk stiff with mud rose from his scalp. Among the tangled hair, a broken feather.

They drank and rioted in their twirling, bumping dance. There were drums all along the shore.

Hot liquid gushed from a skin and burned his throat. The stuff was raw and as he coughed, he couldn't catch his breath. When he did he screamed at the world because he was still alive. The wild-eyed Psychos, leering and toothless, gaped happily at the Boy's reaction.

The men feasted on torn game, greasy and dripping on spits. Women laughed wickedly as they drank and worked the Mohawks of their men into spikes hardened by mud and shining with the fat of slaughtered animals roasting nearby. Their babble was little more than cackles and grunts. Occasionally the Boy detected a stray once-word. A "gunna" or a "sump'in' killah."

Amid the pressing throng, wild with delirium, he asked, "Where are you now, Jin?"

I feel more alone than all those winter nights in the bear cave or cold days on the road.

Or when the lions chased me.

Where are you now?

At midnight the moon was gone and the wind was warm.

A blacksmith worked near a hot fire putting edges to their weapons. The Boy found a saw and set to work cutting down the long barrel of the breech loader.

I won't trust you anymore, he said to his withered hand. You failed me when I needed you most and I won't trust you anymore.

A chieftain howled and the savages fell silent. The babble that passed from the chief's swollen and split lips erupted up from a barrel belly and massive chest, sending the warriors to their boats.

The Boy found himself paddling a canoe loaded with other paddling warriors as they crossed the bay. The flotilla kept a tight formation as it passed the pile of the once city of San Francisco. Ahead, the lights of Sausalito were thin and few. To the east of the Chinese outpost — at its very gates, in fact — MacRaven's armies gathered around campfires that rose along the hills of the little bay.

You don't need to do this, Boy. They'll take your revenge for you. They'll pay them back, if that means anything to you.

'How could they take… her life?' he thought between paddle strokes. The other men grunted and sweated. The Boy could smell the liquor oozing out of their skin.

I don't know, Boy. Maybe I thought I did. But now I don't know anymore. I know that there's good in the world. Good as long as it still exists in people like you. But if you do this… if you get to that place you'll need to go to do this… then maybe all the good that's left will have gone out of the world.

You don't exist, Sergeant.

I did, Boy. I did.

I have to know why. Why did they do this to her?

You'll never know.

You don't know that.

I do, Boy. I do. 'Cause there won't be a reason that ever makes enough sense to you.

The oars and paddles, even the hands that strike at the bay, were stopped. The flotilla laid drifting in the water near a small island just off the coast of Sausalito.

It was cold and quiet. The long night wound toward morning, and even though there was no light to betray the coming dawn, the Boy knew it was close, and so did the Psychos. Arms were flexed, spears laid across knees. The Boy felt his tomahawk at his side. The cut-down rifle was now a long pistol in his belt.

"Ancha!" roared a voice in the dark. The flotilla surged forward as oars and hands struck the water. Every Psycho was pulling hard for the few lights rising above the sea wall of Sausalito.

On land, beyond the eastern gate, on the far side of the little city, torches from the camps of MacRaven's Army surged toward the walls. It was still too dark for targeted gunfire as the torches gathered beneath the defenses.

The Boy's canoe pulled forward, cutting through the still water and low-lying fog. The men about him said nothing. They wanted their surprise to be total. Ahead, the low-lying seawall shielded their advance from any view along the street that led to the gate.

The gate where I first saw Jin. The first time Jin saw me.

And.

Where we began.

The canoe slammed into the rocks and the savages were wading through the water, spears upraised. Someone whooped and they were over the walls.

And what happened next was not the Boy.

A Chinese guard running for the gate fell to the tomahawk as it slammed into his back.

Broken glass.

Screams.

A whistle.

The Chinese gathered about the gate to the inner city. The guards were waiting for orders. They raised their rifles as a pack of screaming Psychos raced into the streets. The guards opened fire. A few Psychos went down but the bloodthirsty tribesmen were on them, hacking and screaming above pleas for mercy.

The Boy wiped the blood from his axe and slipped up through the winding alleyways of the inner city.

He found gardens colored like dull jade in the steaming morning light. Mansions rose up into the fog. Birds sang above the far din of battle on the other side of the gate, on the far side of the wall.

He heard the distant high note of the Space Crossbow. MacRaven's Space Crossbow.

He smelled smoke and heard crashing wood, once delicate, splintering into shards.

He heard the gunfire beyond the walls.

The cannon roared in distant cracks.

He saw the shaven-headed man break from a stand of collapsing defenders as Psychos leapt the hasty barricade, spearing and cutting.

Shaven-head raced farther up the street and disappeared into the drifting blue gun smoke of the falling defenders. The Boy loped after him knowing the man would lead him to the rest; to all the killers, the slayers of Jin. And finally to their tall leader who smiled at him as the roof burned and Jin was dragged away and into the darkness.

Shaven-head raced up and into the quiet neighborhood of stately mansions that rise along the hill above the little city. Servants and the occasional woman peer out into the streets, their questions evident. He darted into a heady garden, crossed a delicate and ornate bridge made of teak. He pulled urgently at a paper door that led into a house, his voice shouting at someone within.

When the man, sweating, turns to cast a worried eye back at the falling defenders, he sees the Boy running hard up through the garden that surrounds the house.

Shaven-head pulls the screen aside and enters, disappearing.

The Boy takes the curving wooden stairs that lead through the garden and hacks the paper screen door to pieces. Inside he smells jasmine and his mind roars red with anger. Anger at Shao Fan, anger that he has carried her scent from the place of her hanging to here.

As if it were his to keep.

As if she were his.

A gunshot cracked sharply across the interior of the house.

In the central court within the house he found Shao Fan, whose pupils are wide above the barrel of a smoking rifle. He seemed not to recognize the Boy.

Shaven-head was dead, flung away like a forgotten rag doll, his arms covering his face.

Shao Fan retreated, running to a far door and throwing himself beyond it.

The Boy pulled his pistol, the cut-down rifle, from his belt and advanced through the courtyard.

The Boy heard his own feet, hard thumps on the soft wood of the walkway that led to the door. In the instant before he heard the gunfire that came from the far side of the door, he heard the metallic sound of a rifle breech being snapped back into place. The Boy threw himself sideways as the paper door erupted in splinters and acrid smoke.

The Boy charged through the screen, breaking what was left of it open with the tomahawk.

Shao Fan, eyes wild and wide, broke the breech of his rifle and slipped another long bullet into the barrel. The assassin snapped the breech back into place. In the space of the moment in which the assassin nodded to himself, assured that the rifle was ready to fire, and before he raised it to fire, the dull silver tomahawk appeared buried in his chest. He stared at the axe in stunned and wide-eyed silence, stared as if in the moment before, it had not been there, and in the moment after, it had always been there.

He continued to try and raise the rifle but his arms would not respond. He felt life leaving him all at once.

He was afraid. He realized how underappreciated this moment before dying was.

'If there were just more time,' thought Shao Fan, raising his head, looking into the eyes of the savage boy charging across his bedroom.

Pistol raised.

Mouth roaring.

There were tears in the eyes of this savage that Shao Fan now recognizes, as his vision surrendered to a closing black circle.

Be careful who you love.

And then the pistol erupted in the hands of the savage and Shao Fan was no more.

The Boy passed through the rape of the last Chinese outpost. It was the same as Auburn and even worse, he thought, as if seeing it all from far away.

He passed the dead guards at the gate, stepping over them. Beyond them, another guard was moving and bleeding, crawling toward the water. Numbly the Boy passed on.

He found a small canoe and set out across the bay.

Alone, the work of paddling the canoe was hard.

His left side was weak. But he did not care about it anymore.

You'll do your work. Same as the other side.

The day was hot and he reached the far side, the southern end of the bay, by noon.

The air smelled of sage and dust.

Behind him, black columns of smoke rose in the north. He could barely see the colony. It was as if it never existed.

He climbed the low hills and found Horse.

They rode south along the old 101.

He was tired and his eyes felt too heavy, but he pushed on until twilight.

At dusk he built a fire near a long, flat bridge over a dry riverbed. He sat staring into the fire.

In time he heard the rider coming up along his trail.

The Boy took up his pack and loaded it onto Horse.

He scanned the murky darkness and saw only the dim outline of another figure.

The big bay horse clattered along the road and the rider drew up just beyond the reach of the firelight. The form was familiar. But the darkness hid everything. It was the hat, the Stetson hat, that gave away the rider, and then the voice, dry and friendly.

"Thought you might be asleep by now," said Dunn. "Figured you'd be all wore out after goin' ashore with them savages last night. All that blood and mayhem and fire makes a man tired, don't it?"

The Boy stood near Horse. The tomahawk was in his hand. The pistol, loaded, waited in the saddle on Horse.

Horse complained.

Easy, boy.

"Been following you since Auburn. Thought I'd catch up to you inside the Chinese base. But surprise, surprise, I found yer horse all staked out and waiting. Figured you'd slipped in among the crazies. But I knew you'd be back for yer horse."

The Boy said nothing.

"So I waited with my new pistols. Just like MacRaven's."

The Boy waited to hear the hammer of Dunn's guns being thumbed back.

Maybe he rode up with them ready to go.

Sergeant…?

"Raleigh was a good man. Didn't deserve what you did to him."

Man's come a long way to talk, Boy. Figures he's earned hisself a speech. He won't do nothin' till he's got it all out.

"Him and I was partners long before you ever come outta…"

So whatever you got to do, Boy. Do it now!

"More'n partners in fact, he was…"

In the moment the Boy threw the tomahawk, he meant it. He threw it not just at Dunn, but at a world that was cruel and made of stone.

Don't let it go unless you mean to, Boy.

The aim was true but it caught Dunn's horse in the throat as Dunn jerked at the reins to protect himself.

The horse screamed.

Dunn fired.

Two thundering roars erupted from Dunn's pistols.

Two wet slaps.

The Boy felt the spray of Horse's blood across his face as he turned and reached for the saddle, a moment later spinning away from Horse, the pistol extended toward Dunn, who rode his mount into the earth, stepping off in one smooth motion, dropping his pistols for the wicked knife he kept on his belt.

The Boy fired and Dunn fell dead, back over his fallen horse.

Flung back.

Put down.

Dead.

The Boy turned back to Horse who looked up at him from the road once more.

That Horse look of contempt.

Resignation.

Forgiveness.

Horse laid his long head down against the cracked and broken highway as his eyes closed finally, firmly, as if to say, I'm done with the world.

EPILOGUE

Where do you go now, Boy?

The road turned south and the days were long and hot. A narrow valley wound its way along the coastal mountains and would continue on all the way to Los Angeles. Or what was left of it now.

But in the days that followed, the Boy turned from the 101, limping, and climbed the smooth grassy hills to the east, soft gentle hills, rising and falling in waves of green grass.

He dragged his body over the hills, his left side aching, withered, refusing to go farther.

He continued on.

On the other side of the hills, he found a wide valley that stretched away in a brown haze to the south.

Who am I now?

He stood in the gusting wind atop the hills.

He continued down into the hot valley.

Ancient roads, ruptured and disintegrating, overrun by erupting wild growth, crossed from east to west. All else was dry and brown, hard dirt and sun-rotten dead wood.

Fires had crossed the valley and there remained little of what once was.

Rusty water towers, fallen and gouged.

Wild tangles of barbed wire.

Fallen walls of blackened stone.

He crossed the old Interstate Five and continued down into the heat of the valley.

The trees here would not grow. They were stunted and sickly and even the ground seemed either unnaturally dark or washed out and spent altogether. Thorns, of which there are many, grew in wicked profusion of ochre, sickly green or pus yellow.

In a village of adobe walls he found misshapen men and women. All of them were blind and dragging themselves along through the dirt. They ate from sickly stands of a dark green kale that gave off a foul aroma when they stewed it inside an old oil drum filled with brackish water.

They knew he was there and they searched for him, but their keening and sniffing in the dusty heat after his scent repulsed him and he went on into the silences beyond their village.

Stands of palm trees clustered in sinister groups as if talking about him and though their shade would be welcome, and maybe even their fruit, he went wide to avoid their dark and fetid clusterings.

In the night he slept in an old grain silo and thought that he should hear birds in its rafters or the bony trees outside.

He could not remember when he last heard the song of a bird.

He drank water from a standing pond because he could no longer stand the ragged dry trench that was his throat. He saw the footprints of the blind villagers in the hard-packed soil.

They too had drunk here.

Blind would not be so bad.

In the still water he saw a monster.

A monster with red-rimmed eyes that reflected no light, no life. A face and chest covered in blood and dried mud. Horse's blood. Muddy, knotted hair and a broken feather. Lips cracked and bleeding.

A monster.

He wandered south, following the twisting ribbon of the once-highway through a silent land of rust and scrub. He caught small things and felt little desire and even less satisfaction in the thin, greasy meals that resulted.

Who am I now?

Dry wood turned to sparks floating off into the night above his fire.

What is left to do and where should I go?

And there was no answer other than his own.

Nothing and nowhere.

In the day all was hot and boiling, dry and raw. In the night tepid warmth refused to surrender until long after the bloated moon had descended into darkness.

The thin road straightened and carved its way into southern mountains.

In the road signs he spelled Los Angeles.

He remembered Sergeant Presley calling it "Lost Angeles."

I should burn the map.

What good is it now?

Mission, not complete.

But he didn't and he continued on toward a crack where the road disappeared into the mountains.

At the last gas station in the foothills he spent the night.

There was nothing left to find here and there hadn't been for forty years.

In the gas station's emptiness he heard the grit of sand and glass beneath his feet. In times past, in all his wandering with Sergeant Presley, he had wondered and even dreamed about the people of Before. What had they done in these places? There had been food and drink, beyond imagining, Sergeant Presley had explained bitterly, all on a hot day such as this, for people to stop and come in from the road.

He spelled I-C-E C-O-L-D S-O-D-A.

I was raised in places like this. It seems as though it should feel like home to me.

But it didn't.

And…

I don't care anymore.

That night, though he did not want to, he dreamed.

Dreams, who can stop them? Who can understand them?

He and Jin walked through the streets of a city. Up cobblestone streets where people live. Happy people. He turned to a fruit stand filled with green apples. It was a market day or a fair, and he selected an apple for Jin.

In that dreaming moment he understood the meaning of the name Jin. Her name meant "precious." In the dream he was glad that he understood this now. It was as though he had found something rare and its ownership had caused his lifelong feeling of "want" to seem like a fading nightmare. As though he had recovered a lost treasure and it changed his future forever. As though his life, their life, would be only good now.

Now that he knew the meaning of her name, the dark times were behind them.

When he turned back to her, she was gone.

A happy villager, smiling, maybe the Weathered Man, told him she was over there, with the man's wife, looking at silk dresses for their wedding. And the smiling farmer handed him the green bottle of Pee Gee Oh full of bubbles, and they drank and the farmer encouraged him to laugh and be happy.

"It's all coming back," said the Weathered Man in perfect English.

And the Boy knew he meant the world from Before. That the days of road and ruin are coming to an end and that there would be homes and families now. That he and Jin would have a place in this new world that everyone was so excited about.

A place together.

He was excited. He wanted to find Jin and tell her about all the good things that are soon going to happen to them.

But his mouth wouldn't make the words to call out her name.

He searched the stalls.

He searched the roads.

It was getting dark in the dream and the market was closing.

"We'll find her tomorrow," said the Weathered Man. "Come home with us and stay the night."

Though he didn't want to be, the Boy was led home and the dream advanced in leaps and starts as the Boy watched throughout the night, looking out a small window, looking onto a dark street.

Waiting for Jin.

He could not wait to tell her that everything good was coming back again.

Soon.

In the dream he could not wait to hold her.

In the morning, the sun slammed into his weak eyes. Tears had dried on his dusty, crusted cheeks. His insides felt sore, as though they have been beaten with sticks.

He sat up and looked toward the road and the mountains.

It was real, he thought of the dream.

The road cut its way onto a high plateau, passing stands of oak and wide expanses of rolling yellow-green grass. In a high pasture he found sheep and a man watching over them.

The man waved at him from the field and the Boy turned off the old highway and into the field.

The sheep, maybe a dozen of them, wandered and bleated absently through the tall yellow grass of mid spring. Beyond the pasture, oak trees clustered at the base of a steep range of hills that shielded any view of the east and whatever must lie that way.

"Stranger, come and have water," called the man over the constant bleating of the sheep.

The man was rotund and dressed in a ragged collection of scraps sewn together. He carried a crooked staff and leaned on it heavily. His hair, gray, sprang from his head in every direction. His voice was a mere rumble of thunder and gravel.

"The road is hard," he said, watching the Boy drink the cool water held in a tin cup. The water was clear and sweet.

"It's a good spring here," said the shepherd when the Boy did not respond.

The Boy handed the cup back.

"I have wild apples near my camp; come and have some."

The Boy followed the man across the pasture and into a stand of wild fruit trees.

They sit in the shade, eating apples.

"Saint Maggie said that food leads to friendship."

The Boy said nothing.

"Who might you be, now?"

The Boy opened his mouth to answer. But he couldn't.

"Can you speak?"

The Boy shook his head.

"Then I'm sorry. The words of man are overrated. Saint Maggie again."

The shepherd took a crunchy bite from an apple.

"I speak too much."

Then, "That's why I'm here. I spoke too much when I shouldn't have. But I love to talk. Love to hear the sound of my own voice. And the sounds of others for that matter. I love talk."

There was more silence for a while.

"Still, my words are overrated."

"Will you stay, or are you determined to go on to the south?"

The Boy rose.

"You will find nothing worth having there!" the shepherd's voice rose in pitched urgency.

"You will find the worst of this world and the worst that the world that died had done to itself."

The Boy began to stumble toward the road.

"If you go west you will find life. Some. But in the south there is nothing but horror. Trust me, stranger!"

As an afterthought the shepherd said, "East. Don't go east into the desert. That is death for sure."

The Boy considered the high sun. Orienting himself.

He turned toward the east.

The shepherd looked at the Boy, eyes wide with amazement and then horror.

A high hill, speckled by a few gnarled oaks, rose up to the east.

The Boy began walking toward the hill.

The shepherd murmured, "No."

The tall grass brushed against the legs of the Boy and he could hear the shepherd hobbling behind him, breathing heavily in the still air.

"Stranger, don't go that way. I told you it was death."

They neared the base of the steep hill as the shepherd pursued the Boy.

"There lies a desert, and it will consume you. A wasteland. You will be no more. Saint Maggie said, 'We must do our best. We must live despite life. God will do the rest.' Stranger, you will find no love that way. Turn west and live."

The Boy fell to his knees and began to climb the hill.

The shepherd fell to his knees.

"I will pray for you, stranger. I will pray for you."

The shepherd was still praying, hours later, when the Boy reached the top of the steep hill and saw the line of hills beyond, descending into the vast bowl of the desert.

What do you find when there is nothing left, Boy?

The days were brutal and there was no water. The land fell into a furnace of burning hard-packed dirt and suffocating dunes.

You left me, Sergeant.

I had to, Boy. The world didn't need me anymore.

I needed you.

And someone, Boy, someday will need you also.

She's dead.

He fell to his knees and wept.

The flat desert stretched away in all directions.

Never give up, Boy. I told you. The world needs us.

You take everything with you.

It's too much, too much to carry, you and the broken places and the evil of the world… and what… and Jin.

He stumbled.

Then he crawled.

How many days?

But to think of them was to think of the pain of all his days.

And still he crawled through the days, deeper and deeper into the burning wastes.

There can't be anymore left of me. Tonight or tomorrow, and that would be the end of the whole mess that is the world, that is me.

In the night, the stars were cold and clear.

He watched them and thought of Jin.

I am done. There is nothing left in me with which to grieve.

He felt empty.

He felt hollow.

In the morning, the sun rose from a thin strip of light.

This is my last day.

You take everything with you.

He reached for the tomahawk.

It felt comforting. As though he had been loyal and faithful to it. As though it stood as a monument, a testament even, to all his loss and failure.

You take everything with you.

His left side would not move.

Curse you then, you never helped me in life and now you won't go with me to my death. What good have you ever been?

Then…

I'll drag you.

He watched the empty wasteland ahead and knew that he would die today somewhere within it.

Five days without water. That's the most a man, a person, can go.

He dragged himself forward.

Sergeant Presley.

Horse.

The bearskin.

The pistol that was once a rifle.

Where did you lose that?

I cannot remember. Somewhere in the poisoned valley.

The Chinese colony at Auburn.

Escondido.

The Chinese at Sausalito.

Jin.

It was a lie.

What?

He had trouble remembering. He was crawling through chalky sand. He had been for some time.

It's so hot now, but at least I'm not sweating.

I don't think that is good.

It depends on what you want to accomplish.

What was a lie?

That you take everything with you. That was a lie.

Oh.

Where are they now?

Sergeant. Horse. Jin.

How can you take everything with you when it is all gone?

I was lied to.

In the end, I don't even know who I am, where I came from. Who were my mother and father? What did it mean to be an American?

Sergeant Presley called me Boy.

The Chinese called me savage.

The savages called me Bear Killer.

All of it seemed to be something that never happened or happened to someone else, long ago.

Who am I?

Jin called you…

"Don't!" he croak-screamed into the dry expanse. "I can't take it anymore."

Hours later, crawling on his knees and pulling with his hand, dragging the side that would not work, he stopped.

He gasped, "Not much farther now."

You got to decide who you are, Boy. Not the world. Don't let people ever tell you who you are. Some people tell nothing but lies. So why ask 'em anyways?

Yes. I remember when you said that.

I'm saying it now.

His hand felt the hard, burning surface of a road.

You're dead.

I'm sorry about that, Boy. I never meant to leave you.

Tell me who I am.

I'm dead, Boy. Said so yourself.

Who am I?

Silence.

In the distance he heard a high-pitched whine and then a loud rumble beneath it.

He was alone in the middle of a desert plain, cracked and broken.

He laid his head down onto the hard dirt and felt it burn the side of his face as he closed his eyes.

My ears are buzzing. This must be death. It has been following me for some time. My whole life even. And now death is finally coming for me. What took you so long?

Who are you, Boy?

I don't know. I never did.

The roar and whine consumed everything. It grew and grew, filling up the expanse of the desert and the sky. Everything was now shadow and heat.

Did you expect to find her in death?

He heard footsteps.

I was hoping to. But I think I will find only death. Who am I to think I might find Jin again? The world is made of stone. Who am I that it should be any different for me?

Death bent down and touched the Boy's cheek.

Who am I? he mumbled to Death.

You should know who I am before you take me.

Or are you just a taker? A taker who doesn't ask.

The Boy opened his eyes.

Death was an Old Man, thin and wiry, gray stubble. His eyes sharp and clear and blue.

"Who is he, Poppa?" A young girl's voice from near-by.

"I don't know. But he needs our help. He's been out here for too long. He's close to death."

"I'll get some water, Poppa," said the girl, and the Boy heard the slap of shoes against the hot road.

The Boy began to cry.

Shaking, he convulsed.

Crying, he wheezed, begging the world not to be made of stone, begging the world to give back what it had taken from him.

"Who am I?" sobbed the Boy.

"I think he's asking, who is he, Poppa!" said the girl as though it were all a game of guessing and she had just won.

The Old Man held the shaking, sobbing Boy and poured water onto cracked and sunburned lips in the shadow of the rumbling tank.

"He doesn't know who he is, Poppa. Who is he?"

"He's just a boy," said the Old Man to his grand-daughter, his voice trembling with worry and doubt.

"Who am I now?" sobbed the Boy.

The Old Man held the Boy close, willing life, precious life, back into the thin body.

"You're just a boy, that's all. Just a boy," soothed the Old Man, almost in tears.

The Old Man held the Boy tightly.

"You're just a boy," he repeated.

"Just a boy."

The End

I'M GLAD YOU CAME BACK. Glad you made it this far. I hope you liked the story of the Boy. I'll be honest. This was the toughest book I've ever written. I was awful to every character. They were good people... Jin, Sergeant Presley, Horse, and even the Boy. They deserved better. But this New American Dark Age is a pretty rough place. And even heroes don't seem to be enough... sometimes. But then there's the Old Man. What did he say in the first book... *"I may not be as strong as I think, but I know many tricks and I have resolution."* Maybe that's what the Boy needs. Maybe, that's what this world needs. There're some people in trouble in a bunker deep beneath NORAD up in a Colorado that got ruined by nuclear fire on that last worst day of humanity. And they need some help. Pretty badly. There's a darkness spreading across the land from the East, and only the Old Man, and his granddaughter, have answered the radio distress message for help. Together, with the Boy's help, they might just make a difference. And maybe, by the acts of a few, civilization might just come back online. We'll have to see. We'll find out in The Road is a River. Which is the final leg of this journey.

Did I tell you I'm so glad you made it this far? On your journey across this apocalyptic wasteland that might be all our tomorrows? I am... Now we're friends in the book, just like the Old Man and Santiago.

Thank you.
-Nick

THE NEW AMERICAN WASTELAND TRILIOGY

THE OLD MAN AND THE WASTELAND

THE SAVAGE BOY

THE ROAD IS A RIVER

WHO IS NICK COLE?

Nick Cole is a former soldier and working actor living in Southern California. When he is not auditioning for commercials, going out for sitcoms or being shot, kicked, stabbed or beaten by the students of various film schools for their projects, he can be found writing books. Nick's Book The Old Man and the Wasteland was an Amazon Bestseller and #1 in Science Fiction. In 2016 Nick's book CTRL ALT Revolt won the Dragon Award for Best Apocalyptic novel. Currently he is writing the bestselling Science Fiction series Galaxy's Edge with co-author Jason Anspach.

Connect with Nick and find out about his latest books. Also you get a Free one.
https://www.nickcolebooks.com/connect/

Made in the USA
Middletown, DE
13 August 2019